WAIT FOR THE LIGHT

Erin Adams
Lo-fi Press

Published by Low-fi Press 2017

ISBN: 0692986200
ISBN 13: 9780692986202

PROLOGUE

The first time I see my mother in me, I'm facedown on the ground, kissing dirt. There's a freedom in not caring what happens to you. I feel calm despite everything that has happened. Maybe tomorrow I'll jump into a paneled van on the offer of candy. If I make it until tomorrow.

I know I should be concerned for my safety. I should be watching the dog instead of the dirt, but eye contact might spook him again. This muscle-bound tank of a creature looks like it could rip me apart, but my need to connect with it is somehow more consuming than my fear.

My mind races with questions as I lie here, holding a treat, something chicken flavored and greasy, in my outstretched hand: Don't most hereditary mental illnesses present themselves around this age? Is this one of those latent genetic inevitabilities that flips on like a switch in young adulthood? Am I going to end up in the hospital—or worse?

I scroll through all the life events that might have driven me to prostrate myself in somebody's mulch voluntarily at the mercy of a large, ferocious animal. Everything goes back to our childhoods, doesn't it? I don't fool myself into thinking that my brand of trauma was special. Different maybe, but we all pay the price for our parents' mistakes, or we add to them, making the cost astronomical.

Maybe life's come to collect everything at once in this moment. *CLICK!* And the light goes out. I am transformed into the crazy stray-dog lady in the bushes.

I hold my breath, willing the animal not to run away or attack me.

If my mother could see me in this moment, risking my life and treating my silk Armani like an old dishrag, she would swell with pride.

PART ONE

CHAPTER ONE

One month earlier

Techno blared through the penthouse all night, taking a thousand tiny jabs at my head, which added up to a pounding headache. Lucy had gone out onto the balcony and I seized the opportunity to lower the music. I glanced through the sliding doors to see if she noticed.

She wasn't there.

"Hey, Luce," I called.

Nothing.

I muted the speakers and called to her again. She didn't answer, so I went to all three bathrooms and found them vacant. I checked the master bedroom next and the walk-in closet. The shoe racks lit up when I entered.

Multicolored stilettos, boots, and sandals cast a rainbow glow on the blond wood floor. But no Lucy. I searched the entire penthouse, even behind the Poltrona Frau in her office thinking she might have passed out from all the whiskey she'd had tonight.

But she was nowhere to be found. She'd left the building.

She must have done it again—snuck past me and the paparazzi camped outside. Now she was most likely walking to a bar. Alone. On South Beach.

But she shouldn't have been able to leave without my noticing this time. I'd stayed close to the balcony ever since she'd gone out there about a half hour ago. It seemed impossible that she could've gotten back inside without me seeing her. The only explanation was that she'd crawled past me on all fours.

I heard the elevator start to whir from below, and I hurried to the metal doors, expecting her to emerge in a minute with a champagne bottle and an amazing story of escape. Or she'd be crying and imploring to me, "Alex, I just want to be anonymous for once. Why can't people treat me like a normal person?"

But she never really meant that. Ever since we were kids, Lucy had wanted to be famous, an A-list movie actress. Instead of pointing out that truth to her, I'd sympathize like a good assistant and friend while plying her with glasses of water.

The elevator chimed and Mushroom, Lucy's little Pomeranian, ran to my side, rasping out excited breaths. The doors opened to reveal Lucy's bodyguard, Frank, holding two brown paper takeout bags in his burly arms. What little bit of hair he had left was damp.

"Have you seen Lucy?" I asked. I was out of breath.

"No. Not since I went out for food." He dropped the takeout on the long glass vestibule table. His head jerked from side to side as he scanned the great room.

I rushed out to the balcony and looked down at the building's entryway. A mob hadn't gathered down there, so Lucy had to have exited through the parking garage. From my aerial view of Ocean Avenue, the people looked like a swarm of pixels dancing along the street in the rain.

"Hey," Lucy's breathy voice said not far from my ear.

I turned, and there she stood on the small ledge, twenty-two stories above the ground. Her red hair was wild, and a satisfied grin cut across her rosy cheeks.

It took a moment to hit me, the terror. It crept in slow motion, and a sour taste scalded the back of my throat. I registered Mushroom's high-pitched yipes coming from the living room behind me. Mushroom knew something was terribly wrong, too.

I had to act. I couldn't reach Lucy from where I stood, so I stepped onto the bottom rung of the rail. She laughed and started to inch away.

"Lucy, take my hand," I said. Holding on to the slippery banister with one hand, I gripped an indentation on the side of the building with the other. I hoisted my right leg up and over.

Hands wrapped around my waist.

It was Frank. "Let me go to her, Alex."

"By the time we switch, she'll fall," I said. "This is the only way."

"Go slow," he said, releasing me.

The drizzly Miami Beach night gave everything the soft edges of a dream, and I felt like I was acting outside of myself. I screwed up my courage and threw my other leg over the rail. Frank leaned over the banister and seized my calf to anchor me. The wind whipped my hair, blinding me for a second. "Come on, Luce!" I called.

"I'm shh-o-wing you what good bla-lance I have." She waved my outstretched hand away. "I'm pr-rooving how undrunk I am."

In that instant, I was filled with deep regret over my comment to Lucy earlier that evening. In the history of partying, telling a drunk person that they're drunk has never helped anything. But who knew those words could be life threatening?

The rough concrete scraped at my jeans as I stretched my arm out to Lucy as far as it would go. It wasn't far enough.

"I've had a couple drinks, too, Lucy," I said. "And I feel pretty buzzed." I tried not to look down, tried not to picture our brains exploding on pavement. The wind threw my hair across my face again, and as I shook the strands away I caught a glimpse of the ground. The world below me reeled. The ant-sized cars drew tiny trails of distorted light that remained in front of me after I pulled my eyes away.

I had to give up my anchor to reach her. "Almost there, Frank," I said. "Just let me go for a second."

He did.

I teetered forward and found my balance by fixing my eyes on the high-rise condo across the street. "Take my hand, Luce."

Lucy closed one eye. "You're no fun." Her lower lip jutted in a pout.

"Now!" I said.

She slowly lifted her hand and placed it in mine. I nodded to her, and she seemed to understand that we needed to move together. We took a treacherous step toward Frank and the balcony. He grabbed my arm and leg. At that moment, Lucy lurched forward. My body acted before my brain could catch up. With the mythical superhuman strength of a mother lifting a car off her toddler, I freed my arm from Frank's grasp and pulled Lucy to me with both arms. We took one more step, and Frank enveloped my waist. Somehow

I carried her weight as Frank yanked us both up and over the balustrade.

We all spilled into a wet, tangled heap on the balcony floor. The sharp scent of whiskey coming off Lucy made my head spin as if I had been the one who had chugged half a bottle instead of her.

I'd saved her life. Now we were even.

CHAPTER TWO

Five weeks after our sky-walking adventure, I was skittering around Lucy's penthouse, preparing for her return from rehab. This was how I shined: making things perfect for her. She would need me more than ever now that she had hit rock bottom, as they say. I was here to cushion her landing. I stocked the fridge with her favorite foods, swapped out wilted houseplants with lush, healthy ones, and sorted all the new freebies from fashion designers and luxury cosmetics companies. I arranged and rearranged them until the spare bedroom resembled an Anthropologie store.

There was more—she would die when she spotted my collage. I hung it on the wall opposite the elevator so it would be the first thing she'd see when she came in. I'd laughed aloud while I'd worked on it, my voice echoing through the vast, empty apartment. I pasted our faces over magazine pictures, my smiling ninth-grade brace-face on the body of an old lady in a rocking chair, Lucy's on Arnold Schwarzenegger's huge physique. I even found a profile image of her bodyguard, Frank, among my pictures and stuck it on a Victoria's Secret model spread-eagle on a zebra rug. In the center of my Art Nouveau piece, I'd glued Lucy's feature in *US Weekly*'s "Who Wore It Best" segment. If she didn't already know, she'd be pleased to learn she'd worn her emerald Dior dress better than Katie Holmes.

I surveyed the front rooms from the foyer. The cleaning service had done a thorough job. The walnut floors gleamed, and the carpet stains were gone. I stooped and ran my fingers through the soft, white shag. Still a little damp but barely noticeable. I lit a jasmine candle (Lucy's favorite scent), and set it on the petrified wood coffee table. Then I began fluffing the dozen or so cushions on the couch. Beneath one pillow was a round black mark, a cigarette burn from one of many bleary nights. I wondered if she ever glimpsed the marred spot and cringed, or if she even remembered.

The appliances had already been scrubbed clean, but I polished them some more, inhaling the citrusy organic cleanser.

When I ran out of things to double-clean, I changed into my favorite wrap dress and let my hair out of its ponytail. I checked my reflection and applied more mascara. Then I tied my hair back up because I didn't feel like ironing out the noticeable crease left by the elastic.

Everything was in place, so I moved to the bar in the dining area and uncapped a bottle of vodka. Midpour, I jerked the bottle upright.

What kind of dumb-ass fixes a cocktail to celebrate her friend's return from rehab? Jesus.

I dumped the contents of my rocks glass in the kitchen sink and returned to the couch, where I sat and waited. I flipped on the TV, but I was too excited to watch anything. A corner of paper sticking out of the console table drawer caught my eye. I opened the drawer and pulled out the brochure that I had studied several weeks prior. I'd laughed when Lucy had handed it to me that day.

"I'm serious this time," Lucy said. "I'm going, Alex."

My laughter had a tinge of bitterness in it as I examined the pamphlet. On the cover was a picture of a woman, her expression as bland as the beige sweater set she was wearing. The caption read, "Did drugs or alcohol take your loved one from you? We will return that person you once knew, healthy, renewed, and sober." I flipped it open.

The woman from the cover was draped in a white sheet on a massage table in front of a scenic desert background. She looked like she was on horse tranquilizers. Hairless man hands kneaded at her back, and the caption below the picture said, "Find Serenity Here."

I stuffed the beige woman back into the drawer.

The elevator chimed and I sprung up, excited to see Lucy's reaction to my "Who Wore It Best" collage. My petite friend stepped through the doors and slowly unraveled her scarf. Her green eyes jutted around, bewildered but clear. She lifted Mushroom out of her tote and set the dog on the floor. Mushroom scampered off to her room.

"Hey, Luce," I said, hugging her. "You look great!" She'd gained a few much-needed pounds, made it to the triple digits probably.

"Thanks," she said, leaning into me and returning my embrace with a limp, jet-lagged arm.

Frank lumbered from the elevator with a cart full of bags.

What came next was startling. A woman emerged from behind Frank, tall with olive skin and a dancer's posture. Immediately I assumed she was the new housekeeper. *Give me a little credit, Lucy*, I thought. *Like I would let you come home to a dirty house.* The statuesque woman swooshed past Frank and Lucy and stretched out her hand to me.

"I'm Tatiana. So nice to meet you, Alex."

Pretty enthusiastic for a cleaning lady, I thought, taking a step back.

The cleaning lady kicked off her sandals and headed to the living room, where she started pacing back and forth, her floor-length skirt billowing in the air current.

"Lucy has told me so much about you, Alex. What a beautiful place!"

She must have known she'd be reporting to me, and that was why she was overusing my name—to win me over. She must have been nervous. Nobody was this annoying. And was she *jingling*?

She was.

A macramé bracelet woven with tiny round bells adorned her ankle. At least she wouldn't be able to sneak up on me like our former cleaning woman. That woman had a terrible habit of stalking into a room like a ninja, scaring the crap out of me on many occasions. As it turned out, our previous cleaning lady also had a habit of talking to the reporters about Lucy. That's why we were in the market for a new one.

Tatiana didn't seem to register that she was ruining what was supposed to be a private, meaningful reconciliation between friends. Of course, it was fine that Frank was there. Despite his formidable size, he was adept at making himself as unobtrusive as a chair in the corner, reacting to nothing going on around him.

"May I please get a glass of water, Alex?" Tatiana asked.

My accommodating Midwestern sensibility stopped me from commenting on her audacity. "Sure."

I headed to the kitchen for bottled water, thanking Frank as he pushed the empty luggage cart back into the elevator.

"So, was it awful?" I asked Lucy as I distributed the waters. "Thirty days without a drink, huh?"

"What? No, not awful at all," she said, edging into the living room and uncapping the water. She moved the container around as if swirling a cocktail to melt the ice.

Tatiana planted herself on the sectional, and Lucy joined her.

"You hired a housekeeper?" I said to Lucy. The two women met eyes and a weird flicker passed between them like they already knew each other.

"Well, that's one thing I can cross off my to-do list," I went on. "So we can go over a few things just to get them out of the way. You're not booked for anything tomorrow or Thursday but I rescheduled your meeting with—"

"Alex, please come sit," Lucy said.

"Sorry, you must be so tired," I said, sitting on the other end of the sectional. "This all can wait."

"No, it's fine," she said, shaking her head. "It's just that Tatiana isn't a housekeeper. She's from the rehab facility, and we need to discuss something with you."

"They fly home with you?" I said. "That's great customer service."

"No, Alex," Lucy said. "She's here as my sober companion."

All at once, Tatiana's presence and behavior made perfect sense. She was one of those people who lived with rich alcoholics to keep them from drinking. Sometimes they would go so far as to sleep in the same bed and accompany their clients to the bathroom.

"Um, that's cool," I said, disappointed. Would she follow Lucy like a shadow and be privy to all our conversations? How long would this awkward arrangement last?

"What am I thinking?" Tatiana bellowed, jumping up. We watched her take long strides to the bar, where she started gathering bottles. Their clangs reverberated through the great room.

"Alex, would you mind telling me where the trash bags are?"

I moved to the pantry to fetch a bag, annoyed with myself at how quickly I'd sprung to attention.

Two bottles in each hand, Tatiana marched to the kitchen sink and started dumping out the liquor. Lucy averted her eyes as if the scene were some grisly car accident. She fixed her gaze on me. "So, how have you been, Alex?"

She sounded as if she were addressing a fourth cousin twice removed.

"Good," I said. I couldn't help thinking Tatiana's being there had something to do with Lucy's distant behavior.

Tatiana. What kind of name was that anyway? She didn't dress like a character from a nineteenth-century

Russian novel, and she didn't have an accent, unless you counted her drawling the last syllable of every word as an accent. A lot of people in LA have that same speaking affectation, like they want people to think they're perpetually coming from a life-changing yoga session. I decided I didn't like her at all.

Tatiana heaved two clanking sacks over to the foyer. "I'll get those later," she said, plunking them down on the marble floor. She came back and sat down, meeting Lucy's eyes. "Do you want to start?"

I felt like I was at a parent-teacher conference.

Lucy took a gulp of air. "Okay, well, Alex, at New Perspectives I learned a lot about myself and how to change the things that are holding me back from being the best person I can be." She wiped the sweat from the water bottle on her yoga pants. "And to do that I need to change people, places, and things."

"Okay," I said, trying to make sense of her statement. What would be left after those changes of hers? We'd leave Miami and go back to LA at some point, so that covered *places*. The *things* must've been the garbage bags full of empties. What did she mean by *people*? Me?

I craved a cigarette for the first time in a while.

"So, about my schedule . . ." Lucy trailed off, and Tatiana moved closer to her and squeezed her shoulder, as if to bring her back.

"I need to take it slow. Tatiana's going to help with that."

"Great," I said. "Welcome aboard, Tatiana."

They exchanged looks again. I couldn't help but feel jealous. I was the one who exchanged looks with Lucy.

"She'll live here while I get back on my feet. I won't be working at all for at least a month."

"That's cool. Probably a good idea. Whatever I can do to help—"

Tatiana broke in. "That's the thing, Alex. Lucy needs to take this journey alone."

I looked back and forth between them. Tatiana dipped her head. Lucy, doe-eyed, spotted the collage that I'd made for her. She didn't even comment on it.

"Are you guys serious?" I asked, wondering if this sanctimonious hippie woman had brainwashed Lucy, convinced her that I was part of the problem.

Tatiana nodded and pulled her knees to her chest. Her ankle jingled again.

This was not how this was supposed to go. I'd imagined a glorious reunion, the promise of renewed friendship, and perhaps a raise. I so deserved that after putting up with Lucy's drunken shit. We'd go back to how it used to be. Movie nights with Ben & Jerry. Stumbling and laughing through the latest fitness crazes. Staying up late and bitching about our mothers. I wanted that all back.

"I'll pay you until you find something else," Lucy said after a beat, finally meeting my eyes. Tatiana whispered something in her ear.

"Alex, I'm beyond grateful for everything you've done . . ."

Tatiana must've fed her that line. *How nice of her.*

"Right," I said, getting up and starting to pace. "So you're going back to LA without me?"

"I might have another movie deal here, so we're in a holding pattern."

"Congratulations," I said flatly.

"Don't think of this as a bad thing." Her voice hitched. "We're still friends, and this isn't necessarily forever. I just need help staying sober right now."

These were things that people said when they dumped someone. "I was trying to help you," I said, scraping my toe into the carpet and staring at the indents I'd made.

"I know you were trying to help," Lucy said. "It's just—"

Tatiana broke in. "Alex, what Lucy needs is someone who's as committed to sobriety as she is."

"Well, that's me," I said with conviction. It was true. I had demonstrated this commitment on many occasions by watering down her drinks and hiding her cocaine.

"And that's great to hear, but I'm not sure someone outside the program is equipped to give her the support she needs. For instance, getting rid of all the booze in the house."

I stiffened. Dumping perfectly good liquor had been a nonthought. Even if Lucy didn't drink it, she entertained guests who would drink it. I thought about the cocktail I'd almost had. What would Tatiana have said then?

"Alright, guess I'm still learning about how this all works." I tried to give her a good-natured grin, but I felt my face forming into a grimace.

Tatiana cleared her throat. "If you ever were to come back, you couldn't drink."

"No problem."

"Maybe you don't understand," Tatiana said, her eyes narrowing on me. "You were one of Lucy's drinking buddies, were you not?"

She made us sound like a couple of fifty-year-old Teamsters instead of twenty-five-year-old women. I didn't answer her. I knew enough to know anything I said at this point would just sound defensive.

"Alex, if you want to continue with Lucy, you need to be one hundred percent sober."

"Okay, well that sounds a little extreme."

"It probably does sound extreme to you," Tatiana said. "But you'll have plenty of time to search your soul, figure out if it's something you're willing to commit to."

I couldn't listen to this anymore. I took off down the hallway. They called after me, but I shut myself in my bedroom suite. I couldn't believe I really had to leave. This had been my home, my room. Where would I go? My first thought was a hotel, but that was a stupid idea for someone who just lost their job. I had an apartment—a crappy one where I kept some of my things. Had I ever even slept there? I would have rented a better place if I knew I would need to sleep there.

I threw open the closet and hurled clothes into my suitcase. I moved to the bathroom and regarded the multitude of jars and tubes on the counter, swag that flowed from Lucy to me. My suitcase wouldn't hold it all.

Fuck it. Frank could send me the rest later. The only thing I needed was the pack of Parliaments that I would be purchasing shortly.

I struggled down the hall with my luggage, concentrating on how incredible that first nicotine head rush would feel. I'd pick up something at the liquor store, too, just to make the cigarettes taste extra good.

Lucy hurried toward me, but I sidestepped her and hit the elevator button.

"Alex, are you alright?" Lucy asked. She sounded like she was about to cry. "Please just sit down for a second."

"I'm fine," I said, my voice rising an octave. I was trying not to cry, too. "I'll talk to you later."

Lucy stuck her arm between the doors, keeping them from closing. "Listen, I have another job for you."

If this was temporary like she'd said, why would she be finding me a new job? And if she said "housekeeper," I was going to lose my shit.

"What's that?"

"It's a little sensitive, and it would be a big favor." The elevator doors chimed as they tried to close again. "It's totally understandable if you want to shoot it down," she said. "Rottie Wiles just got out of jail, and he needs someone on a temporary basis. Even if you do it for a little while, it would be a big help. I can email you the details."

"The dog-fighting guy?"

She nodded.

My mind flashed to my mother's face. Whenever I saw an image of her in my head, she was crying. This time she was having a full-on temper tantrum, on her stomach, kicking her feet and pounding her fists. That would be her worst nightmare. My mother would rather announce to her friends that I'd taken up residence on a stripper pole than tell them I was working for a man who abused animals.

I told Lucy I'd think about it, stepped into the elevator, and pressed the button that would take me to the lobby.

The doors eased shut. Lucy's collage caught in their breeze and slipped to the floor.

CHAPTER THREE

Rob and I sat on Nexxt Café's patio sipping mojitos. "There's an opportunity for me to make a lot of money fast," I said. I hadn't told him that Lucy had cut me loose indefinitely. I put it in the best possible light, that she had a sober assistant living there and she had been kind enough to give me some time off. As I waited for Rob to stop looking at his phone, my eyes followed a ridiculous vision—a woman teetering in five-inch heels while pushing a stroller. A beefy child, well into his walking years, overflowed from the carriage's seat.

"More money?" Rob echoed, shooting me a quick glance over the top of his Ray-Bans. He held his finger up. "Hang on. Let me finish this email real quick, babe."

I went back to swirling the little bit of ice left in my drink, sneaking glances at him as he typed. Sometimes it was hard to contain my giddiness for him, perhaps because he was the first person I'd dated who could be classified as an actual adult. He didn't cut his own hair or have his frat brothers cut it for him. He didn't believe that turning his baseball cap forward was making an effort. He wore pocket squares. Sure, we'd hooked up the first night after we'd met at a club, but he called two, not three, days later to take me on a real date.

On top of that, he turned the heads of *models*. Maybe it was how his aqua eyes and sandy hair made you think of the beach. Or his perpetual smirk, like he was savoring a piece of irony that nobody else got. "Do you think he's douchey?" I asked Lucy when she met him for the first time, fishing for approval. "He's so hot, he gets a douche pass," she said. I'd detected a hint of envy in her voice and I'd latched on to it, been bolstered by it.

At least I had Rob.

Sometimes I wondered if people thought Rob and I were a mismatched couple. I'm not bad looking, but I don't have any features that are particularly striking. Nobody has ever said, "Wow, I'd kill for those eyelashes, girl!" No one has ever remarked on any one part of me, beyond complimenting my chestnut highlights (fake). But people have told me I'm pretty. My skin is clear for the most part, if a little on the pale side. I'm taller than average, but not statuesque. I'm slim, but not willowy.

Rob, finished with his email, shrugged off his tan linen jacket and arranged it on the back of his chair. "Wait—why would you leave Lucy now? I thought things would be better once she got back from being hospitalized for exhaustion," he said, throwing up air quotes around "exhaustion."

I chuckled into my straw. Some of my rum drink splashed over the top of the glass and speckled the white paper covering the table.

"Guess that sober police woman's going to perform my duties in between slapping gin from her hand."

"No gin? That sounds like a toxic work environment," he said deadpan.

I laughed again. "Anyway, so you know Rottie Wiles?" I asked.

He took off his sunglasses and nodded.

"I'd be working for him."

"Rottie *fucking* Wiles?" Rob paused for a moment. "Wait—isn't he in jail?"

"He just got out."

"Holy shit. That whole thing seemed like it went down yesterday."

"Right?" I said. Actually, it felt to me like it had been a long time ago, perhaps because my life had been so different then. Lucy and I had been living in LA. That was before her romantic comedy, *Running from Love,* brought us to Miami.

"Damn, I love his new song. It's so dark," Rob said. Lifting his hands over his head, he started rapping:

"*Wish I could play the victim/ Claim it as a ghetto symptom/ He was gone but I still didn't contradict him.*"

He was singing Rottie's latest single, released under the name "Reginald Wiles." It smacked of apology: *Doin' like my daddy did befo' he up and ran/ Now the blood of the innocents is on this nigga's hands.* The record label must have timed its release so it came out less than a week before Rottie's prison sentence ended.

Rob plunked his mojito down and palmed his forehead. "I bet his crib is sick."

His gangsta speak was cute, but I rolled my eyes anyway. He had a bevy of hair-twirling secretaries in his law office who doted on him, and I didn't want to be slotted in with them. The truth was I thought I might be falling for him. But it was too soon—we'd only been seeing each other for a few months.

He raised an eyebrow in response to my eye roll, and I fought to keep the sides of my mouth from turning up again. It was a constant struggle, keeping my cool with him.

"I don't know if I'm even going to bother," I said. "He just needs someone to fill in on a short-term basis. I'll go back to Lucy when Russian tundra or whatever calls that sober zealot Tatiana back home. Or the mountains, I guess. She lives in Ariz— "

"If you're going to bother? Are you crazy?" He grabbed my hands, leaned into me. "This is Rottie *fucking* Wiles."

"Well, I mean he's basically a violent criminal, right?" I said. "He pissed off like half of the population, not least of all my mother. That whole thing was pretty ugly."

"Shit, I'd quit the law firm right now to work for him," he said. "Tell your mom to get over it. Tell her this is Rottie *fucking* Wiles."

If Rob only knew my mother.

Rottie Wiles lived on Star Island. Anyone driving on MacArthur Causeway took in its gleaming palaces that lorded over Biscayne Bay. I'd been to plenty of opulent homes in LA, but these residences seemed more implausible somehow. I couldn't pinpoint why. The only thing I could come up with was that you had to cross a special bridge to get to them.

But security at the neighborhood's edge was looser than I had imagined. The booth operator asked me where I was going as he pressed the button to lift the thin access bar. That was it.

"You're two minutes from your destination," said the British lady on my GPS. I had hoped to get a closer look at the island's homes, but they were far less visible from the inside. Story-high hedges carved into perfectly flush ninety-degree angles obscured my view. Every so often the green sentinels gave way to gated entrances, solid and too high to see over.

I ogled a barrier that looked like a passage to a Tibetan monastery, arched with a grand pagoda-style roof. The British woman's voice on my GPS told me to turn right at the next address.

I had reached my destination. A thick stone wall bordered the rapper's property, and a man in a black suit paced along its barricade, bringing old Mafia films to mind. He glared at me, covered one ear, and spoke into a walkie. A moment later the iron doors parted. My heart sped up, and I tapped the gas.

Golden rays broke through paddle-like leaves flocking either side of the residence's easement. As I drove, the foliage parted to reveal more of a compound than a house, with two sprawling ivory stucco buildings, one a mansion, and the other perhaps former horse stables converted into a two-story garage. Through its wide doors I saw at least a dozen cars and enough space left over for a hockey rink.

I checked my reflection in the visor mirror and blotted my face. The front door opened and out walked a giant man wearing a black tracksuit and a steely expression. He stood with his feet hip width apart, hands folded. He averted his eyes from me in a respectful way, but it still felt like he was watching my every move.

I flipped the visor back into place and stepped out of my car. I wished I had blotted my armpits, too.

"Welcome, Ms. Rader." The man's deep voice matched his stature, and I recognized it from the Rottie Wiles tracks that I'd listened to in preparation for the interview. I could hear him rapping, *"Lucky number's thirteen / Dat playground shit don't irk me / Drink another Flirtini / Yo' only friend's imaginary."*

"Terence Warner. But you can call me Ham."

Did he just say Ham, as in the pork product?

"Like a Christmas ham," he said with no trace of humor.

"Pleasure to meet you, Ham."

He gestured for me to enter and then lumbered after me into the ceramic-tiled foyer. My eyes followed a polished wood staircase leading up to a railed walkway. White baroque columns stretching from the main floor supported the promenade.

"We'll be in here," Ham said. "Watch your step." The recessed living room rug was a pale-cream color. I scrambled to remove my heels, swaying to keep my balance while clutching my bag and holding my knees together so as not to split my pencil skirt.

"You fine. Leave your shoes on," he said. Relieved, I followed him into the room, which was so massive that even with three overstuffed leather sofas it was mostly empty space. Solid windows made up two of the walls, one facing the backyard and the bay, another separating an atrium bursting with so much greenery that it looked like the plants might break out and fill all the negative space in the living room.

I felt the need to comment on something, anything. I zeroed in on an asymmetrical floral bouquet in a vase on the low glass coffee table. "What an artistic arrangement," I said. "Do you have a regular florist?" I leaned into the arrangement. It was made of Calla lilies, tall spindly twigs, and some periwinkle blooms I didn't recognize.

Wait . . . Is that a bong holding those flowers?

I turned and shot Ham a conspiratorial grin.

He frowned back at me. "Sometimes we use a florist, but mostly the gardener brings stuff in," he said. "Take a seat." Ham cinched up his pants at his tree-trunk thighs and lowered himself onto the couch opposite me. The leather wheezed beneath him.

"Thirsty?" he asked. As if on cue a slender, middle-aged Latina woman with pursed lips marched through an archway to our right. She set out glasses and an iced tea pitcher with floating sprigs of mint.

"Tea would be great. Thanks."

The pitcher and glass looked like a child's tea set in Ham's huge hands as he poured it.

"Gracias, Marcia," he said.

"So, you come highly recommended by Reggie's boy Dwayne. How do you know Dwayne?"

I didn't know how to respond. First of all, I didn't know who he was talking about. Second, I thought Lucy had recommended me directly. Then I remembered seeing pictures of Reggie with Dwayne Smith, the basketball player. Was I supposed to act like I knew him? I'd met his wife once, at a fund-raiser with Lucy, but I didn't realize that she was anything more than an acquaintance. Lucy didn't seem to like her, referred to the dress she'd worn that night as skanky. So it was news to me that Lucy wanted to do a solid for Dwayne Smith's wife.

Unless she was trying to get rid of me.

An unmistakable gravelly voice saved me from having to lie to Ham. "I didn't expect you to be white," Rottie Wiles said from the balcony above us.

I could sense his cold appraisal of me.

He didn't know I was white? Would my whiteness count against me? I'd seen the guard and the maid, and they weren't white. Through the large glass windows a gardener worked in the yard. He wasn't white either.

"Well, I didn't expect you to be black, Mr. Wiles," I said. Immediately I realized what a stupid thing it was to say.

He took his time down the steps to the foyer and moved toward us, stony faced. "I'm so sorry, Mr. Wiles," I said.

Rottie turned his baseball cap forward and settled on the empty couch, his face still stern. Then a huge grin spread across his face.

"I'm just playing with you." Rottie laughed and flicked his fingers in the air.

Ham crossed his arms and dipped his head, chuckling into his chest, the first time he'd cracked a smile since I'd arrived.

I'd never thought of Rottie Wiles as handsome, but now, without his trademark grill to distract from his bright-almond skin and lean six-foot frame, I reconsidered. His features were more delicate up close than I realized, but not womanish. Interesting flecks of hazel lit up his dark eyes.

Rottie's smile faded, and he studied me. I struggled to maintain eye contact with him. I felt a giggle forming in my chest, as if we were playing the staring game and I was losing. I wanted to win this guy over.

"Thanks for having me here today, Mr. Wiles," I said.

He leaned in, pressed his palms together, and spoke slowly. "You can call me by my first name. I go by Reggie. Rottie don't exist no more. Want to make a clean break from my past."

That made sense. Rottie Wiles . . . Rottweiler. Smart of him to disassociate from anything dog related.

"Sounds good, Reggie," I said.

He brushed a dreadlock from his eyes and splayed his arms across the back of the couch. "You come highly recommended," he said. "I know all about you. Can I call you Alex?"

"Please do," I said, taking a deep breath and pulling my skirt down over my knees. "We actually met a few years ago in LA."

I sipped the tea, and it shocked my taste buds. I wasn't expecting it to be sweet.

"I don't remember that. Where'd you see me?" He glanced down and brushed something invisible from the shoulder of his white T-shirt, bored already at the prospect of having to relive our meeting.

"Video awards after-party," I said quickly. "It was brief. If you were someone off the street, I probably wouldn't have remembered you either."

Shit. That made it sound like I didn't find him memorable.

He raised an eyebrow. "Well, I *am* from the street." He looked at Ham, who chuckled again. "Alex, you from Cleveland, too, right?"

"Born and bred," I replied. That might have been the first time I'd ever used that phrase. He brought out an eagerness in me that made me uncomfortable. He reminded me of the disruptive kid that the teacher never seriously punished because she was either taken with his cleverness and charm or she was afraid of him.

"But not from the *streets.* Me and Ham, we came up in East Cleveland. Ever been there?" He glared at me as if my fate hinged on my response. What could I say? Like any white girl from the suburbs, I'd been warned to avoid that area. In fact, I had driven through once as a scared teenager after taking a wrong turn on my way home from a downtown bar that didn't card. I ran a red light when I spotted some kids, probably harmless, congregated on a street corner.

"Yes, I've been there," I said, hoping he wouldn't quiz me further.

"What were you doing there?" He smirked at me.

"Just driving through," I admitted.

He looked satisfied, as if I'd confirmed his hunch.

"Are your parents still in Cleveland?" he asked.

"Just my mother. My dad died when I was thirteen."

"Aw, man. I'm sorry."

"Thanks. It was a long time ago."

Reggie smacked his palms on his thighs. "Alright, I like you," he said. "I just have one more question for you."

"Shoot. I'm an open book." (Another saying I'd never uttered.)

Reggie leaned forward and stared at me. "Do you think," he said, putting strong emphasis on each word, "that I am a monster?"

"I can't answer that question," I said without a beat.

He leaned forward. "Why not?"

"Because I don't know you at all."

His eyebrows raised, and he turned to Ham, who returned his gaze with an almost imperceptible dip of his chin.

Reggie turned back to me. "When can you start?"

CHAPTER FOUR

Reggie's wall guard greeted me with a Taser-gun stare. *How does this guy not remember me from yester-day?* I asked myself. The gate slid open, my cue to drive forward.

I watched the guard, unmoving, in my rearview mirror. His back was to me. Beyond him on the street were two parked cars, a lone man in each one. Paparazzi. I hadn't noticed them in my nervousness. The guard's death stare was for them.

I'd never experienced first-day jitters before. None of the previous three jobs I'd held were anxiety induc-ing. Coffee shop barista in college, an internship at a county newspaper in Ohio that I was pretty sure only old people and shut-ins read. Then after graduation I went to visit Lucy in LA just as fame found her. I ended up staying there on the payroll as her assistant.

Ham met me in front of the house as he did the day before, in a military at-ease stance.

"Nice to see you again, Ham," I said, hopping out of the car.

'Mmm-hmm." His face was wary, annoyed. I wondered if he disliked me especially or if he treated everyone he met like a poker adversary. And I still wasn't clear on Ham's role: Security? Driver? Chief of staff? Was he my boss, too?

He rubbed his hands together. "Reg's recording today, so you gonna be with me." We stepped into the foyer, sunlight beaming down on us from a second-story window.

"That's exciting. Where does he record?"

"There's a home studio," he said. "It's on the main floor."

"How long has Reggie been here?" I asked.

Ham's mouth pulled to the side, and I realized it was a dumb question to ask. Reggie's nine-month jail term had ended two weeks ago, so he'd been here for that amount of time.

"He bought the house a year ago, and that's when we started renovations," he said. From the look on his face, I could tell he was already growing impatient with me.

"C'mon," he said, and led me to the kitchen. It was more modern than the rest of the interior, lit by a dozen exposed filament lightbulbs above concrete slab countertops. A picture window faced a shady stone patio and shimmering aqua pool that seemed to disappear into the bay. The smell of sugary dough and berries floated in the air, and Ham went right to the source, a cloth-covered basket. He helped himself to three muffins.

"Want one?"

I shook my head. My stomach was too turbulent for food.

Marcia, the woman who had served us tea the previous day, scrubbed the huge Viking stove. "I get you something, Miss Alex?" she asked, not turning around.

"Just some water, thanks," I said. "If you tell me where the cups are, I can get it myself."

"That is my job," she said, reaching into a cabinet. After she handed me a glass of water, she took her washrag and left us.

Ham pointed to an iPad and iPhone on the countertop. "Those are yours," he said, tearing into the second muffin. "You sign the forms?"

I retrieved a binder from my bag.

"Any questions?" he asked. His heavy eyes told me I should make my questions brief.

Rob had studied the contract the night before. He'd told me to ask for clarification on one item. "Can you explain what 'not engaging picketers' means?"

"Lots of people coming at Reggie and the crew. When you go out with him, you'll see it. And you need to stay cool."

"Oh, sure. I've dealt with that sort of thing before."

"Doubt you did," he said, narrowing his eyes. "This is a whole new level."

His seriousness made me squirm. "Are we talking about like PETA throwing red paint on us, or are we talking about bombs here?"

He didn't laugh. "Just keep your head down, don't talk to anybody, do what security tells you."

Was this why Reggie compensated so handsomely? Hazard pay?

Ham finished the third muffin in two bites and then slapped his palms on the counter. "C'mon. I'll give you the tour."

"You and I in charge of staff," he said, leading me out of the kitchen, past the cluster of couches in the living area. "I'm mostly focused on security, but I'll help you handle the rest until you know what to do. You met Marcia. She good. You don't have to babysit her." He shoved through a glass door to the atrium, and we stepped onto a marble walkway cutting through the mini jungle. The air was humid, like a rainforest. I gazed up at the cloudless sky through the glass-paneled ceiling, grazed the waxy oval leaves with my fingers.

"There's the garden and pool man, Xavier." Ham pointed to a little man on his knees trimming a hydrangea. Xavier waved at us. "If you walk around the property, you'll know if he's doing his job. I'll introduce you around to everybody else later." Ham stopped walking and turned to face me. "And I'm just showing you this stuff once, got it? I figure you know all this already. Me and Reg are busy and we don't have time for every little thing. You need to solve problems on your own, anticipate needs."

"I got it," I said.

A palm frond swished above, and then there was a beating sound, the batting of wings. I jolted when a giant bird came into view—yellow, blue, red, and orange—and landed on a branch a few feet away.

"That's Biggie," Ham said. "If anybody asks you, we don't know how he got here."

Biggie swooped after us to the indoor pool, where lazy waves of light bled along turquoise tiled walls. At the far end of the room, a garage-style glass-paneled wall separated the outdoor and indoor halves of the pool.

"Other than that you just answer to Reg and me. Whatever he wants. Shopping, handling his schedule, doing his parties—you know the drill."

Did I know the drill?

Lucy had plenty of money to throw at a party, enough to hire Miami's top chefs to cater. But with Reggie's net worth in the hundreds of millions, I couldn't imagine the extravagances his event budget would allow. Would he ask me to hire Cirque du Soleil to perform in his back-yard? Should I just go ahead and put a party planner on retainer? Did he already have one? And what did Ham mean about not bothering them with every little thing?

Reggie's voice broke in. "Ham, come to the studio."

My eyes searched around the pool area, but Reggie wasn't there. Ham thumbed in the direction of an in-tercom unit on the wall behind him. "Didn't think we'd get through the whole house. I'll fill you in on the rest later. But one more thing. You signed the nondisclosure agreement, but I just want to make sure. We know you wrote for a newspaper in Ohio. Don't think it needs mentioning, but you ain't here to write a book about Reggie or anything like that, are you?"

"Not at all."

He stared at me.

"It goes without saying."

"Good, because we might need you for some media stuff later."

"Sure. Anytime," I said, grinning despite myself. Lucy had never consulted with me on media relations matters. I'd offered my services, but she'd declined, say-ing she needed a publicist who specifically handled ce-lebrities. Her argument made sense. Nonetheless, her lack of confidence in me stung. I hoped my tenure with Reggie would be short, but if I could handle the de-mands of public relations for this mogul, perhaps Lucy would reconsider and give me a shot someday.

Ham and I meandered farther down the corridor to a passage with a horizontal traffic light above it. The light changed from red to green, and we entered yet another room that was larger than my entire apartment. Hundreds of white pyramid-shaped panels lined the walls. Beyond several rows of seating, two men in shiny suits and drivers' caps manned a long mixing board.

Reggie perched on a stool in a glassed-in box at the front of the room. When he saw Ham and me, he slid the headphones from his ears. "We ready to lay down the track," he said, his voice booming through the speakers in the room.

Several bandana- and jersey-clad men lounging in low white chairs swiveled their heads around. Their eyes traveled from my wedges to the preppie headband in my shoulder-length hair. I grinned and lifted my hand in a wave. Only one person acknowledged my gesture, with the tiniest of nods. Everyone else turned back to the booth, as if I were invisible. I shrunk into the empty seat next to Ham, feeling like the new kid nobody wanted to play with.

The producers adjusted some knobs on the soundboard and then pointed to Reggie. There was a beep, beep, beep, followed by an aggressive beat, all drums and bass, enveloping my ears. Reggie twisted to the music, his fingers twitching and his mouth moving as if he were counting beats. After a few measures, he cupped the headphones over his ears, closed his eyes, and began rapping.

I stay clean for a minute / But then I'm back up in it
The past comin' back to haunt me / Can't take refuge
in my luxury
Take this bitch I knew from a long time ago / I ain't
proud but my story's apropos
I talked sweet to her / Put diamonds on her
Knew she was obsolete/ Not like I stole her honor
Still gave that ass one more tap / Took that necklace
back
And gave it to her daughter

He jumped with the force of a pogo stick, twisting and landing with his feet together, dreadlocks following a beat later. His voice sounded crackly and smooth at the same time, perfectly in tempo with the music, not fumbling a word.

I got it all on tape / So she can't call it rape
Deleted my number / When she was under / Made a
clean escape
Years go by then I'm back up in da club / You know the
kind—two-drink minimum
This bitch jumps off the stage / Puts her phone up in
my face
Showin' me a picture of some kid that I don't know /
Said I fucked her and her momma three years ago

I couldn't help but move with Reggie, with the heads thrumming in front of me. I forgot my desire to disappear a moment ago and only felt the bass, which made me want to dance, work out really hard, or drive really fast. I wished I could film the performance for Rob, but I'd have to settle for telling him about it. He was going to be superjealous when he heard about this.

> *That kid don't look like me/ She just want my money*
> *Said I caused her ruin / She just spewin'/ Lies and*
> *treachery*
> *It's so hard not to sweat the small stuff/ All a sudden*
> *this club soda ain't strong enough*
> *I stay clean for a minute / But then it's just too tough*

"Hell yeah, Reg!" the bandana and jersey guys yelled. "This shit gonna go octuple platinum!" Their energy ran through me, and I clapped and whooped along with them. Despite being the only woman and the only white person in the room, I felt a sense of belonging. Reggie's lyrics were misogynistic, but I got it. It was tongue-in-cheek, a social commentary.

"Can I get a water?" Reggie asked, emerging from the booth, taking a towel from Ham and mopping his neck with it.

I launched myself toward the door, ready to perform my assistant duties. "Water. Got it."

I was so pumped that I was bursting. I called over my shoulder, "That was incredible, Rottie. You're so talented."

Reggie didn't reply. He probably hadn't heard me through the sound void. But when I turned around to say it again, he was staring right at me, hovering over the audio mixer. His mouth hung open in a mixture of disbelief and disgust. He looked at me like I'd just puked on his pristine white sneakers.

"Sorry," I said in a whisper, my cheeks heating up.

Had I broken his concentration? Spoken out of turn? Why had my compliment offended him?

I tried to make a quick exit, but the door didn't budge.

"Hold up," Ham said from across the room. He was standing in front of an open fridge with a frosty bottle of water, holding it at his side like a club. Silence permeated the room, too eerie even in this noise vacuum. Reggie's friends, who hadn't acknowledged me until this moment, now burned holes into me with their eyes.

I pulled, not pushed this time, and slunk out. Ham swung out of the door a second later and glowered at me.

"What the fuck is your problem?" he asked. He sounded like a subwoofer.

"I'm sorry." I found myself apologizing for the second time, though it wasn't clear what I'd done wrong.

"Do you even want this job?"

"Yes," I said, not knowing whether I meant it. I wanted my old job.

"Then get your shit together," Ham said.

How? I wanted to ask. *By learning where all the refrigerators are?* But I just stood there dumbfounded.

He crossed his arms and huffed out a breath. "You don't even know what you did, do you?"

I didn't want to answer him. His nostrils were flaring, and anything I said would just anger him more. I pursed my lips, waiting for him to tell me.

"You called him muthafucking *Rottie!*"

Christ. I was a fucking idiot. He'd told me to call him Reggie. He'd told the world to call him Reggie or Reginald. His friends, his crew hadn't even called him Rottie.

Existing in Lucy's orbit, even when it oscillated wildly, wasn't nearly as stressful and confusing as this. I never had to think about choosing my words carefully. I couldn't wait to get back to that safe place, where I could say whatever came to mind without offending because we were "Lucy and Alex," and it didn't matter.

This territory belonged to Ham and Reggie. I was on the outside.

CHAPTER FIVE

My phone blew up as I drove to work the next day, tightening my already wound nerves. Having no desire to go inside and face Reggie, who was probably going to fire me, I stalled in his turnaround beside a fountain with a statue of a topless woman. I checked my texts. Reggie needed me to get him some shoes and a gift for his four-year-old daughter. Good. I had an errand. *At least the shoes will be easy,* I thought. But what did four-year-olds play with? Would she choke on Legos? Maybe Reggie figured I could magically tune myself into the whims of a small child because I had prior experience assisting a celebrity. I didn't want to ask him about it in case this fell into the category of "every little thing."

My phone rang again five minutes later, just as I reached Bayside Marketplace. I shouldn't have answered, but my mother would just keep calling until I picked up. If you asked her about our relationship, she'd say we were close and that we'd clung to each other after my dad's death when I was thirteen.

I called her Mom to her face but thought of her as Denise.

Denise's voice assaulted me in stereo through my car speakers. "Honey, why are you working for that man? Are you in financial trouble?"

"Hi to you too, Mom," I said as I patrolled the parking garage, searching for a spot. I pictured her sitting at her kitchen table like she usually did when she talked on the phone, fingernail scraping dirt off her vinyl tablecloth with pictures of fruit on it. "My finances are fine. Why do you ask?"

"I don't care how famous that Rottie Wiles is. He's scum," she said. "I'm friends with some animal groups on the Facebook. Do you know about all the horrible things he did to those poor defenseless animals?"

"Yes, I do. But he served his time, and the job pays very well. Also, he goes by Reggie now."

"Well, money isn't everything, dear. And I don't see how you can be so callous. Does he think that if he starts calling himself Reggie everyone will just forget what he did?"

I didn't respond.

"Speaking of the Facebook, why won't you let me be your friend?"

I groaned and slammed my SUV into reverse to make way for a gold Lexus pulling out of a spot, its sparkling finish burning my retinas. I pressed on my temples and imagined what would happen if Denise became my Facebook friend. She'd jam my wall with teddy bear memes that said sappy shit like "Share If You Love Your Daughter."

"Um, I don't really check Facebook, Mom," I lied, charging into the parking space before a bald man in the Corvette convertible across from me could take it. I shut my car off and put my phone to my ear. "I'll accept your friend request next time I'm on there if I don't close my account. I've been thinking about doing that." I needed to remember to block her from my page.

"What about your job with Lucy? I thought she was done with the drugs," Denise said, her voice lowering to a whisper at the word "drugs." I wondered if she had a guest at her house. Did anyone ever come to her house anymore? I didn't bother asking. If I stayed out of her business, maybe she would stay out of mine.

"It's a long process," I said. "You wouldn't understand."

"What's there to understand? You two have always been attached at the hip! What happened?"

My insides tightened. *That's what I would like to know, too.*

"I really don't have time to go into it right now," I said, hurrying down the walkway toward Foot Locker.

"Well, why don't you try to get a job where you can use your degree? It's been three years since you graduated and you haven't done a thing with your college education."

"A lot of people don't end up in the fields they majored in," I said, trying not to let her rile me. "And anyway, I'm going to go back to work for Lucy when she's ready."

"Alex, do you really want to keep working for these self-absorbed people?"

Again, I kept silent, let it slide that she called my best friend self-absorbed.

"Do you know what kind of man your new boss is?" I could hear her anxiety dialing up as she talked faster and faster. She was on her feet now. I could hear the familiar sound of her mannish clogs squeaking against linoleum. "If he could torture animals that way, you can be sure it doesn't end there. You know, there are studies that prove—"

Anger bubbled and rose in me, and I interrupted her. "Would you stop for a minute and calm down? Look, this thing with Reggie isn't permanent, and why should his past concern me? He had a different upbringing. He grew up in East Cleveland with his dad doing that stuff, and now he's done with it."

I spotted the Foot Locker sign a couple stores down. "Listen, I have to go."

"Alright, Alex. But I don't see how you can say that man's atrocities don't *concern* you. Especially after how you were raised."

A ball of fury, the kind that only Denise could mold so round and tight, burned its way up my esophagus. I flung myself down on a cement bench in front of the shoe store, banging my tailbone hard. She'd just referred to the torment she'd inflicted as *raising* me.

And why was she telling me how to live my life? Hers was a disaster that bled into mine while I was growing up.

"I have to go," I said. "I have another call." Before she could get one more word in, I hung up.

I pushed my wallet and sunglass case aside in my purse, searching for my pack of Parliaments. They weren't there. For a second I was tempted to go back to my car, but that would waste too much time. All I had to do was run in and get the shoes. I'd be smoking angrily soon enough.

The only person on the Foot Locker sales floor was a kid with an asymmetrical haircut who looked like he smoked weed under the bleachers while his more clear-eyed classmates played sports.

"I need the new LeBrons in a size eleven, please."

The kid hunched forward, placing his fist over his mouth. His narrow shoulders started to heave with silent laughter. "Yeah, they sold out like three seconds after we opened," he said when he caught his breath.

Well, crap.

This gig with Reggie was starting to look even more temporary than I'd imagined. If Reggie were to fire me, Lucy might decide that I'd failed her again.

CHAPTER SIX

I felt a low rumble when I set foot in Reggie's. Either I ate something that didn't agree, or my sense of foreboding now had a soundtrack to accompany it. I figured it was best to tell Reggie right away that I'd failed to obtain the new LeBrons. I followed the reverberating noise, figuring he was in the gaming room. The pulsing tweaked on my nerves, giving me the sensation that my entire body was shaking.

I found the gaming room empty and silent. But what else could cause the walls to shake? I continued following the sound. The thundering grew more intense until I spotted a door with a blue sliver of light shining through the cracks. Knocking would be futile over the racket, so I just stuck my head inside.

The room was concrete and bare, like a drained Olympic pool or an Area 51 government lab. In the center was a giant shell, an oscillating pod that appeared to have been sliced in half. Reggie and Ham were sitting inside it, their backs facing me. They wore headsets, surrounded on three sides by screens and hundreds of buttons and levers. I watched for a minute as they worked the controls.

Then in unison they threw their hands in the air. The machine and the blue lights powered down. Ham stood and turned, ripping his headset off. He spotted me.

"What?" he hollered.

I wanted to disappear. "Sorry to interrupt," I said.

"We fireballed the motherfucking reentry, anyways," Reggie said, spinning in his seat and gesturing for me to come closer.

Moving toward him, I noticed the NASA logo on the side of the pod. It was dizzying to think about the money one must have to commission NASA for a space shuttle simulator.

And I couldn't even get him a stupid pair of shoes.

"They sold out of the new Lebrons," I said. "But they're expecting another shipment next week."

Reggie sighed.

"That don't make no sense," Ham said. "We'll talk about it later."

"Sure," I murmured, trudging out of the room.

I busied myself sorting Reggie's vitamins and supplements, placing them in trays for the days of the week like Ham had showed me the day before. Would they fault me for not getting in line at 5 a.m. to purchase the latest signature Nikes? I scanned the wheat-colored ceramic tile for an Omega-3 pill that had slipped out of my grasp, wondering how I was supposed to know those shoes would be so popular. Of course I should know, I told myself, snatching up the supplement and tossing it into the trash drawer. That was my job.

A throat cleared behind me, and I whisked my head around to see Ham standing beside the long kitchen table, arms crossed.

"Did you talk to our guy?"

Nobody had mentioned a guy.

"No," I said, embarrassed to look at him.

"You didn't check your email then."

My email. I didn't remember seeing a message from Ham. I pulled my phone out and checked my Gmail. Nothing.

"Sorry, but I don't see anything here. Maybe it went to my spam folder."

"Ain't likely. I set it up myself."

He set it up? That would mean . . . *Oh shit.* I found the iPhone he had issued me the day before. Sure enough, there was a different email account on it with several messages from Terence Johnson. I opened the first one.

Terence Johnson, yesterday, 7:55 p.m.: *Look at yachts to charter.*
Terence Johnson, yesterday, 7:57 p.m.: *Or he might buy a yacht.*
Terence Johnson, yesterday, 9:12 p.m.: *Go to Aventura Mall Finish Line and ask for Samuel. He's holding Reggie's Lebrons.*

This was my strike two. But why so many portals of communication? It seemed like they were setting me up for failure. I hadn't done a single thing right since they hired me.

"I'll go get them now," I said.

When I returned, Ham met me at the door. I handed him the $400 shoes that Samuel at Finish Line had given to me for free. Ham reeled off a list of tasks for the day, so I guessed they weren't firing me for now. Reggie wanted a tiki bar installed in the middle of the outdoor pool; he needed me to pick up his new commissioned jewelry piece from a store downtown for an upcoming video shoot; and Biggie the parrot hadn't come down from the rafters above the indoor pool all night.

What did they expect me to do? Climb up there and somehow persuade a bird to do my will? Was the bird supposed to hop on my shoulder like I was Snow White? My fingers jumped to my teeth, but I stopped before chipping into my fresh gel polish.

He handed me a set of keys. "For the panic room," he said. "Once you get the new bling, go put it in there."

Cool, but what about the wild animal trapped in the ceiling? I wanted to ask. He left me in the entranceway before I could better formulate my question.

I headed toward the garage, where one of Reggie's employees was bent over a yellow Ferrari, buffing it in circular strokes. He pulled a giant headphone off one ear when he saw me.

"Is there a ladder in here?"

He shook his head. "Check the garden house."

I didn't know there was a garden house.

He told me it was behind the garage. I followed an uneven stone path around the huge structure to find yet another white stucco building. This made four separate buildings on the estate—the house, pool house (bigger than my childhood home), the mansion of a garage, and now a garden house. Perhaps I'd find a hospital or a museum beyond that.

I located a stepladder and a rake in the well-organized space and dragged them inside to the pool area. A smattering of bird poop on the cement told me where Biggie was hiding. Grateful that the ceiling wasn't as high as most of the other ones in the house, I unhinged the ladder and climbed it with no plan whatsoever. The parrot watched me with its beady eyes and flapped one azure wing.

"C'mere, Biggie," I said without conviction, holding my hand up like a perch. His feathers puffed, and he buried his head in his chest. I climbed back down the ladder and googled "things parrots eat." The results were seeds, pellets, fruits, and vegetables. I headed to the kitchen, helped myself to a dish of Marcia's fruit salad, and popped a mango slice on the way back. It exploded in my mouth, sweet as candy. If this didn't bring him down, nothing would.

Once at the top of the ladder beyond the rung that warned not to go any higher, I held up the entire bowl of fruit. Biggie puffed up even fatter and turned his yellow head away. My only other option was to scare him from the rafters. I went back down for the rake and climbed again. His head popped out from the mound of feathers when I slashed the air with the prongs just below him. When I waved the rake again, he started flapping. One more swipe and he went airborne, diving straight at me.

I ducked, dropping the rake on the ground. It hit the floor with a loud clang that echoed through the tiled room as the bird descended on me. His beak, which was hard as stone, pecked me on the top of my head. I clambered down the ladder and ran, hearing the beating of wings behind me.

The bird was screaming now, a war cry. Not knowing what else to do, I jumped into the deep end of the pool. The chlorinated water soothed the sting on my head, and I sunk down and down, wondering how long I could hold my breath. The tips of my pointy flats touched the bottom, and I let myself hover there. In the silence, I felt trapped. I made bad choices in these situations.

Pressure started crowding my lungs, and I chose scalping over drowning. I pushed up to the surface, gasped for air.

Ears popping, I heard a chittering sound that I assumed was the bird gnashing his beak before he dove for another chunk of my skull. I treaded water and scanned the air above me, ready to go under again. Then I saw two figures, Reggie and Ham standing side by side at the edge of the pool. Chlorine blurred my vision, and I couldn't make out their expressions right away. But there was a tie-dyed blur of color on Reggie's shoulder. Biggie.

I paddled to the pool's edge and hoisted myself out.

Standing there sopping before them, I realized the water had rendered my linen shirt transparent. I threw my arms across my chest.

Ham's face was vacant, of course, and Reggie wore a smirk. He stroked the bird's head and gestured at the ladder sprawled on the ground. "You should've had Xavier get him for you," he said. Biggie's creepy black tongue waggled, as if he were making fun of me.

"You gonna mix the cement yourself to build that tiki bar next?" Ham said, one corner of his mouth pulling up.

This was the third time I'd made an ass of myself in three days. At least they seemed more amused than pissed. But still, I looked like a moron.

I mumbled an apology and left. On the way to get Reggie's custom bling, I drove with the windows down, trying to dry myself off. But it was so humid out that my clothes were still damp when I returned with Reggie's jewelry, a diamond-encrusted medallion in the likeness of an old Super Nintendo remote.

Grasping the key Ham had given me, I tried to remember which hallway housed the panic room. It would be barely visible because the door blended seamlessly into the wall. I had to feel for a difference in the plaster. It was in the second corridor that I chose. I turned the key and pushed inside, metal creaking. A light flickered on automatically, and my breath caught.

Surely, they did not want me to see this.

Along the cement walls were hooks holding thick chains bearing more precious metal medallions: an alien head with emerald bug eyes, the Mr. Hero logo, and what appeared to be a miniature gold urn holding ashes. These items were probably worth more money than my dad had made during his entire tenure as a Ford salesman. But the Egyptian tomb–grade treasures weren't what shocked me. Long racks held a large arsenal of handguns, shotguns, and even an automatic-looking rifle.

Was this some kind of initiation? A way of making sure I wouldn't be easily scared off? Reggie's wall guards carried weapons, and I could deal with that, but being confronted with this stockpile was different. Reggie was letting me in on a secret. As a felon, he couldn't own guns, and he would go to jail if the authorities found out. After my blunders, it didn't make sense that he would trust me with this knowledge.

Maybe he hadn't given it a thought. As rich as he was, maybe he took for granted the implications, figured he was above the law. Or perhaps he figured the intimidation factor of this room was enough to keep me quiet.

My rational mind knew that none of these inanimate guns could shoot me. But my baser instinct told me to get the fuck out of there. I hung the new piece of jewelry on an empty hook, hurried through the metal door, and sealed it shut.

This was enough for one day. I'd deal with the tiki bar tomorrow. I wanted to talk to Lucy, tell her about the military bunker, ask her if it was crazy that I didn't want to go back there. Explain myself in case I had to quit, since I was supposedly doing this for her. I didn't have the courage to ask Reggie and Ham how much longer they would need me. Maybe Lucy knew. I fought the urge to call her because I'd promised myself I'd give her space.

CHAPTER SEVEN

I ended up texting Lucy. Nothing needy, just *Hey, wanted to check in and see how you're doing. Miss you!* I hoped she would text me back and tell me Tatiana was annoying her and was doing a terrible job filling in for me, but she didn't text me back at all.

I also had a couple cocktails that night, tried to forget about the day's events. That might have been the reason for my weird dreams, one of which involved Biggie holding me up with a tiny pistol. He talked to me, his wormy tongue working hard to form the words. I don't remember what he said, but it must have been funny because my own laughter woke me up.

But the guns weren't so funny. Still, I couldn't picture Reggie shooting someone. He didn't strike me as an impulsive, rash man. He seemed to be in complete control, deliberate in the way he carried himself and spoke. He refrained from tweeting ridiculous or insulting things—that's a tall order for a lot of stars.

Then I thought of the clip of Reggie I'd watched right after I interviewed with him for my job. It was an appearance he had done on a nighttime show before the dog-fighting scandal broke. He came across as extremely likeable. He seemed to genuinely like the talk show's host, and they had the chemistry of two guys hanging out at home, shooting the shit, seeing who could make the other laugh the hardest. Reggie told a story about his childhood. He said he was runty until high school, and the meanest kid in his fifth-grade class challenged him to a fight.

"Well, you know I had to go meet that kid behind the school or I'd just be scared of my shadow forever. So I hired the biggest brother I knew to be my bodyguard."
The host broke in: "So you've always been flush with cash?"
Reggie [deadpan]: "You saying you think I stole the money? I earned it at my job at H&R Block. Way to stereotype a [bleep]."
The host chuckled.

Reggie: "So after the bell rings, I'm waiting for this guy with my hired security, hoping he won't show. But he comes around the corner, running straight at me, and his eyes are pure evil, like a mad dog. My bodyguard jumps out of the way. I'm ready to die, but the dude stops right in front of me, smiles, and picks me up. Then he carries me about ten feet to the dumpster and throws me in."

Host: "So he humiliated you. Wasn't that worse than getting beat up?"

Reggie: "Hell no. I wouldn't have gotten my iconic name without him. Everyone started calling me 'Rottie' because I stunk like rotting trash."

Most people assumed his rapper name was dog fighting related, but it wasn't. I wondered if he minded changing it.

I wondered if Tatiana was holding Lucy's phone hostage, because she still hadn't texted me back by eleven thirty the next day when Ham, Reggie, and I piled into Reggie's black Mercedes SUV. Reggie wore an unexpected ensemble, a lilac button-down and chinos. Good for him, I thought.

The paparazzi on the street in front of Reggie's estate trailed us off the island. Reggie and Ham talked to each other, not to me. I demolished my manicure, wishing for a cigarette. I gathered the little chips of crimson from the seat and floor and dropped them in my purse.

The paparazzi followed us to the parking station outside the glowing white Shore Club, where Reggie's supervised visit with his daughter, Mackenzie, would take place. There was only one attendant at the valet stand, a young kid with bleach blond hair and cargo shorts. I figured by the time that kid could valet the paparazzi's cars, we'd already be inside.

But as soon as we pulled up, the men tailing us skidded to a halt and ditched their cars right in the middle of Collins Avenue. They hurried toward us, scrambling with their oversized cameras. Horns blared from all around. People on the sidewalk stopped and squinted at our dark windows, trying to see who was inside.

"Stay close," Ham said. He pushed out of the SUV and opened the door for Reggie. "Back off," he said in a low roar to the photographers, who were now crouched on one knee between us and the hotel. I snatched Mackenzie's gift and let myself out as the valet jumped into our ride. I scurried around the car after my bosses.

Ham wrapped himself around Reggie and funneled him forward. I stayed at their heels. Behind us a girl shouted "Murderer!" I spun around to see a petite college-aged brunette in a hippie dress. She looked straight at me, her lip curled. "How does it feel to be an accomplice to murder?"

I froze and clutched Mackenzie's present in front of me like a shield.

"What you doing?" Ham called from the entrance. "C'mon."

I reeled around and dashed into the hotel.

"Why'd you stop?" Ham asked once we were in the elevator. I shrugged, trying to shake off that woman's harsh words. I had wanted to point out to her that I neither participated in, nor covered up, any murders and therefore I couldn't technically be an accomplice. I had wanted to tell her it was just a job. But that wasn't true. Slinging ladies' sportswear was just a job. Waiting tables or working a reception desk was just a job. Those vocations meant carefully budgeting to make rent and buying a used economy car. I didn't have to do any of those things, because this was not just a job.

We reached our floor and stepped off the elevator. A young bellhop stood waiting for us outside a room. He fidgeted, trying to suppress a shy grin as we walked toward him.

"Hey, man," Reggie said to the kid. He tapped Ham on the elbow, and Ham passed a hundred-dollar bill to the hotel worker.

"Thank you so much. I'm such a fan, Reggie," the kid said, knocking twice and inserting a key card into the door's slot. He had to be a big fan to know to call him Reggie.

"Good to know. I'll be back and I'll ask for you next time we here, Daniel," he said, reading the kid's name tag. Daniel swung the door open and we stepped inside.

A black woman and a white woman, both stylishly dressed in neutral tones, stood side by side in front of a picture window overlooking the turquoise ocean, as if posing for our arrival. Mackenzie jumped from a squatted position on the floor, Barbie in one hand, Ken in the other. The girl's hair, startlingly long and full for such a young child, poured out from a bow at her crown in a shimmery, dark fountain. She dropped her dolls and scuttled toward the women.

To my surprise, Mackenzie went to the white woman. She grasped her legs and peered at Reggie with big, alert eyes. The black woman strode up to Reggie and shook his hand. "Mr. Wiles, good to see you again."

Just like me to misread a room.

Kim, blond and compact, stroked Mackenzie's hair. "It's okay, baby." She shot Reggie a dirty look. "She wouldn't be like this if you'd been around."

"Or if you let me see her more," he retorted.

Kim rolled her eyes. "That's the court's choice, as you well know." Her skin was like bronzed velvet, but the effect stopped just above her neck. "I guess you found a suitable assistant," she said, her hazel eyes traveling from my head to my Chanel flats. "Interesting choice."

What does that mean?

She turned to Ham and her expression softened. "How's it going, Ham?"

"Oh, you know, same old same old," he replied, rubbing the back of his neck.

Reggie puffed out a sharp breath and turned to me. "Where's my girl's swag?"

I handed him the package, and he stooped down to Mackenzie's level. "You want to open your present?"

She unpressed her face from her mother's rear, but her feet stayed put.

"Here you go, baby," Reggie said in a gentle voice, setting the gift on the floor halfway between them.

Kim patted Mackenzie's head. "Go open it."

Mackenzie emerged from her hiding space, the squares from the carpet pattern still indented on her tiny knees. She tentatively worked at the Disney wrapping, letting little paper feathers drift to the floor. As she revealed more and more of the colorful box, she began ripping with vigor.

"A puppy! Look, Momma!"

Kim's thick, partially drawn-on eyebrows raised.

Reggie whirled around and glared at me, and I recognized his expression. It was the same way he'd looked at me in the studio when I'd called him Rottie—like I'd barfed in his hot tub.

A sick realization came over me. I had chosen the most inappropriate item from the toy store. I purchased one of those robotic dogs that could sit, roll over, and bark. Not the best gift from a man trying to distance himself from an animal cruelty conviction.

"I just thought she would like it," I said in a small voice.

Kim let out a sour laugh and started slow clapping. "That's rich. I like her."

All eyes were on me. Even the pants-suited social worker observed me with interest from the desk chair. I held my breath. A random thought came to mind. If they threw me out, I'd have to fend off protesters alone out there while waiting for an Uber. They had looked like they were itching for a fight.

Mackenzie, forgotten in the moment, scampered over to her father and pushed the box into Reggie's legs. He froze in surprise as she beamed up at him. Then, with a big grin, he started flapping his arms, pretending to fall backward, catching himself at the last second. Mackenzie giggled and hopped up and down on bare feet. "Can you open it, Daddy?"

Reggie went to work on the dozen or so twist ties securing the toy to its cardboard packaging, while Mackenzie bounced around with excitement. He freed the plush white puppy and flipped a switch on its underside. The toy crouched down on its hind legs and let out a mechanical yap. Mackenzie shrieked with glee and imitated the puppy's yoga pose. One of her rainbow hair clips dislodged and slid down a wavy strand of black hair. Kim sauntered over and pulled it out.

"Well, guess she likes it," Kim said, dropping the barrette into her purse.

"Yeah, guess so," Reggie said without looking at Kim. He lurched downward, joining Mackenzie in imitating the toy's every move.

"Daddy, thank you!" she said, leaping up and charging him. Reggie caught her and hoisted her above his head. "You're welcome, sweet girl," he said.

"Again," she cried, and he flipped her over his shoulders, dipping her until she was inches above the floor.

The social worker looked up from her tablet and smiled.

After they'd played for a couple hours, Mackenzie and Reggie lay in bed next to one another eating room-service quesadillas and watching cartoons. Kim reclined on the other bed, engrossed in her phone, snapping a couple of selfies. I sat on the sofa next to Ham, going over Reggie's schedule on my new iPad. Ham nudged my arm, an actual smile on his face. "I ain't seen them like this in a while," he whispered.

CHAPTER EIGHT

I wanted to celebrate the unexpected home run I hit for Reggie. Rob didn't answer when I called. No matter. It would be fun to surprise him with Chinese takeout. I knocked on his door, bearing chopsticks and dumplings.

Rob, shirtless, threw his door open. He looked tired, blotchy, and bloodshot. "Hey, what's going on?" he said.

"Did I wake you up or something?" I asked. "Are you feeling okay?"

"Yeah, why?"

"You look a little run-down," I said. I tried not to be too obvious about inhaling his hairless chest as I scooted past him into the apartment.

"Thought I'd surprise you with dinner," I said, heading over to his Restoration Hardware bar that resembled a copper submarine, where I chose a bottle. "This okay?" I asked, holding up a Syrah.

"Uh, I'm sorry, babe," he said. "I actually have to write a brief." His voice was higher than usual, and he was talking fast. He wasn't tired at all.

"Really? You seem kind of buzzed," I plucked a corkscrew from one of the hooks inside of the pod.

"Just found out about it."

"That sucks." I poured the red liquid into a stemless wineglass. "You work like twelve hours a day, and then they spring this shit on you. Do you have to work all night again?"

"Probably."

I took his stubbled chin in my hand. "Well, there are noodles and dumplings on the counter for you. I'll go into your room and watch a movie while you work." I didn't mind. His place was the perfect escape, with the cool slate blues and clean lines of a spa. It smelled like a spa, too, because he kept expensive aromatherapy candles around to mask the ashtray scent that drifted in from the balcony.

He pulled my hand away from his face. "This is for a pretty big case. I should probably concentrate."

"You want me to make you some coffee?"

"I can't focus if you're in the next room."

"Awww, thanks," I said, planting a kiss on him. "I think I'll watch a Jason Bourne movie." I liked watching action movies in his bedroom because the sound system was set up so the gunshots came from every direction.

He grabbed my forearm, startling me, and a drop of wine spilled from my glass onto the sofa. I picked up a paper towel that was sitting on the coffee table, sending a puff of white dust floating in the air.

I looked down at the table. Where the towel had been, there was a little mountain of more white powder. A Platinum American Express card and a few long, telltale smudges told me that the pile had started out bigger.

"You don't have to hide this from me," I said. He knew I didn't partake anymore after Lucy's habit got out of hand, but I didn't care if he did it now and then.

He threw his hands up and plopped down on the chair beside the coffee table, then rolled up a one-hundred-dollar bill and put it to his nose. He used large denominations because they hadn't circulated as much as the ones and fives.

"What's wrong?" I asked.

He stopped mid-dive and waved the money. "It's just—I really need to concentrate."

"I can see that." For a split second I wanted to join him there, hovering over the table. There was nothing like that first bump lighting up your brain like a Christmas tree. But somewhere around the fifth bump, the tinsel wraps itself in knots. You could chase it with booze, but then you end up going back and forth from one substance to another, trying to get the levels right, until finally, inevitably, you overdo it to the point of being sick and depressed. I'd seen Lucy go through the same thing many times, but on a grander scale, over days instead of an evening.

"Okay, then. Some other night," I said, slugging down the rest of my wine and setting it on the coffee table.

He leaned back and pinched his nose. "Now you're mad."

I thought about wrapping my arms around him, asking him what was really going on inside his head, but I stayed put. "No. You're the one who seems angry," I said.

He leapt up, squeezing his fists and gritting his teeth. "Why are you being so fucking condescending?" His eyes were pinned, flashing.

"What the hell—?"

His cell rang, and my eyes followed the sound to the kitchen counter. The caller ID read "Waverly," the name of his building. Rob strode across the room and snatched it up. He took it to the bathroom and shut himself in.

I stood there, feeling stung, confused. Maybe he was just in a bad mood. I didn't need to make a big deal out of it. He'd probably be calling me later to apologize. I picked up my things and trudged out of his apartment.

As I stepped from the elevator to the lobby of Rob's building, my eyes were drawn to a Latina woman wearing a halter top and denim shorts unbuttoned and folded in a slutty game of peek-a-boo with a lime-green bikini bottom. A phone was glued to her ear, and she shouted and stomped, changing direction every few steps like a sexy robot gone haywire. It was hard not to stare because her presence took up the entire sitting area. She whirled around and came right at me, head down, absorbed.

I swerved out of the way.

"You don't tell somebody to come over and then just leave," she said in a shrill Colombian accent. For a second I thought she was talking to me. I slowed my walk and pretended to search for something in my bag while I stole little glances. The front desk worker was watching her, too. Her nostrils flared, and she tossed her raven shampoo-commercial hair. "What does that mean, you 'have to write a brief'?"

Oh my god. She's talking to Rob.

That asshole didn't even know that I had left. He was probably still shut up in his bathroom trying to calm his mistress down. Or was she a hooker?

If I were the fearless female that *Cosmo* magazine told me to be, I would have walked right up to her, calmly tapped her on the shoulder, and informed her that Rob was in fact upstairs. But it was all I could do to get out of there before I turned into a puddle on the mosaic tile floor.

The door leading outside felt lighter than I remembered. It slammed into the side of the building as I left.

I got in my car and drove with no destination in mind. Just not home. I liked to take my depression public so it didn't taint my everyday surroundings. After my dad's funeral, when everyone had left our house looked dirty, though it was spotlessly clean for the guests. The gravity of life without him settled in like a thick layer of dust.

Not that I considered my apartment home. Up until recently it served more as a catchall for my things while I pretty much lived with Lucy.

I scrolled through my mental list of people who might meet me for a drink and realized I'd never hung out with any of them without Lucy. I piggybacked on her friendships just as I piggybacked on her life. That left my former next-door neighbor, Isabelle. When she'd moved out she'd given me her phone number, but I never thought I'd use it.

CHAPTER NINE

I sabelle agreed to meet me at The Abbey, a rare unpolished gem in glittery South Beach, where most drinking establishments had the atmosphere of a glamorous street riot. But here, with its hops-infused, wood-paneled walls and a long row of colorful taps as its most decorative feature, it reminded me of the unpretentious bars in my college town of Athens, Ohio. Living in Miami made me appreciate bars where patrons left their shirts on and respected each other's personal space.

Heads turned, and I followed the gaze of nearly every man (and a few women) to Isabelle's frame in the doorway. I waved and she spotted me, her face igniting as she clasped her hands and did a little leap. I felt like a jerk. Until now she didn't exist to me outside of our tipsy evenings together on our shared balcony. We were friends by proximity, not real friends.

"I am so glad you called," she said in her heavy Swiss-French accent, hugging my neck.

"Me too," I said, patting her forearm.

"Were you crying?" she asked, pulling back and searching my face. "You sounded upset when we spoke."

"Ugh, it's nothing. Just a long day." I swiped under my eyes to catch any makeup that might have migrated downward.

We ordered drinks from a grisly-bearded bartender. I didn't want to talk about Rob. "How have you been since you moved out?" I asked.

"It has been difficult, but I must stay away from Jean-Marc."

I nodded as if I understood, but I never got her fatal attraction to my next-door neighbor, Jean-Marc. He was about twenty years too old for her, overweight, and always seemed to be covered in a layer of grease. One time he asked me if I was "down with the ménage." It made no sense. She couldn't have been with that sleaze for money, because he lived beside me in a mirror of my own bare-bones, one-bedroom apartment.

"You're probably right to just cut him off completely," I said. "It'll get easier." My words felt empty in the wake of my fresh heartbreak. I wanted to call Rob.

She twirled her hair and gazed at the row of backlit liquor bottles across from us. "Things are getting better because I have received some good news. *Marie Claire* magazine chose me for a photo shoot."

"Whoa. You're perfect for that magazine."

"Do you think so? This is the best job I have ever received, so I hope you're correct," she said. "They are flying me to a location."

"Seriously? Where do you get to go?"

"The great state of Kansas," she said matter-of-factly.

I had been expecting her to say something like Venice or Belize. "Wow . . . Kansas."

"The theme is called 'prairie goddess,' so they are taking me to the prairies." I pictured her decked out in gingham, surrounded by romantically fading sunlight and overgrown dead grass, her wheat-colored hair done in messy pigtails.

Isabelle batted her lashes and ordered shots from the misplaced lumberjack behind the bar.

"*Tequila?* Guess I'm not driving," I said.

She waved her willowy arm. "We will take the Uber."

We watched the silvery liquid stream into the tiny glasses, and we downed our shots. The smooth burn felt good in the back of my throat, and the sour lime paired well with the bitterness inside me. I hoped that Rob was feeling that same burn but knew he probably wasn't. He was probably feeling what was under that girl's short shorts right now.

Isabelle plunked her glass down and turned to me, her blue crystal-chandelier eyes all a-sparkle. "We should go clubbing."

"I don't know." I was more in a bar-stool-slumping state of mind than a dancing one. And I remembered how wasted she would sometimes get on the balcony. I didn't want to be responsible for someone tonight.

She jumped up. "I have to go to the toilet."

The liquor started to kick in while she was gone, softening the music and conversations around me, but bringing with it a pervading sense of loneliness. I started ruminating about Rob, how he'd turned out to be just another guy after all and not a man. None of it made sense—I'd thought we were well on our way to falling in love. How had this happened? I felt pathetic. My thoughts sounded pathetic inside my head.

I glanced around the pub. A college-aged guy with baby smooth skin and a square jaw caught my eye and raised his pint to me. Too young, I thought, shaking my head to make sure he didn't get inside it. He lowered his glass and turned back to his buddies. He wouldn't have looked at me if Isabelle wasn't in the bathroom. She was one of the three gorgeous women on earth who could pull off straight-across bangs.

Jean-Marc had once remarked we could be sisters, and I'd joked that it was the nicest thing anyone had ever said to me. Then he took it back.

"Ah, cousins perhaps."

He was right. Isabelle and I have similar coloring and bone structure, but put us side by side and you'd see she has gotten the best genes of our imaginary shared bloodline. Taller, thinner, shinier.

Isabelle returned from the bathroom. "How about we grab some dinner?" I asked.

"Dinner sounds awesome." She was a little too enthusiastic about my suggestion for someone who by the looks of her would be ordering a side salad with no cheese.

We had another beer and chatted some more about her modeling gigs.

It was dusk when we stepped out of the bar into the balmy tropical air. A hazy streetlight illuminated a 6 a.m. tow zone sign that I didn't remember being there before. "Damn it," I said, pointing at the sign. "I'm in no shape to drive right now."

"I have an extra spot at my new place," Isabelle said.

I paused and tried to set aside my tipsy optimism that was telling me I'd actually rise at five thirty the next morning to walk back here and retrieve my car.

"It is only three blocks that way," she said, pointing to our right.

We hopped into my car. Rap music blared when I started my engine, an old Rottie Wiles song that was playing on my iPod.

You actin' all street with them hoes and that big stack/
Playin' like you know
You just playin' with yo' ball sack

"Sorry," I yelled, fumbling for the volume.

"It is okay, I like it," she hollered back after I had muted the stereo. We looked at each other and burst into giggles.

"This is my new boss rapping," I said.

"Pardon? You no longer are with Lucy Adler?"

"Not at the moment," I said. "But I'll be going back to work for Lucy soon. She's going through some changes right now."

Isabelle raised her eyebrow. "So you have a new job?"

"That's how it goes when you work for megastars."

"What an interesting life you must lead. I always want to ask you questions about your famous people, but I know that you are not allowed to discuss their affairs." A coy smile spread across her face. "Can you tell me just one detail about what you do? Something that will not get you into trouble, of course."

"Mmm." I gazed up at the sunroof and opened it while I thought. Isabelle watched me like I was a magician about to show her a mind-bending card trick.

"Okay, here's a good one. You know that movie Lucy did called *In Too Deep*, where she lived on the lake? The one that ended in a boat chase?"

"Yes. I remember it. The boyfriend turned out to be a terrorist, correct?"

"That's the one," I said. "When she got cast for it, she told the director she could water-ski, but she'd never water-skied in her life. We were living in LA back then, and a couple weeks before shooting started we went and stayed at her friend's house on Lake La Quinta so she could learn how to water-ski."

"She looked like a professional. She learned very quickly."

"Yeah. She was nervous being out there by herself and she needed a boost to get up on the skis when the boat started pulling her. I spent five days in the lake, treading water with her ass in my face so I could push her up when the boat started going. I was submerged for so long that I broke out in this awful rash all over my legs."

"That sounds horrible."

"It sucked," I said. "But she felt bad about it. She had me hire someone else to bob around in the water with her for the last couple of days."

"How nice of her," Isabelle said dryly.

"No, it wasn't like that at all. She didn't order me to stay in there for the entire time. I wanted to do it. I wanted to do everything I could to help her."

"Hmm," Isabelle said. "So what about Rottie? I would guess he makes crazy requests."

"Let's see . . . Well, he just had me rent out the entire Miami Dolphins stadium to throw a bachelor party for one of his friends. And he's paying the entire team and their cheerleaders to be there."

"Incroyable!"

"If you tell anyone what I just told you, I could get sued you know."

"But of course." She pulled out a cigarette. "This is okay?"

"Yeah, I started smoking again," I said.

She lit up and passed it to me. "Do you think Rottie Wiles is truly reformed now?"

"I don't know. And I don't really care."

I shoved my SUV into drive and turned the music up again.

This shit about to blow
When I read my riot act
Heat coming off me like a radiator
Get right with God, 'cause you meetin' your creator
There's a reason niggas say I'm a muthafuckin' gladiator

Isabelle pumped her hands through the open roof, and the night swirled around us as we rode, a dark living thing that seemed to breathe in time with the music.

I saw it at the intersection of Sixteenth and Michigan—a white streak bolting from the shadows toward us. I slammed the brake, my tires screeching on the concrete. A thump rattled the car and shot through my body. I pulled over and muted the stereo, my heart picking up where the hip-hop beat left off.

We sat frozen, plastered against our seat backs as if we could rewind time by holding still.

"What was that?" Isabelle said, facing straight ahead.

I squinted in the direction where the streak went. "I have no idea."

The streetlights barely penetrated the thick canopy of trees above, but my vision, sharpened by adrenaline, caught movement on a corner property across the street. "Be right back," I said, opening my door and stepping onto the quiet residential roadway. Palm leaves crackled in the distance, coming closer and seeming to chase me as I rushed across the pavement. A soft squeal wafted on the current, and a hedge came to life at the yard's border.

I hit an animal. Never before had a day started so great and ended so disastrously.

I could almost hear the animal rights protesters shouting at my new boss. Their favorite chant—"No redemption for a murderer!" Denise's voice rang in my head, too, clearer and more immediate: *How can you work for that awful man?*

The voices drove me forward. I wasn't going any-where until I made sure this creature wasn't gravely hurt. I crept a few more feet and made out the silhou-ette of a dog in the dark foliage, crouching with paws stretched forward, ears pricked, rear end pointing at the sky. I moved slowly toward it. If it was scared, it could flee—or charge at me.

Its movements were cautious, but its mouth seemed to be turned up. Animals don't smile before they attack, I reasoned, offering out my hands, palms up.

A familiar ding sounded. I turned to see the interior light flash and Isabelle's head popping up from behind the car door. "Isabelle," I whisper-called as best I could, flagging her back, hoping she wouldn't spook the pos-sibly injured animal. She sunk back down and pulled the door shut, scrunching her face and mouthing, "I'm sorry." I turned back to see the animal lope away with a lopsided gait.

"Shit," I said under my breath, racking my brain for ideas. My experience with dogs was limited to Lucy's dog, Mushroom. I could never get that dog to do a damn thing unless I bribed her with food.

Then it came to me. Treats! There must be a pro-tein bar or something in my car. Better yet—I hap-pened to have these chicken jerky treats that I'd been meaning to throw away. They'd been meant for Mushroom, but Mushroom only liked liver biscuits. The jerky had been fermenting in the back of my car forever. I ran to the lift gate and found the grocery bag containing the treats while Isabelle watched. "I'm going to try something," I told her. "Just hang on." I hurried across the street, ripping at the package and pulling out an oily strand of something that resembled meat. I started shaking the bag. The sound of treats jostling brought Mushroom out of hiding on many occasions.

Rounding the house to the backyard, I stooped down but didn't avoid a low-hanging tree branch. The switch whipped me in the face and sprayed water droplets at me, stinging and cool at the same time. I shook it off and kept going until I saw the dog. It stood still in the center of the yard, a nub jerking back and forth where its tail should have been. It was large, maybe eighty pounds, but low to the ground, wide and sturdy. That smile still cut across its face and up the sides of its jaw like the Joker.

A neighbor's porch bulb blazed on. I looked over, holding my breath. A man glanced through the window but didn't come outside. I turned back around to see the dog's face lit from below, the light glinting off inch-long metal spikes around its neck, creating a halo effect. I could see that the animal's coat was two-toned, a light tan and white, and other markings were visible as well—lines along the jaw, under the eyes, spanning the body. Did my car do that? A front paw hovered a couple inches above the ground, injured.

I moved closer to try to get a better look at the leg, and the dog took a step back. I froze. We were in a stalemate. I knew somehow that I should get low to the ground, and I dropped to my hands and knees. The dog's nostrils flared in and out as it shifted from its back legs to its one good front leg, and from this new vantage point I could see he was a boy. His nose twitched faster the closer I got. He'd caught a whiff of the chicken-flavored snack. "Here, buddy," I said in a high-pitched tone. I was stricken by the sound of my voice in that moment—it sounded eerily similar to my mother Denise's.

The dog snorted and leapt back.

I set the box down and, stretching out on my belly, nose touching the ground, I became aware that I was treating my designer shirt like one of Denise's disheveled flannels.

I held my breath. A few seconds passed, and then the treat slid from my fingers.

CHAPTER TEN

S till lying on the lawn, I lifted my eyes to the dog. He was smacking his jaw, grinning, asking for more.

I smiled back at him. "Good boy," I said, hoisting myself up and heading back toward the street, shaking the bag. I wondered what the hell I was doing. Up until I started working for Reggie, I probably would have kept on driving. The dog scuttled after me to the car and leapt right in when I opened the back hatch.

"HIIIIYEEEE," Isabelle cried, reaching out. He maneuvered around the junk in the back to get to her, his nub of a tail wagging. He gave her a quick lick on her face, but when she moved to pet him he slipped out of her reach, grunting like a pig after truffles as he searched for something else to eat.

"He's limping," I said.

Under the interior light, I could see he wasn't bleeding after all—those lines on him were pink, not red. Old scars, forming a winding, incomplete road map along his body. Isabelle furrowed her brow, her eyes tracing the marks on him, too. I passed the bag to her so she could give him a treat. He chomped it down and licked her again.

My throat shrunk. Allergies, I thought at first. But nothing itched. This was emotion hitting my body before my brain caught on.

The dog perched on the armrest between Isabelle and me. I sat for a moment, stroking his head. His eyes rolled up toward the sky. This animal, so nervous just five minutes earlier, was the picture of contentment now.

"I don't know what to do," I said. I couldn't drive home in my condition, and I couldn't abandon this animal, possibly injured by me.

"Just park up there and we will figure it out," Isabelle said, pointing farther down the street.

"Okay," I said, putting the car in drive and pulling slowly forward. "Wonder if a cabdriver would be cool with a dog."

Isabelle's head shot around. At first I thought that the dog had thrown up or bitten her. But when I looked down at him he was still sprawled out as if settling for a nap.

That's when I saw the red and blue lights.

Isabelle and I uttered the word in a long breath at the same time: "Fuuuuuuuuuuck."

Gum. There was gum in the center console. I gently shooed the animal aside and lifted the armrest lid. He started to pant, and I patted his chest. I was still searching when a jarring knock and a bright-white light assaulted us.

I lowered the window.

"License and registration, please."

As I fumbled through the glove compartment, the dog retreated to the back and started whining. Isabelle made a move to follow him, and the light shone in her face.

"Stay where you are, please," the officer said.

She leaned into the light, letting her spaghetti strap fall off her shoulder. "I'm sorry, sir. We will do whatever you say." Her voice was husky.

The officer's face remained stony, and as I handed him my records I didn't even bother flashing my cutest smile. It might have gotten me out of a speeding ticket once, but if Isabelle didn't do it for him, there was no point.

The cries in the back grew more frantic as the cop studied my documents. Then he regarded me. "Miss, have you been drinking tonight?"

"Only one, sir," I over-enunciated.

"Step out of the car, please."

He had me follow his finger with my eyes, and I willed them not to cross.

The cop instructed me to touch my nose with either index finger while walking in a straight line. The street was quiet, with no gawkers to distract me, and the wind had stilled. I felt steady. *This will be over in a minute,* I told myself. I'd borrow a belt or maybe some rope from Isabelle, walk the dog home with me. Lesson learned.

A shrill cry pierced the silence—the dog was panicking. I lurched forward and stumbled.

Then the Breathalyzer came out. The dog's cries continued, anguished and climbing, as if he understood that our situation was getting worse.

I couldn't remember if I was supposed to comply with the test or refuse it. Rob had once talked about what to do in the face of a DUI, but my memory wasn't working. Was it that if you refused, they'd automatically arrest you? But was that the preferred course of action because the charge would more likely be dropped after the fact?

I'd forgotten everything he'd said.

I took the risk and blew into the mouthpiece. I passed. My heart leapt. The dog's whining grew softer. But then the officer told me I had to do it two more times.

I failed two out of the three tests.

The officer gripped my shoulder and told me to turn around and place my hands on the hood of my car. The handcuffs clicked into place like a bad dream, and I shouted to Isabelle, "Can you take the dog?"

Dizzying shadows spun light and dark as a Vespa with an angry muffler growled by. The cop guided me into the back of his cruiser and Isabelle yelled something, but I couldn't make out what she was saying.

CHAPTER ELEVEN

A crisply uniformed man with a face like a crumpled piece of paper took my information, and then someone else led me to a narrow room to wait with the other criminals. A female guard paced, snapping gum, watching us with distrust even though there was nowhere for us to run. It smelled like pee. I shivered as I wiped my clammy hands on the underside of the long bench we were all sharing. I'd always heard jail was cold, but this was bordering on unbearable. I guessed nobody would be adjusting the air-conditioning for my comfort or come floating down the aisle offering blankets and hot towels.

But if TV and movies were accurate, I should be entitled to a phone call. I asked the guard about it.

"It's not a question of if," she said, as if my inquiry had just roused her from a deep sleep, "it's a question of when. You're not getting out of here until morning anyways, so settle in."

My mouth tasted like burnt toast when I swallowed. I longed for a big glass of ice water and a toilet—I could almost feel myself contracting a UTI from holding it too long. *Is anyone else this uncomfortable?* I gazed down the row of bodies, and my eyes stopped on a Rorschach ink-blot on torn denim. On the floor below was a small but expanding puddle. "The fuck you looking at?" said Ms. Pee Pants, glaring at me through smudged purple eye-liner. She looked about fourteen and crazy enough to kill me. I sat up straight and focused on the dried gray paint drips on the wall.

I had been drunk tonight. I'd never done anything like this before. I'd never tried to save an animal. I was the person at the party who gave the house pet an obligatory pat on the head when people were watching and shooed it away when they weren't. I was the designated driver.

Still, in this sobering, bright place, I couldn't help but wonder about that smiling dog, worry about whether he was safe and comfortable. What if Isabelle opened the car door without thinking and let him run off? How far would he get on a bad leg? Could I have stopped my car in time? I felt responsible for him.

Okay, you're just not thinking straight, I told myself. *Maybe it's the alcohol.* But I didn't feel drunk anymore.

There had to be another explanation. Perhaps after losing Rob and Lucy I was searching for something to ground me. Lucy and I hadn't even spoken since then, and it was weighing on me. I didn't understand why we couldn't see each other. I missed my best friend.

Was this why people were so in love with animals? Did they glom onto their pets because people let them down?

The guard called us to our feet. I hugged myself as our group weaved like a giant caterpillar through the corridor. "Aw, you cold?" said a skinny girl with blond cornrows. Her sleeves were rolled up to expose raw, red forearms.

"I'm fine, thanks," I said.

"Too bad. I was going to give you this here hoodie." She scratched at her blotchy arms, and her beam was so intense that the whites of her eyes and teeth were practically jumping from her face. I wondered what drugs she was on.

"Why?"

She yanked her zipper down and revealed another sweatshirt. "I dressed in layers."

It was hot outside. Did that mean she had planned on being arrested tonight?

"I don't have anything to trade you for it." Another thing movies had taught me about jail—inmates bartered.

"Hey, no talking," said a high but stern voice behind us. We were at the tail end of the caterpillar, and another guard was bringing up the rear, a tiny woman with perfect posture and a stiff walk. If she were green, she would have been a plastic action figure.

My new acquaintance whispered, "You *will* have something."

"What's that?"

"Your food."

"Oh." Not the response I'd been expecting. I pictured gray meat with slimy sauce, and it was an easy decision. "Deal." I took the hot-pink hoodie from her. It had a fermented smell, like a baby's spit-up milk, but I zipped it right up over my grass-stained blouse.

We were led to a windowless cell with one toilet and a dirty sink. I watched where Ms. Pee Pants went and I chose a cement bench on the opposite side. Isabelle had to be asleep by now. Hopefully she would answer when I finally got to make my call, and the dog would be with her.

I jolted awake at the sound of my name, not knowing if I'd slept for five minutes or five hours. On instinct I reached for my phone to see what time it was, only to remember that it was locked behind a metal grate—along with all my contacts. I didn't know Isabelle's number, or even Rob's. The only number I knew was Lucy's.

Calling her wouldn't bode well for my chances of getting my job back.

Little Miss GI Joe led me to a phone on the wall, and my shell-shocked brain tried to think of someone else—anyone else.

"If you're just going to stand there, there's plenty of other people who need to use the phone."

Lucy picked up on the second ring. I tried to make my voice sound like everything was breezy, but another voice broke through at that moment, announcing that the call was coming from an inmate of a Miami-Dade correctional facility.

"Oh my god, Alex. Are you alright?"

"Yeah, I'm fine, thanks," I said, as if this could still be downplayed. "Listen, I'm sorry to ask, but can you get me out of here?"

"I'm on it right now," she said without hesitating.

A sob heaved in my chest.

CHAPTER TWELVE

The back of my head throbbed as I walked out of jail, but I felt buoyant without the watchful eyes of the prison workers weighing me down. Strange how quickly you get used to being herded like cattle. Puddles were evaporating in the parking lot, and I soaked up their steam. I peeled off the pink hoodie, scrunching it into a ball and doubling back to the trash can near the exit. A twinge hit me as I left it there among cheese-crusted wrappers and wet Styrofoam. It had been my most prized possession for a night.

Just as I was opening my Uber app, I heard a car horn. Frank was circling Lucy's white Range Rover to open the back door for me. My chest squeezed. I'd told her not to wait for me after she posted bail. One of my new prostitute acquaintances had said it would take hours for the jailers to process my release. I'd told Lucy I didn't want to inconvenience her any further.

But really, I didn't want to face her.

Lucy was sitting in the cream-colored leather back seat. Tatiana wasn't with her thank God. She threw her arms around me when I climbed in. I turned my head away so she wouldn't catch the stench of old beer and two missed appointments with my toothbrush.

"That must've been terrifying," Lucy said, pulling back to meet my eyes. "I'm so glad you called me instead of some bail bondsman. Are you alright?"

Holy shit. I could have called a fucking bail bondsman.

"I'm fine," I said, feigning interest in the featureless jail building outside the window. "But I wish you wouldn't have waited all that time."

She waved her hand. "Don't be ridiculous. Think of all the times you bailed me out when I was in trouble."

I looked at her straight-on now. She was beaming, her red hair coming off her in rays.

Was she enjoying this?

"I did what anyone else would've done," I said.

"Well, you saved my life. I don't think just anyone would've done that."

She had saved my life, too, a long time ago, but I let that point slide by.

Lucy and I said little as Frank whisked us along the bridge to the beach. She asked how it was going with Reggie, and I told her it wasn't terrible. But I didn't offer any more information. I couldn't help but take some delight in being on the "outside" again. I lowered the window all the way, took in the salty air, which seemed purer than it did yesterday. I traced the shapes of the cruise ships along the causeway with my hand. The water surrounding the massive boats glimmered with fresh possibilities.

I wondered about the women I had met the night before, whether any of them were riding away from jail with this same gust of optimism right now. It didn't seem likely. Most of them had seemed far too comfortable there, greeting each other with a "Hey, girl" as if they were old friends or colleagues gathered for a monthly happy-hour date. They'd been in and out before and I doubted they were lucky enough to be going home to a beach property, even if it was a modest rental.

I wanted to tell Lucy about the ladies, especially Keesha.

Keesha, a heavy woman, had sauntered into our airless holding cell announcing she was "fixin' to recreate Hiroshima." Then she dropped her sweat pants and plunked down on the steel toilet in the center of the room. Her forehead seized, and she grunted. Someone shouted, "Aw, *hell* no," and someone else called, "You nasty, Keesha!" I moved to the farthest corner of the room, which wasn't very far. My gag reflex kicked in, and I tasted acid and tequila coming up. If only I had learned to meditate like I promised myself, I thought, shutting my eyes and waiting for the bottom to drop out—literally.

"Naw—I'm just playin' y'all!" Keesha hollered. "I got you, dumb bitches!"

When I realized she was joking, I had fallen into a long convulsive laughter fit, the kind that shoots through your body like morphine. The next thing I knew I was waking up to a gross food tray being shoved in my face.

I didn't think Lucy would find any of this funny. This wasn't the Lucy I knew, the one who would eat up seedy jail stories. She hadn't even reacted to my welcome home collage. Her mischievous smile and sarcasm were gone. Her new, more sensitive approach to life seemed to have sucked all the humor out of her.

Lucy's voice pulled me from my melancholy thoughts. "I bet you're absolutely starving! Did you eat anything? You want to come over and have some breakfast?"

"Thanks, but I have some things to do before I head to Reggie's."

"Well, maybe you want to meet up later? I'm going to an AA meeting tonight if you want to tag along. There will be good food." Her inflection was casual, like she was dropping the invitation as an afterthought.

She thought I needed help for my drinking. I had proved Tatiana right in Lucy's mind.

"I actually have something going on at home that I need to take care of," I said.

"Maybe another night?"

"Sure," I said. "Another night."

She took my hand and squeezed it. "This is really brave of you, Alex. It'll be hard at first, but you'll see. Things will be so much better."

As she looked at me, her expression warm and hopeful, a realization hit me: this was my way back in.

Maybe if we shared this twelve-step "journey" she'd want me at her side again. Quitting drinking would be worth it, and it wouldn't be for long. No way would Lucy keep up this sobriety thing forever. I hoped she'd go at it with less gusto when she started drinking again, that rehab taught her to slow down at least.

"Later this week for sure," I said, pressing my lips together, feigning the somberness of a person at rock bottom.

"So, what's going on at home?" she asked.

"I found a dog last night that got hit by a car. Isabelle took him to my place." I left out the part about it being *my* car.

"Is it hurt badly?"

"No, I think he just got clipped. But he was limping a little and I couldn't just leave him there in good conscience. I need to take him to a vet."

Lucy tilted her head and studied me, her face crinkling as if she were trying to recognize me. After decades of friendship, we were strangers.

"Well, well," she said. "Taking in strays, just like Denise."

I let out a guffaw. There it was, that spark, the Lucy I knew, making a tasteless joke. That's who we were—nothing was too sensitive a subject.

We stopped at the complex's entrance, and Lucy asked Frank to park in the lot.

"We're coming inside with you," she said, pulling on a baseball cap and threading her hair through the opening in the back. With her oversized sunglasses, she wouldn't be recognized unless they had a sharp eye. I shrugged and led them up the back way to my apartment, wondering what kind of damage the dog had inflicted on it.

Frank stayed on the balcony, and Isabelle opened the door and greeted us with bed head, wearing my sweats and my dad's frayed Grand Canyon T-shirt. I blinked at her.

"This is okay?" she asked, pulling on the shirt. "I am sorry."

"Yeah, of course it's alright," I said, smiling at her.

The dog jumped from the couch but kept his distance, his nose jutting back and forth in the air. I held out my hand and kicked off my shoes.

"Is he friendly?" Lucy asked from behind me.

"Once he gets to know you."

"Well, he doesn't look hurt anymore," Lucy said, moving toward him, dropping to her hands and knees and sticking out her palm.

The dog sniffed her. As I watched her crouched there on the ugly pine-green carpet, I realized this was the first time she had seen my apartment. It wasn't her fault. I'd stayed at her place almost every night, and she'd never had a reason to come here. I was glad it looked like a storage unit. Glad I didn't bother to unpack most of the boxes, buy some decorative throw pillows, or even hang a picture. The unlived-in surroundings made it seem like I was holding vigil for my old life—and that was exactly what I wanted her to see.

"I'm going to go change. I have to get home," Isabelle said, bending and reaching for her ball of clothes on the floor. Worry lines appeared on her forehead. "Did you see Jean-Marc when you came in?" she asked. "I made sure I did not run into him last night, and I do not want to do so now."

"Coast is clear," I said.

Lucy offered her a ride.

"I can't thank you enough," I said, hugging Isabelle goodbye.

"But of course," she said. "Me and Oliver had a lovely time. He is such a nice boy. He enjoys the eggs, and he peed outside."

The moniker took me aback. "You named him?"

"Oh, no." Isabelle's eyes widened in apology. "I just call him that for now instead of Dog."

I smiled. "Oliver sounds much better than Dog."

Oliver padded over to me as if he recognized his name already and leaned into my legs. My bones hadn't completely thawed from the cold night in jail, and his body heat felt good.

"Awww," Lucy said, placing her hand over her heart. "He loves you."

"Well, shit," I said.

CHAPTER THIRTEEN

I drove to Publix on South Beach, figuring a dog couldn't live on eggs alone. The dog food varied from five pounds to fifty, from four dollars to sixty. I stood there blocking the aisle for a long time, contemplating whether he needed salmon, beef, or chicken. And then there was the question of grains or grain-free. I googled "best food for pit bulls." The results said uncooked protein was best. That wasn't going to happen. I couldn't remember the last time I had cooked, let alone handled, raw meat. The search results also warned against fillers, so I settled on an expensive wheat-free, corn-free, all-natural brand. Fifty pounds should do him, I decided, heaving the bag into the cart. Then I picked up some accessories: a leash, plain green collar, and a cute navy bandana to replace the scary S&M monstrosity he was wearing.

Oliver was frantic when I returned with the food. He plowed into my torso with his front legs, thrusting me backward into the flimsy closet. One of the laminate sliding doors separated from the track with a bang. I reached up and caught myself on the closet frame, dropping the dog food. He pounced onto the bag, and with a swift, forceful jerk of his head he tore a hole in it. Kibble poured out, and he started munching. "No!" I yelled.

His demeanor changed in an instant. He stopped eating and cowered to the floor, head low, trembling.

"Aw, man. I'm sorry, Ollie." The nickname came out naturally, like I'd said it a million times before. He was still shaking, and his nails chattered like teeth on the linoleum patch in the entryway. I knelt beside him. He flinched at first but stayed put, letting me scratch his back. Soon his nubby tail began flitting again.

I didn't mind sitting there, petting him, but I needed to move things along in order to get to work by noon. "Ready to go for a walk?" I asked, unfastening the too-tight spiked collar around his neck. He rolled his eyes and heaved a great sigh as if he'd just unbuttoned a pair of skinny jeans after Thanksgiving dinner. I pulled the new collar and leash from the grocery bag, and he held his head still while I attached them. He'd done this before, only he probably hadn't been going anywhere good those other times.

The moment I led him outside he let out a deep bark.

"So, I see you had a visitor last night," said a booming voice.

"Shit!" I said, jumping and spinning around.

Jean-Marc was leaning against the balcony rail, a smirk on his orange face. Did he mean the dog, or did he see Isabelle last night?

Ollie yanked at the leash, a low rumble sounding from his throat. "It's okay, buddy," I said in this new pitchy voice of mine. I leaned down to give him a reassuring pat and noticed his ears were slanted flat against his head, and his tennis ball tail had gone dead still. He glared at Jean-Marc, who raised his palms and took a step back.

"I'm sorry," I said, tugging the leash. "I'm just watching him until I can find him a home." I told Ollie to sit, and he obeyed without taking his eyes from my neighbor. Jean-Marc backed into his apartment and peered at the dog through the cracked door. Ollie shuffled back and forth on his front paws, hovering his butt a couple inches above the ground as if awaiting a "kill" command. "I don't think it's personal. He's been through a lot," I said. "Listen, I really have to get going."

"We'll talk later, Alex." The way he said it struck me as sinister, as if he meant, "We need to have a talk" versus, "Talk to ya later!"

The relationship between Jean-Marc and Isabelle had been dysfunctional at best. I had heard them fighting on several occasions, voices raised, doors slammed. At first I assumed it was a cultural thing, those frequent, heated exchanges. Maybe it even spiced things up for them. Usually they ended up on the balcony sharing a bottle of wine a few hours after a brawl, practically fondling each other under the table.

But then one early morning I ran into Isabelle on our shared walkway. She must not have gone to bed yet, because she was decked out in a sequined Band-Aid of a skirt, drinking cheap beer from a can at 7 a.m.

"Alexandraaaaa," she drawled, waving her skinny arm as I advanced toward her. I gave her a limp half wave, trying to think of a way to shut her down.

"Hey, I'm in a hurry to get to work," I lied.

She clip-clopped up to me in her wedge shoes. Her nose was red, and navy mascara streaked her apple cheeks.

"I am done with Jean-Marc," she said. "He is a monster, and I think he is cheating on me." Alcohol thickened her Swiss-French accent.

"Seriously?"

"Would you like a beer?" Isabelle asked, turning her can over and watching a few lonely drops fall to the cement.

"No, thanks," I said.

"Be right back," she said, tottering inside to get another. I watched her unstable gait, expecting to have to run to her aid at any moment. That was when I noticed a bruise on her back below her right shoulder. She must've already fallen last night or collided with something.

I leaned against the banister, letting the key ring dangle from my middle finger, staring across the glassy bay at the Miami skyline rising and disappearing into the morning fog. A few early risers lounged by the pool. One woman had removed her bikini top and was greasing up her bare, unnaturally round breasts while a small child zipped past her feet. Typical for South Beach, but I'd never get used to seeing that.

Isabelle returned with a fresh beer.

"So, are you okay?" I asked.

She nodded, and her eyes flashed. "Hey, can you get me some coke?"

"Nooooooo," I said, glancing around to see if any pool dwellers had heard her.

"Just give me a little bit of yours then."

What? When did I ever give her cocaine?

Jean-Marc had always seemed to be holding, and he'd shared with me a couple times before I stopped doing it. Jean-Marc must have run out. I wondered if Isabelle was an addict, too.

"Sorry. Don't have any," I said, patting my pockets like that was some kind of proof. "So, why do you think Jean-Marc is cheating?"

"He did not come home all night, and there was this girl."

"What girl?"

She turned to me and stumbled. I grabbed her arm to steady her. "She said 'good morning' to him on Facebook yesterday."

"That could be anything," I said. "Maybe you should go to sleep so you can talk to him when you're in a better headspace."

"What does that mean, 'headspace'?"

"When you're able to think better."

"I do not want to sleep!" she said, loud enough that her voice carried down to the pool loungers. "I want to fuck over Jean-Marc like he did to me!" A few people glanced up from their reclining chairs.

"I know," I said, almost in a whisper, patting her arm, hoping she'd mirror the level of my voice. "But maybe you need to think about how to do it, come up with a really good plan."

"I think I know where she lives."

She looked around like she was getting ready to take action.

"Going over there is the worst thing you could do," I said. "We'll figure out how to really hit him where it hurts."

Isabelle bobbed her head and swayed. "He hit me where it hurt." She spun around and pointed to the bruise I'd noticed on her back.

"Oh my god. He did that?" Now my voice was getting loud, too, and I didn't care who heard us. "Has he done this before?"

She blinked at me. "I hit him first. He pushed me away and I fell into the table."

"Well, he pushed you pretty fucking hard. Do you have a friend you can stay with?" Her head tilted, and the thought struck me that she might ask me. "Somewhere he can't find you?" I added before she could speak.

Isabelle shut one eye as if deep in concentration. "Yes. Monique. I called her already, but she did not answer."

"Just grab what you need for right now. I'll help you."

I escorted her inside, swatting the air as we entered. It smelled like feet. In the kitchen an unwrapped half wheel of cheese sat on the counter with a swarm of fruit flies hovering above. This was normal for their household. Leaving food out to rot was a highly cultivated practice, according to Jean-Marc. Americans, he had said, manufactured subpar cheese because we didn't allow our dairy to age.

She bent down and fumbled with the buckles on her strappy shoe. I grew frustrated watching her and offered my help, but she wanted to do it herself. After an eternity, she freed her foot and kicked the sandal across the room. Then she swung her other leg, but the shoe was still fastened. She reeled back, all gangly arms and legs, and I rushed over to catch her.

"What do you need for the next couple days?"

"My toothbrush."

"How about some clothes?"

"Yes," she said, plunking down on the floor.

"No, no, no. Don't go to sleep yet." I put my arms around her and pulled her up, careful to avoid the bruise.

"You can borrow whatever you want from me. Let's just get you out of here."

I helped her stagger to my apartment and tucked her into my bed. "Listen," I said as I rifled through my closet for my flip-flops. "Do not go back home under any circumstances. Do not open the door for anybody."

She didn't respond, and when I turned to glare at her imploringly, I got my answer. She wouldn't be going anywhere or talking to anyone. She was dead asleep.

I'd expected Isabelle's resolve to vanish when her hangover kicked in. But she showed up at my door two nights later, breathless, with a guy who appeared more appropriate for her than Jean-Marc, closer to her age, probably another model.

"I could not have done this without you," she said, hugging me. "Give me your digits." She held out her phone and had me enter my number. Then she called me so I would have her contact information.

"I'll call you," I said.

I didn't mean it at all.

CHAPTER FOURTEEN

During the week after my jailing, I established a semblance of a routine between my responsibilities for Reggie and Ollie. After exercising Ollie in the mornings, I'd drop him at Isabelle's for the day. I didn't know what I'd do with the dog when she went to "The Great State of Kansas" for her modeling gig. I'd taken zero steps to find him a permanent home, too exhausted from work and making sure Ollie burned off some of his limitless energy.

I would arrive at Reggie's sometime around 9 a.m. and head to the kitchen for one of Marcia's pastries and a second cup of coffee. Then I'd fix Reggie a blueberry smoothie.

One morning my jaw dropped as the blender began to whir. The scene outside the picture window looked like the aftermath of a Civil War battle, minus the dead bodies.

I blazed through the back door and across the patio wondering what possibly could have happened. Did some animal rights people come in the shroud of night to defile Reggie's home? If so, how in the hell did they evade security?

Faint odors of whiskey morning breath and bonfire mingled together. But there was no fire pit in sight. The ground squished under my feet even though it hadn't rained in days. Plastic cups, plates, chips, and charred rib and chicken bones were mushed into the grass. The pool was worse, with more cups, a neon bikini top, cigarette butts, and an amoebic orange mass floating on the surface. I stood there, scanning the refuse-filled yard until I spotted the source of the smell—a hedge, charred black and leafless, beside the pool house.

A hoarse voice from behind made me jump. "They was burning that bush like Moses last night!"

I turned to see an older man grinning at me from beneath a straw fedora. "Didn't mean to scare you," he said, extending a lanky arm for a handshake. "Sorry. I'm Reg's Uncle Marvin."

I shook his hand and introduced myself. "Do you have any idea what happened here, Marvin?"

"Guess you'd call it a last-minute gathering," he said with a wink.

"They had a *party* last night?"

"And what a party it was!"

We were both staring straight ahead at the detritus. My mind was racing. Wouldn't they have wanted me to help with a party? I was never not on duty for one of Lucy's soirees, sometimes making wild last-minute arrangements. Once we had a peyote tent erected in her living room on an hour's notice. And she usually wanted to do giveaways, hundreds of bags of luxury skin care or candles, not to mention the party favors that came in smaller baggies—the illegal kind.

"Why didn't they call me?" I said, more to myself than Marvin.

Marvin shrugged. "Reg probably didn't want to bother you so late."

Didn't want to bother me? That sounded ludicrous. Stars didn't shy away from inconveniencing their assistants. That was why we existed.

"I don't get it," I said in a bewildered voice.

He turned to me. For a second, it looked like he was about to put his arm around my shoulders, but then he must have thought better of it.

"Hey, what's got you all worried?" he asked. "If they didn't want me here for this"–I gestured at the yard— "something must be wrong."

He drew back, put his hands on his hips. "Now why would you think a thing like that, young lady?" His voice was friendly, unlike the stern tone Denise would use when calling me *young lady*.

"Because I was hired for things like this."

"So you think he purposely kept you away last night for some reason," he said, stroking the wisps of hair on his chin.

I gave him a look that said, *Duh—it's obvious.* In the next moment, I regretted my attitude. This guy was trying to make me feel better out of the kindness in his heart. He didn't need to stand here and listen to me moan.

Marvin didn't seem offended. "Listen," he said, fanning a finger, still grinning. "It's no secret that boy has had his troubles. He's impulsive. He goes to dark places. But underneath it all he's a good kid, and he learned how to keep his demons away. Last night was nothing more than a case of blowing off steam."

I was confused for a second until I realized we were talking about two different things.

"No, I wasn't worried about *that*," I said. "It's just events are supposed to be one of my duties. I'm wondering if they thought I couldn't handle it."

Marvin's eyes bulged out. He bent at the waist and straightened again.

"Are you kidding me? Reggie told me he likes you. He ain't never said that about one of his assistants before." He grew more and more animated as he spoke. "The party just kind of happened, and I guarantee the reason he didn't call was that he didn't want to wake you up."

Really? Was it possible that this gangsta rapper, who had known me for less than two weeks, was being considerate of my time? More considerate than my best friend had been?

"Okay, well, thanks," I said, actually feeling better.

Marvin gazed out at the yard, hands on hips as if he were surveying crops. "Mmm-hmm. They sure messed shit up last night."

"Yeah, it looks like everyone had fun," I said.

"Guess I'd better go get some trash bags and start cleaning up."

"Sure, sure." Marvin adjusted his hat. "Just remember what I said, and keep your chin up."

I smiled, grateful I'd run into Marvin. I'd never seen anyone move like him—herky-jerky, dramatic, and the motion never stopped. If his arms weren't gesturing, his head was bobbing or his legs were twitching as if he were fending off an invisible swarm of bugs. It was entertaining to watch, when I thought about it later. I think he meant it to be. He was like a magician performing misdirection, trying to take the focus off my anxiety.

I heard my name being bellowed. I turned to see Ham standing at the back door, hands cupping his mouth.

I jogged over to him. "We'll get this cleaned up by the end of the day," I said.

He shook his head. "Never mind that. Xavier got a crew coming. You got bigger things to do."

"What's going on?"

"Reggie needs to get his fans back."

"What happened?" As of eleven o'clock the previous night, Reggie had more than twenty-one million followers on Twitter. Ham had told me to alert him if that number dipped below twenty million. Some scathing news story must have broken to make that happen in a ten-hour period. I pulled up the app on my phone.

"Nothing. He just knows he lost people after everything. Maybe they won't buy his next album, but that ain't what he cares about."

Reggie's Twitter feed came up. He still had twenty-one million followers. "What's he thinking?"

"He just doesn't want people to see him as a monster."

There was that word again, "monster."

"I understand."

"Good, because he wants you to create his new image campaign."

CHAPTER FIFTEEN

D riving Ollie home from work that evening, my mind raced. I'd been charged with crafting the new public persona of one of the most notorious men in the country.

I daydreamed about Lucy's reaction to this news, pictured the look of astonishment on her face when I told her about my promotion. She'd realize that she'd underestimated my skills. Even better, she'd be stricken with the fear of losing me. She'd kick Tatiana out and ask me back right then. She'd regard me as an equal, or at least a professional.

The problem was I had no idea where to begin. The only input Ham and Reggie had given was that they wanted to make a major donation to the ASPCA. I'd get that news out . . . and then what? The world would magically love him?

And on what did Reggie base this monumental faith in me? The robot dog?

I was grossly underqualified for this task. There was no way.

I'd thank my bosses for their faith in me and turn down the opportunity. I'd recommend that Reggie and Ham hire a real expert—no, a team—and I'd be happy to be a part of it by fetching coffee for the brighter minds.

Ollie whined as we pulled into my apartment's parking lot. He was raring to go, pawing at the passenger door. When I let him out, he yanked me toward the street, ready for a walk. "Don't you want to eat first?" I asked. He answered by charging forward.

Ollie delighted in smells on the ground, and every block or so he would send me reeling backward when he stopped to consider the grass and the bushes with his nose. I'd let him snort around for a few seconds, and then I'd say, "Okay, let's go!" He would lift his head and move along until another scent captured his attention.

It was prime dog-walking time. A woman about my age linked to a little black-bearded mutt gave me a look of mock exasperation as our animals circled each other, wrapping their leashes into a military-grade knot. We chatted as we worked to untangle them, and she asked me if Ollie was a rescue. I considered the question for a moment before answering yes.

"See you around," she said. "Like your shoes!"

I smiled to myself as we parted, not noticing a middle-aged woman promenading a guinea-pig-looking thing until she was nearly on top of us. When I responded to her slight nod with an exuberant "How's it going!?," she sped her pace a little. A beach-bodied Latino man in cuffed capri pants strolled toward us with a retriever of some sort, and I toned it down with a cool nod. The man smiled at me.

I'd never had this much interaction with strangers living on the beach, let alone friendly encounters. People always seemed worlds away in this diverse city, tucking themselves into their respective cultural pockets. I had always identified more with the spring breakers than the locals. I often wondered if other South Beach dwellers experienced this same sense of disconnection, but not on this night. Not us dog walkers. We were practically a community—meeting on the streets, exchanging knowing looks, sharing our poo bags with a bewildered new dog owner who forgot theirs (I had been that bewildered person last week).

A Rottweiler pranced toward us, and Ollie lunged as if a trigger had been flipped in him. I held firm and led him across the street. "Thanks!" the Rottweiler's owner called, unbothered by my dog's show of aggression. I was getting the hang of this, feeling light as Ollie trotted up the street. The traumas and stresses of the past weeks—the breakup, jail, my work life—all fell away like scabs, revealing shiny pink skin.

"You know I'm going to find you a nice home, right?" I said to him. He deserved that.

I breathed a sigh of relief when we got back and I saw that Jean-Marc's window was dark. Somehow I had managed to avoid him ever since he'd threatened to have a talk with me. I opened my door and heard my computer playing familiar tones, a Skype request.

I clicked the mouse, and my Uncle Paul's dimpled face popped up on the screen. "Hey, stranger," he said, his salt-and-pepper hair shooting off into little peaks that resembled whitecaps on the bay. The sight of him lit me up into a big grin that was reflected in the little box at the right with my picture in it.

Uncle Paul, Denise's younger brother, was my favorite family member. Less than a month after my dad had died, he and his partner, Edward (Uncle Eddie), had packed up and moved to Cleveland from Columbus, Ohio to be near us. Paul's Shih Tzu, Greta, barked from his lap. Ollie scrambled up, wrenching into my foot and jumping into my lap, trying to get at the screen.

"Ow, dude!"

"Holy shit!" Paul said, eyes widening. "Who's this?"

"This is Ollie. I hit him with my car."

Ollie started barking. "That's just Greta," I said to the dog in a tone that could have been a voice-over of an old lady in a cartoon.

I told Paul the story of the night I found Ollie (leaving out the DUI). "Do you think I'm crazy?"

He smirked. "Yes, but not for rescuing that cute dog."

"I didn't rescue him. I almost ran over him. And I need to find him a home."

Ollie licked my cheek.

"Your mom didn't mention this to me. What did she say when you told her?"

"I didn't tell her."

His head jerked back. "Why not?"

I had been avoiding Denise since she'd given me shit for working for Reggie. Every time she called or texted, I thought about that virtuous stance she took from the safety of her paid-for house with her paid-for electricity and cable. She'd expected me to give up my livelihood for her chosen cause. She had no idea what it meant to worry about making money. First Dad put up with her and provided for her, and after she ran Dad into the ground, Paul had taken the conductor's seat on her crazy train.

"It'll just remind her who I'm working for, and she's not too happy about that," I said.

"But she would love to hear about her daughter taking in a wayward animal. You know what a big heart she has."

I disagreed. If she had a big heart, it didn't extend to me. A memory popped into my head, the thing I always thought of when I started to feel any sort of tenderness toward Denise—her yelling at my dad over and over,

"You love her more than me." What kind of mother is jealous of her own daughter?

"I just don't want to upset her," I told Paul.

"It's true that she's been through a lot, a hell of a lot," he said, as if he didn't realize she brought most of it on herself. "But that doesn't mean you can't share what's going on in your life with her."

"That's what you're here for, Paul," I said, trying to redirect the conversation. It made me uneasy, talking with him about Denise. I had to bite my tongue to keep from saying something that I shouldn't. He was a light-hearted, jokey guy, but he never joked when it came to her. He shined a halo of light around her faults so she looked like an angel to him.

To Paul's credit, he did talk to Denise about her "open-door policy," as he delicately put it, after my dad had died. I had been spying when I'd heard Paul say, "This is causing real damage. It's not good for either of you." Nothing good came from that conversation—she didn't change her ways. I wished he'd tried harder to convince her, or whisked me away from that house. Maybe he would have done more if I'd told him what happened that one night in my bedroom, my atrocious secret. But I had been too ashamed. He still didn't know.

"Yes, you know I'm here for you," Paul said, pulling me back from my shitty memories. "I feel so lucky that we have such a strong relationship, kiddo."

I had shared a lot with him over the years, things that I had hidden from Denise. My first period had made a huge blot on my robin's-egg-blue skirt, and everyone at school knew about it before I did. I came home, threw the garment away so Denise wouldn't see it. Then I'd cried to Paul about my humiliating experience.

"Yeah, I probably overshared with you," I said.

"No way!" Paul said. "I loved it. I still remember the name of the boy you had your first kiss with. Abraham."

The kid's name was actually Todd, but Paul's memory impressed me anyway.

Paul was the one who got me through those awkward, dramatic teen years, not my mother.

"Abraham, that's right," I said, rolling my eyes.

Ollie started lunging at the screen again, sniffing it and leaving wet pixelated streaks that distorted Paul's face. Greta yowled, and Ollie joined the chorus.

"Just give your mom a call when you can," Paul said when the clamor died down. "She'll be tickled about your little development." He gestured at Ollie.

"I will," I promised, even though the last thing I wanted to do was bond with Denise over anything. It would be like telling her that everything she did was okay.

CHAPTER SIXTEEN

It wasn't okay. A year ago it all caught up with Denise. That was the most recent time I'd gone home. Paul had pleaded with me to take a few days off from Lucy to support Denise after the tragic incident.

I remember sitting in my rental car, looking at the tan brick Parma, Ohio ranch where I grew up. It matched every other house in the 99.98 percent Caucasian Cleveland suburb. The rusted iron trellises supporting the porch's overhang looked ready to give up on the task. I didn't want to go inside.

I breathed in through my scarf, spritzed with herbal aromatherapy spray for this very reason, and stepped onto the crackly bed of dead leaves covering fractured blacktop. Denise appeared, ghostly behind the storm door's smudged panes, gazing out. Bolts of white hair surrounded her face, giving her a witchy aura. She always waited too long between touch-ups, neglecting her roots until her head resembled a skunk's pelt. But she must've stopped going to the salon altogether because just the ends grazing her shoulders looked like they'd been dipped in a bucket of espresso-colored paint.

A waft of ammonia and floral air freshener hit me as she threw the door open. She pulled me into an embrace.

"Hi, Mom."

"My dear, dear Alexandra is finally here," she said. She stroked my hair like I'd just been rescued from a well and handed back to her after three days. I stood there, waiting for her to let go of me. In the living room, dark stains and piles of baking soda speckled the salm-on-pink carpet. The mantel, where many of her collect-able figurines had sat in the past, was now bare.

And the smell was something more than ammonia. It stunk like someone had been violently ill.

She started talking, and her words garbled together against my shoulder. I cringed, thinking about her tears and snot seeping into the fabric of my Burberry coat. I started patting at her back slowly and then more rapidly, hoping she'd get my hint to wrap it up. But she just held on, her sobs reverberating with the thumps.

I pried myself out of the hug, and she hinged her hands onto my shoulders, keeping me there in front of her. We'd always stood eye to eye, but now she had to tilt her head up slightly. I sensed she wanted me to say something comforting.

"Where'd all your Precious Moments go?" I asked, craning my neck to examine the puddle on my shoulder.

"Oh dear. I didn't mean to mess up your pretty jacket." She pulled a wadded Kleenex from some fold in her rumpled clothing and held it out to me.

"It's fine," I said, not taking the Kleenex. The coat would have to be dry-cleaned.

"Well, let me throw it in the wash then."

"I'll do it later," I said, trying to distract her from defiling my coat further. "What happened to your little statues?"

She blinked a few times. "They kept getting knocked down, so they're boxed up in the garage. I'll glue the salvageable ones back together while you're here and then I'll pass them down to you."

I pictured disembodied porcelain baby heads. Those figurines gave me nightmares when I was a kid, and now they were even more nightmarish. And how did she expect me to lug them through an airport?

She rubbed the small of my back, and I stiffened. "I know you always loved them, dear," she said. "I'm sorry you don't get to have the whole set."

I'd been there for three minutes, and I already wanted to smack her. Where did she get this stuff?

I heard footsteps. "Is someone here?" I asked.

Uncle Paul's treelike frame appeared in the dark hallway. As he ambled into the light, I could see the surgical mask on his face.

"I thought you'd be at work!" I said, rushing to him.

He lifted the mask, and the elastic popped into place on his forehead. Bending down, he lifted me into a bear hug. "Thank you," he whispered. "This means so much to your mom."

I pulled his mask and it snapped against his head again. "Got one of these for me?"

Denise waved her hand. "Really, you guys, it's not that bad. I can't even smell anything."

My mother warmed up lunch. We convinced her we should eat on the porch. We hunched against the chill in lawn chairs, giving our respiratory systems a break from the ammonia. I stared out at the front yard of my childhood. The older house, not part of one of Parma's many developments, sat back from the road, the lawn thick with oaks and maples bursting into fiery fall colors. Evergreens lined the long, narrow property, muffling the traffic noise.

Honking geese interrupted the vibrating silence. I watched the gaggle flicker dark and light through red leaves, jealous that they got to go south.

I examined the lasagna for foreign objects.

"I have cleaners coming, and then we're having the house recarpeted," Paul said. "We picked out a nice taupe with a raised leaf design."

"That'll look nice," I said, setting my forkful of Italian fare down without eating it.

Denise folded her cardigan around her, her untouched plate teetering on her knees. "Honestly, Paul, we really could just leave it bare. There's decent flooring underneath."

She pushed her crooked glasses up and turned her attention to me. "How's your glamorous life treating you, honey?" she asked in that singsong cadence she used when she inquired about my state of affairs. Her tone implied that my life was one big vacation when, in fact, being a celebrity assistant required a small series of miracles every day. Denise couldn't possibly understand how difficult it was to find an antiaging crème with responsibly sourced diamond flecks and then get it overnighted from France.

She liked to set me up so she could respond with that favorite phrase of hers: *Must be nice.*

"Is Lucy traveling anytime soon?"

I'd say, "Yes, to the South of France," and yes, I would be accompanying her.

And then, BAM! *Must be nice.*

It wasn't as if Denise worked. She'd quit her administrative job years ago and let Paul take care of her.

Must be nice.

My phone buzzed with a text from Lucy.

Tell those fuckers at Ferragamo that I won't take less than $20,000 to sit in the front row at their show

I blew out a sharp breath and pocketed the phone.

"Who were you texting with, sweetheart?" Denise asked.

I felt myself regressing to my teenaged self: slumped shoulders, drawn in, trying to guard what little shreds of privacy I could. "Work stuff," I said. "You know, sitting on boats with umbrella drinks."

Before she could start with the questions again, a mewing sound drifted from a nearby bush. She shot up from her chair. "Bitsy! They didn't get you. Good girl!" She shuffled to the edge of the cement slab. "I think Elmo is still around, too," she said, more to the shrubbery than us. A ghostlike wisp of a feline sat in a thicket of brambles a few yards away.

"How many were there?" I asked, touching the cylindrical inhaler in my breast pocket and willing the cats to stay back. The medicine in the canister was so old that it would likely do more harm than good, but it comforted me.

Denise didn't answer. Paul lifted his hands while her back was still turned, holding up four fingers and two fingers. *Forty-two cats.*

Denise made her way to the house, jabbering about how hungry Elmo and Bitsy must be. The storm door banged behind her, and the electric can opener revved up after a couple seconds.

Taking my plate of food, from which I'd extracted four cat hairs, Paul gave me wink. "Keep watch for me," he said. I saw Denise through the window, her back to us as she prepared a kitty feast. Paul strolled on his long legs toward the evergreen line. He dumped our food and kicked leaves over the evidence.

I shot him a thumbs-up as he walked back empty plated. "Bless you," I said.

"I'm absolutely loving that coat," he said, retaking his seat. "Maybe you need to take me shopping with you. I'm starting to think I'm dressing too young for my age."

"We could have fun shopping in Miami," I said, admiring his chocolate suede chukka boots and navy cashmere sweater.

He reached out and took the fabric on my arm between his fingers. "Oh shit, there's a stain," he said, pointing at the spot on my shoulder where Denise had gotten emotional earlier.

"She tried to put it in her washing machine."

"That's my fashion-forward sister," he said, shaking his head. "It's so wonderful of you to be here for her," Paul said. "You should've seen her three days ago. She's doing much better now. I think you had something to do with that."

I didn't see how my presence improved Denise's outlook—I hadn't given her a pep talk or even expressed sorrow for what had happened. "Well, that's good," I said, pulling a cigarette from my pocket.

"We just need to keep things positive, you know what I'm saying? She's pretty traumatized."

"Seriously?"

He raised an eyebrow at me. "Well," Paul said, "imagine if a bunch of people came into your home with a court order and took something you cared about deeply."

I tried to imagine it, but the only things at my place that I came close to caring about were the designer clothes, most of them gifted to me by Lucy. I pictured humane society agents raiding my apartment, sifting through my suede shoes and calf-skin handbags that overflowed from my closet. Had I inherited Denise's hoarding tendencies? I made a mental note to put everything I didn't wear on eBay as soon as I got home.

The next day was spent helping Denise, Paul, and the hired crew clean up the house. Before I left to catch my flight home, Denise handed me a paper grocery bag. I peered inside to see my naked American Girl doll staring up at me with vacant eyes. "I couldn't find the clothes, but I kept her bagged so she wouldn't get dusty." Denise smiled proudly as if she'd just given me a sack full of money. Something else weighed the bag down. I reached inside, pulled out a bag that read

"Chicken Jerky," and held it up to her questioningly. "I bought dog treats by accident," she said. "You can give them to Mushroom."

"Okay," I said. "Thanks for the doll."

She attempted a smile, but her face twisted, ready to wring out more tears. "They took my babies!" she wailed. "They invaded my home and took them to that awful place where they'll probably die!"

Paul's eyes started watering. I tried to feel something, too, but nothing came. I do remember thinking that even though this mess had been her fault, I would never wish this pain on her. That was the best I could do. I wrapped an arm around her shoulder, knowing I wouldn't see her or this brick box again for a long time.

"Well, at least you still have Elmo and Bitsy," I said.

CHAPTER SEVENTEEN

The morning following my Skype conversation with Paul, I skipped my pastry and coffee and headed directly to Reggie's screening room. I would tell him to hire someone else to run his campaign.

I couldn't help but catch my reflection passing the mirrored walls that housed the barbells, Stairmaster, and treadmills. My neck was blotchy, and the spots were advancing up to my cheeks. *That's just the way it is,* I told myself. My redness was something that I had to deal with. Not long ago I'd conceded that no amount of cold water or self-talk would calm it, and therefore I either had to go into uncomfortable situations face blazing or never go out in public.

The screening room was situated in a loft above the home gym. As I climbed the stairs, I heard Reggie's voice and another voice that I couldn't place right away strained in argument. The carpet must have muffled my footfalls because they kept talking as I ascended. I halted before my head would be seen in the gap between the railing and the floor.

"I'm just worried history's repeating itself," Reggie said. "It looks bad."

"It's not the same thing, but you're right—it doesn't look good," said the hoarse, tense voice that didn't belong to Reggie. "And that's exactly why you can't be anywhere near it." At that moment, a face popped into my head: the fedora-wearing man I'd met in the backyard, Marvin.

"I know," Reggie said.

"You're on probation, man," Marvin said. "Let me help you."

"We both know it's not that simple."

"It's simple if we make it simple. But if you give the police a reason, things could get very hard for you."

It was silent for a moment. I debated whether to turn back or keep going. All they had to do was come closer to the railing to see me lurking there like a snoop.

Reggie made the decision for me by changing the subject.

"Let's talk about it later. You good on cash?"

I heard the crinkling of money, and I climbed the stairs, holding my breath. Whatever Reggie was involved in, I couldn't impress upon him enough how uninterested I was. Or "uninterested" wasn't quite the right term—I couldn't help but wonder.

An ex-girlfriend of his from years ago, before jail, came to mind. She had been pregnant at the time, and she had alleged he'd assaulted her when she asked for child support. She was photographed with a black eye. When the police took Reggie in for questioning, he showed them security footage of what went down at the front gates of his old house. There was no sound, but you could see them arguing. The only time he touched her was to put a hand on her shoulder. It looked like he was trying to calm her down. It seemed to work because she went still.

And she stayed still—for far too long. You knew something was coming, and it did. Slowly, as if in a trance, she lifted her hand. Then she started hitting herself in the face over and over.

Somebody had gotten ahold of that video, and it went viral of course.

His only statement to the media was "God help me, I'll always love that woman."

Had he taken up with her again?

That was more likely than him getting back into dog fighting, wasn't it? Reggie would have to be pretty stupid to make that mistake again. As far as I could tell, he was smarter than the average person.

In my mind, anything would be better than dog fighting—drugs, guns, the black market art trade. *Then again it could be nothing at all*, I reminded myself. *It's not my business. Better not to know.*

Plausible deniability, I think they call it.

Reggie's face was serene after such a stressful-sounding conversation. He sat in a high-backed red leather chair. His Uncle Marvin sat in one, too, folding bills into his wallet. There was an empty seat between them.

They both smiled at me.

"Whassup, whassup, Alex?" Reggie said.

"Not much." My pulse raced.

Blackout shades adorned the windows in the room, and it smelled like salt and butter. A pop-pop-pop sound erupted from the corner, and I turned my head to see an old-timey glowing popcorn machine.

"Help yourself," Reggie said, pointing at it. "It's fresh." He lifted a red-and-white-striped bag from his lap.

A movie was paused on the giant screen, and I recognized the scene where a young Vito Corleone, played by De Niro, is tricked into stealing a decorative rug for his wife.

"*Godfather II*, huh? That's a great movie."

They didn't say anything. Reggie had an odd smirk on his face.

They must know I heard them.

For a second, I let my mind go to worst-case scenarios. Would Reggie deal with people who knew too much in the same fashion as a mafioso—exchanging niceties, sharing a drink, and then shooting them in the head? I didn't think he was literally going to shoot me, but he might let me squirm for a while before firing me. Or maybe he would threaten me with the terms of our confidentiality agreement.

I walked over and scooped some popcorn into a bag even though I didn't want any. I just needed something to do with my hands.

"Never met a girl who likes this movie," Reggie called after me.

The vise on my chest loosened a bit. I tossed a piece of popcorn into my mouth.

"I can come back later if you want."

"Your time's as valuable as mine," he said. His smile seemed genuine, and I relaxed. They didn't realize I'd been lurking.

"It's about your image campaign," I began.

"Yeah. You got some ideas for me?" He waved me to the middle of the room. I went and stood in front of the screen, their new entertainment.

"Well, actually I wanted to talk to you about that," I started again. "See, I'm not sure if I'm exactly qualified to be in charge of the whole thing."

"You don't want to do it?"

"No, that's not it at all. It's just that this is an important job, and if it's not done well, you could end up looking even worse." I fiddled with the Tiffany charm on my neck. "You need someone who's more savvy and experienced in media relations. My experience only goes as far as writing small-town articles and a few press releases."

Marvin looked back and forth between Reggie and me. "I'm going to get a sandwich from Marcia," he said, heading for the stairs.

Reggie didn't take his eyes off me. His expression was intense and perplexed. "How could you possibly make things worse?" he asked me. "All I want to do is find some way to help animals so people will see I'm not that person who did those awful things."

"I'm sorry, but I don't think the public's ready to see you working with animals. It could be spun negatively."

"How so?"

I hesitated, unsure if it was wise to share the what-ifs with him.

"See, you're worried about nothing," he said. "You can't even think of anything."

"Okay, say you're photographed with a dog."

He shrugged. "Yeah, so what?"

I hesitated.

"Give it to me straight. Real talk."

"Well, anyone can make a meme from that image. And memes usually aren't kind. No matter how pure your intentions, people will twist that. I'm imagining something right now: you with your arm around a Rottweiler or a pit bull, and the caption under it reading something like, 'Right before he choked the dog out.'"

Reggie's eyebrows slanted down. "Damn."

"I'm sorry," I said. "I was just going for the worst-case scenario."

"No need to apologize. That's exactly what I asked for."

"And that's why you need a seasoned professional, a big firm maybe, that would consider every angle, no matter how farfetched."

"Sounds like you're considering the angles."

"Yeah, but there's more to it than that."

"How so?"

"I could miss something else."

"Like what?"

"That one chain you wear. Not the braided gold one, but the one with the thick links. It's like a dog chain."

He steepled his fingers, nodded at his lap.

"Sorry," I said. "I'm probably being paranoid."

"Ain't that how you supposed to be in this business?"

"But they would—"

"They would try and make me a cardboard cutout, remove all my personality. That ain't what I want. You wouldn't do that. You see these problems, but you would fix them and still let me be me. Those people don't know me."

"And you think I know you?"

"Well, you ain't pissed me off, and you treat me like I'm just a regular guy."

I chuckled. "Maybe I need to try harder."

"Try this campaign then," he said. "You can hire some savvy, experienced people, as you say."

It was flattering the way he was trying to talk me into this.

"Okay. On a trial basis," I said. "And then we can reassess."

"Good. Now we need an idea for a foundation."

"Have you given it any thought?"

"The only idea I had was to train animals to help people—you know, like seeing eye dogs for blind kids, or the ones who can tell when a kid's about to have a seizure or something." I could tell this idea excited him. "They had a program in the prison where the guys worked with the dogs to get them ready for that. I heard that like one in fifty families who apply get one. It's because they don't have enough facilities and whatnot on the outside. So I thought I could open a service dog facility."

Shadows darkened his expression. "But it sounds like there ain't no way to do that."

I tongued at a popcorn shell lodged in my gums. I felt his disappointment. It was a wonderful idea, but it *could not happen*. Public perception wouldn't change if his new initiative associated him with his old crimes, even in this positive light.

"I love your passion," I said.

"But?" Reggie said.

"We need to . . . redirect it. Let me look something up."

I did a quick search on the iPad. The top results included kids with cancer, the environment, children with birth defects. Something popped out at me—a theme. The service dogs he'd described were helping children.

"You love kids," I said.

"Well, yeah. Who don't?"

"But you really care about them. Why don't you do something with young people? Something that uses your strengths?"

Marvin returned with a sandwich and offered half to Reggie, who waved it away.

"Yeah, I could teach them how to break into houses or steal cars," he said, nudging Marvin.

"You're joking, but we can use that," I said. "You have a unique voice that could speak to at-risk kids."

"Hold up," he said. "Last time I checked, parents don't want their kids listening to my music. You think they're going to let me anywhere near youths?"

"Good point. Your role could be kind of behind the scenes, but people will know this is your thing. You'll have a big say in what goes on, and you can participate, but licensed counselors and volunteers can work with them day to day."

His attention shifted to his pant leg. He scraped at a small spot on his thigh with his nail, then licked his finger and continued rubbing it.

"Look, you've been there, so you're not like a police officer or some teacher who can't relate to them. You'll know what kinds of programs will get through to them."

Marvin looked up. "She right, Reg," he said through a mouthful of meat and bread.

I began pacing as the idea took shape. "I've seen you with your daughter, Reggie. You know how to relate to young people."

"Fuck yeah, I can relate," he said, turning his attention from the stain on his pants to me. "Because I'm a kid in a grown man's body, after all."

I smiled. "Well, the sum you're willing to commit would allow for an ample donation to animals in need, which is definitely important. But you could also purchase a building and refurbish it with that money. If you're supplying the funds, people are going to let you decide how the youth programs are run."

Reggie dipped his head and ran a hand through his dreadlocks. "You're giving me all kinds of thoughts, you know," he said. I could see his mind working. "Yeah. I see basketball courts, and music lessons, maybe even a recording studio for these kids." He gestured in the air, painting his ideas on an invisible floating canvas. "That'd been sick if I had that shit growing up."

"Hang on. Let me write this down." I started taking notes on the iPad.

"We can have school supplies there for them, too. I never had tablets or nice markers and shit."

"These are all great ideas," I said, grinning.

"Yeah. What do we got to do to get this thing popping?"

"Ahhh. I've never started a nonprofit before. We'll need a location, volunteers, and some kind of committee to make sure we do things right." My head felt like a balloon ready to float away on a mixture of his excitement and my anxiety.

Reggie stood and moved toward me, placed a hand on my shoulder. "Alex, I know you can do this the right way. Hire whatever people you need. Just get it done."

CHAPTER EIGHTEEN

I got going on the foundation right away, spending hours on the phone with media consultants and then a nonprofit attorney, whom I hired on the spot.

Now I was sitting in Reggie's screening room surrounded by what must be close to two thousand loose Blu-ray discs. I knew I needed to call Denise, and I was procrastinating by taking on this monumental task.

I held the phone with my shoulder as I continued to organize the discs. Denise sounded like she'd had four cups of coffee. First, she told me about her cats, who had been gone for a year. Or maybe she got new ones—I wasn't really listening. Then it was the lady at the humane society who yelled at her for no reason. I put the phone on speaker so I could make faster progress with the Blu-rays.

"I just can't figure out what's wrong with the one burner," Denise said. "It lights sometimes, and other times it doesn't, and the flame is a weird color, like something's stuck down in there. If my hair's singed off next time you see me, you'll know why."

"Mmm-hmm. Maybe have Paul take a look at it."

I picked up a pile of loose discs, found *Steel Magnolias* stashed among several Bruce Lee movies, and wondered if Reggie had watched them all in one sitting.

"It's just the darndest thing," Denise went on. "I have no idea what it could be. Can a gas line have a short? No, it can't, can it? Maybe it's your father come back to haunt me. I swear it's going to explode in my face one of these days."

One can only hope, I thought, feeling particularly annoyed by her rambling.

I never broached the topic of Ollie.

By the time I hung up with Denise, I'd sorted maybe fifty Blu-rays. It was a tear down and rebuild kind of mission. I'd barely scratched the surface.

The NBA clock on the wall read Lakers/Pacers o'clock, or 11:15 p.m. as far as I could tell. After confirming Reggie would not be watching a movie this evening, I abandoned the Blu-rays. Ollie was waiting for me.

When I got to Isabelle's to pick him up, Ollie was looping in figure eights around her living room, his nails clack-clacking on the hardwood floor. I bent down, and he raced to me. As I was petting him, I noticed his toes. "He placed his paw in my lap when I was painting my nails," Isabelle said. "He asked me to do it." She held out her matching manicure, a bright plum.

"I can't believe he sat still for that," I said with a laugh. "Did he give you any trouble otherwise?"

"Not at all. He was a gentleman."

"You have to let me start paying you."

"Your money is no good," she said with a wave of her hand. "And remember, I am not going to be available very much in the coming weeks with my work schedule. Do you know what you are going to do?"

"I'll work something out."

She sunk back on her couch, pulled her legs up, and wrapped them to her side. "What about the doggie day-care?" she asked.

I let out a laugh. I'd seen one of those places on Collins Avenue a few weeks before I got Ollie, called Leave Ur Retriever. I remembered thinking it was a ridiculous concept.

"Maybe we'll try that," I said, swiping up Ollie's leash. Ready to go, he started dancing again. "Or maybe I'll find him a new home by then."

On the ride home, Ollie tried to crawl into my lap, head down, creeping, as if I wouldn't notice eighty pounds of dog on my thighs. I shooed him away. *I'm going to miss him,* I thought. My heart twitched as I pictured him with a new owner, his mournful eyes watching me leave him. What if this new person fed him food with corn as the first ingredient? What if they didn't take him for enough walks?

The more I thought about it, the more I realized I couldn't do it.

But I couldn't take care of him alone either.

Isabelle's career kept her nearly as busy as me. There was always doggie daycare, and if he didn't get along with the other animals at Leave Ur Retriever, I could get a dog sitter. The thought surprised me. Was I one of *those* people?

I guess I was.

But this wasn't me being crazy. It felt sane and right. I'd never been religious, and I was wary of the platitude "Everything happens for a reason." But in this moment I questioned nothing. An awareness had come over me, maybe for the first time in my life: I was supposed to take care of this dog. Perhaps I was even chosen to take care of him.

Would I even have considered taking him in at any other time? Before I started working for Reggie? You couldn't be associated with a convicted dog fighter without considering the plights of animals.

I'd put off looking for a home for him because his home was with me. It was a win-win. He was always overjoyed to see me, and not in an annoying, needy way like Denise. Before him, I used to find myself thinking about Rob during the day and smiling. Now I found the corners of my mouth turning up recalling one of Ollie's antics: the way he'd let me pick him up halfway and walk on his hind legs like a person; the time I'd given him a baby carrot and he liked it so much that he collapsed to the floor and groaned. And the other day he'd gotten stung by a bee on one of our walks. He'd glowered at me. I swear if he could talk he would have said, *How could you let this happen?*

Someone to come home to was someone to come home to, whether that came in a package of skin or fur. I guess Denise hadn't ruined me for animals.

Ollie and I bounded up the stairs to his forever home. Even Jean-Marc waiting outside my door, shirtless, didn't puncture my joy bubble.

"Hey," he said, scratching his protruding belly. "I have been trying to catch you, but you are always with that animal." His eyes were creased with disdain and years of sun damage. Ollie hunkered low, mouth curled in a snarl.

"Be nice, puppy," I said. My silly voice did nothing to cut the tension—the two males continued to stare each other down. "Um, okay. We can chat now. Just let me just put him inside."

"Yes, please."

I gave Ollie an organic chew treat and skirted back outside. Jean-Marc had disappeared into his apartment, leaving his door cracked. I propped myself onto a chair at his high table, where he, Isabelle, and I had shared many drinks and conversations before I'd noticed that bruise on Isabelle's back. My palms were sweating. No matter what, I had to stay tight-lipped. He couldn't know I was in communication with Isabelle or he'd press for information. He'd probably try to find out where she lived.

I jiggled my leg, waiting for him to come out and join me at the table. He appeared on the patio with a bottle of red and two wineglasses. I was grateful to see that he'd put a shirt on, though his coral shorts needed a few more inches of fabric. They were fine standing up, but when he sat down they would reveal more than I wanted to see.

He set a glass in front of me and tipped the bottle, offering me some.

"No, thanks," I said. I'd been taking to this alcoholic thing like a method actor. Maybe abstaining made me feel like less of a liar.

"You're saying no to my wine?" He raised an eyebrow at me and filled his glass. I tried to keep my eyes on his face, because if I gazed down at the glass table I would see right up his Daisy Dukes.

Muffled scraping and whining came from my apartment door. Apparently, the organic chew wasn't as long lasting as the package had boasted.

Jean-Marc placed his elbows on the table and intertwined his fingers. "So, how is it going, Alex?"

I pulled a cigarette out and rummaged through my bag for a lighter. A loud click and a flash of light startled me. Jean-Marc's ignited Zippo hovered in front of my face. I leaned toward the flame and inhaled.

"Good, good. Busy," I said, blowing out the smoke. "What's new with you?"

"You know what's new," he said. "Isabelle is gone. But tell me all about you—I haven't seen you since she left. I like to think I am your friend also." He reached across the table and touched my forearm for a second, and then he let his hand rest too close to mine. I couldn't help but recoil slightly. He didn't seem to notice.

"Of course you're my friend," I said. "I'm sorry. It's just that this new job has me crazy busy." I pulled my hand away from his, waved it around to show him how all over the place I was. Ollie continued to make noise. The palm leaves, almost at eye level on the third floor, started jangling, and I smelled rain coming. Ollie still needed his walk, and he wouldn't go out in a thunderstorm.

"New job?"

"Yeah."

"With whom?"

"For this musician, Reginald Wiles." I didn't think he would recognize the name because it hadn't caught on yet. Most people still referred to him as Rottie.

"That rapper who fought the dogs?" Jean-Marc said.

Damn.

"I'm just helping out as a favor," I said. "I should be going back to my old job soon."

He pointed in the direction of Ollie's scraping and squealing noises. "That is one of his dogs?"

"No! Reggie's done with that."

Jean-Marc gave me an incredulous look. "You would have to say that whether he is or is not doing that."

"I haven't seen a single animal at his place." I didn't account for Biggie. Then again if Reggie ever decided to start a parrot-fighting ring, Biggie would be a strong contender.

He took another long gulp of wine and topped his glass off. "Speaking of Isabelle, I am having difficulty reaching her. Do you happen to have her new telephone digits?"

I widened my eyes. "I know! I can't get ahold of her either. I was going to ask you for her new number."

He answered me with a glare.

"I guess you don't have it either," I said with an exaggerated shrug.

He didn't respond.

"Well, it's been good catching up with you, but I'd better go," I said, pointing at my door. "He'll keep you up all night if he doesn't get his walk."

A strange smile came across Jean-Marc's face but didn't make it to his eyes. "Is a little strange, no? You with a dog now."

"Yeah, well, I hit him with my car, and I just felt so bad that I brought him home with me."

"And you have had no other visitors lately?"

I grinded my cigarette butt hard into the ashtray.

"Um, I don't think so. Why?" I asked. My lie swirled around in the air with the cigarette haze. We both saw it.

"No reason," he said with a wink.

"Okay. Well, I'd better go," I said, pushing back from the table.

In a flash, he reached across the table and grabbed my wrist. "Are you telling me the truth?"

I forced myself to meet his eyes. "I swear. Isabelle and I weren't close."

He continued his death grip on my arm.

"You're hurting me," I said, pulling away.

He released me, and my eyes traveled down to my wrist, a band of pink where he had clamped it.

"I apologize. I am just very distraught, as you may understand," he said.

"No problem. I get it."

"Go, Alex," he said, waving me away. "I'll talk to you later."

"Uh yeah," I mumbled. "Before it rains." I hopped down from my chair.

"You had better keep that dog away from your new boss," he said after me with a dry chuckle. "And the authorities, no?"

The hairs on my neck stood up as I fumbled with my lock.

I turned to look at him. "What do you mean?"

"It is illegal to own a pit bull in Miami-Dade County. Did you not know that?" He had a toothy grin on his face.

"No, I didn't."

"You should be careful. They will take away that vicious thing if anyone were to inform them."

With all the lightness I could muster, I said, "Well, you won't have to worry about him much longer because I'm moving soon anyway."

CHAPTER NINETEEN

I'd expected a grim church basement with metal folding chairs, stale donuts. Skid-row types. Not a butler straight out of eighteenth-century England bowing and welcoming me to a three-story brick mansion on North Miami Beach.

"Right this way, miss," he said, his gloved hand making a sweeping gesture. My boot heels reverberated as I gazed up at the Tiffany chandelier in the grand foyer. We reached a great room drenched in white, where two dozen people chatted on a large wraparound sofa upholstered in a black-and-white cow-pelt pattern. About half of these people were famous. There was a local news anchor, a comedienne who liked to talk about her vagina, and a formerly muscle-bound action star who had turned bloated and yellowish. They were smiling and chatting, none of them appearing downtrodden or broken except maybe the action movie guy. My heart fell when I saw Lucy sitting beside Tatiana, the Birkin bag at Lucy's feet contrasting with her sober assistant's patchwork hobo purse.

Scents of shellfish and lemon mixed with coffee in the air. Lucy had said there would be good food. She hadn't noticed me yet, and I was starving, so I beelined to the buffet.

Somebody said, "Welcome!" as I swooshed past them. I pretended not to hear. Before I could tong the giant prawns, arms enclosed my waist. It was Lucy. I turned and hugged her, facing the room. A dark-haired actor whom I'd always thought was hot winked my way. A jolt of electricity went through me. His knees were pulled up to his chest, a hole in the big toe of his sock.

A woman with a dark bob and sinewy arms padded to the center of the room. Lucy grabbed my hand and led me to the sofa, for which a dozen cows had sacrificed their lives. The chic woman introduced the gorgeous movie star with the old socks. I stopped shoveling crab dip into my mouth and paid attention. This wasn't going to be as boring as I'd thought.

"I'm Wade and I'm an alcoholic."

"Hi, Wade!" said everyone in unison.

Wade told us he'd been sober for 1,902 days, or a little over five years for those of us who were doing the math in our heads. I was not one of those people. He was even better looking in person than on the screen. His trademark dimples flashed as he spoke.

"I am here by the grace of God," Wade said. "There's no reason I should be alive right now. I attended my first meeting when I was released from the hospital after my motorcycle accident." He paused and ran his fingers through his raven hair, creating instant bed head. "I was high off my ass on cocaine, heroin, and booze, and I don't remember a thing. But I sure do remember being in traction for five weeks."

I sat motionless, forgot about my hors d'oeuvres. The media had said Wade had lost control of his bike and crossed four lanes of traffic. There was no mention of intoxication. How had his people kept that out of the press? Who did his lawyering and PR? I needed them on Reggie's team immediately. Would it be vulgar of me to ask him about it after the meeting?

"And then there was that time I played Russian roulette with a Mexican drug lord tweaked out of my mind on peyote."

Everyone laughed.

Lucy looked at me, her eyes alight with amusement. I smiled as if I were in on the joke when I really wanted to ask, "How is this funny?"

"The fact that I'm alive today tells me there's a God," Wade continued.

Heads bobbed in agreement. Did they all identify with his story? Did they think that some god had intervened when Wade had chosen to give himself a one-in-six chance of living?

"My dad died of a heart attack that night while I was playing with live ammunition in a basement." The mood flipped in the room, and a twinge of emotion nipped at me. This I identified with. I knew what it felt like to lose a father suddenly. Wade paused and looked up to the skylight as if gathering strength from the heavens to continue. "Nobody could get ahold of me. I didn't get to say goodbye to my father, and he never got to see me grow into a semi-decent person. But now I talk to him every day, and I hope he can see my living amends wherever he is."

I scanned the room. Everyone was silent. A few people had tears in their eyes.

Wade talked about AA and the twelve steps for a while, and my eyes wandered back to the buffet table. After several minutes everyone clapped, and I gathered the meeting was wrapping up. But the attendees stayed seated. Then one by one they stood and launched into their own monologues. The first person to do so was an older man, maybe in his late fifties.

"I'm Pete and I'm an alcoholic." ("Hi, Pete!") He scratched at a murky bluish tattoo on his forearm. "I went from a perfect GPA to turning tricks on the streets for ten bucks," Pete said. "Just wanted to say your story really resonated with me, Wade. I've also cheated death many times. I know that God kept me alive because he has a plan for me."

Everyone had a crazy story. "I woke up on a boat with men carrying automatic weapons," or "I lost my virginity when I was eleven," or, "I ate a watermelon naked in the middle of the produce aisle."

Was everyone required to spill their most embarrassing moments? They were so dark, and none of my drunken experiences even came close. My skirt got tucked into my underwear in front of a lot of people once. Should I make something up when my turn came? No, Lucy would know if I was lying, because she knew everything about me. I'd go with my straightforward, boring DUI when my turn came. I felt like a fraud.

The true confessions fizzled out before they made their way around the entire room. I was off the hook.

Our hostess resumed her post in the middle of the room, hands folded in front of her. "Do we have any newcomers this evening?" she asked.

Lucy patted my knee. I hovered over my cushion like a dirty public toilet. "Hi, I'm Alex . . . and I'm an alcoholic." The words felt lumpy, like a pill stuck in my throat.

A wall of noise rose up in front of me: "Hi, Alex!" Tatiana's voice was the loudest. I got the feeling they'd cheer at anything:

"I like to eat babies!"
"I have painful diarrhea!"

"Thanks for having me," I mumbled, lowering myself back down to my seat.

The group joined hands in prayer and chanting. Lucy kept her grip on my hand after the mantras died down. Tatiana came over and grabbed my other hand. "You just did the first step," she said.

"How are you feeling?" Lucy asked, her eyes jumping back and forth as if my face were a page in a thriller novel.

"I have to move," I said.

They both nodded. "This stuff can be pretty intense for a newcomer," Tatiana said.

"We can go for a walk," Lucy said.

"No, I mean I can't stay where I'm living anymore. Neighbor stuff."

"Those French people?" Lucy asked. "Oh yeah, they were your drinking buddies, huh?"

What Jean-Marc had said about owning a pit bull was true. I'd googled "pit bull laws in Miami-Dade" after I left him on the porch. They were banned. I couldn't leave the county, but I could move away from the man who threatened to report me for having Ollie.

"I have to get out of there fast."

"Come with me," Lucy said. "There's someone here who might be able to help you."

She marched me up to Wade, the Russian roulette player, who was chatting with Pete, the guy who used to be a ten-dollar hustler. Unless Wade owned an apartment complex and a moving company, I doubted he could help me. Up close his face appeared older, creased, but still attractive in a swarthy kind of way.

"Welcome," Wade said, regarding me as if he already knew me. "Glad you're here."

"Thanks. I've never met a group of people more excited to see me."

"Well, count me as the most excited of the excited people," he said, stepping closer to me. Was he flirting?

"Leave her alone, Wade," Lucy said, taking my arm and spinning me away from the actor. "We came over here to talk to Pete."

It turned out Pete owned rental properties—a lot of them. He asked me what I was in the market for. I told him I needed one that allowed dogs. "I have the perfect house for you. One and a half baths, three bedrooms, and a nice deck out back," he said with a grin. When he told me what the rent was, I made plans to meet him there early the next morning.

As Lucy, Tatiana, and I were walking out, I felt a tickle on my palm. I turned, and Wade was behind me, finger to his lips. I clasped the piece of paper he was handing off to me and slipped it into my back pocket.

CHAPTER TWENTY

Pete and I met at 7 a.m. His rental property was a yellow bungalow with a clay-colored roof. The scent of chocolate-chip cookies wafted at me when he opened the door.

"It's kind of early for baking, but I hear that's what you're supposed to do when you're showing a house."

The cookies were delicious and melty but unnecessary. The house seemed welcoming all by itself. I could envision where every piece of my furniture would fit in the open interior with wooden beams running across a vaulted ceiling. And then I spotted my dream feature: a bench in front of a bay window that I could use as a reading nook. I imagined the musical sound of Ollie's feet clicking across the ceramic floors as I pored over a dark mystery.

"This is what I call the airplane lavatory," Pete said, showing me the tiny second bathroom, where the toilet almost touched the vanity. Size didn't matter; I was thrilled because I'd never had a home with more than one toilet.

He led me out to the deck and pointed out the flora in the backyard: a spray of yellow goldenrod flowers; a stout red and green plant called rushfoil; a giant wax myrtle tree in the center, shading most of the area. The tree's winding limbs reminded me of the tree that used to be in the front yard at Denise's house. It had been a sycamore, tall but with low, frequent branches that allowed me to climb higher than the house when I was little. One of my earliest memories was Denise yelling at my father, "Get her down from there right now!" When she disappeared inside, my dad winked and told me to climb a little higher.

Some guys came and took their chainsaws to it right before the one-year anniversary of my dad's death. I watched the whole process, crying while Denise explained that the tree was diseased. For a while the stump had remained, and I would sit on it and read. Over time it decayed and became a circle of rot in the grass.

"Your dog will have a little room to run," Pete said. "What kind is it?"

I pictured Ollie bounding down the wooden stairs to his new, mostly fenced-in yard. We'd run around and play fetch, being careful to avoid the canal. When he got tired, he'd nap under the wax myrtle.

"He's a mutt. He's really good, not destructive or anything."

"I have a great dog myself. If you want to fence that last section, I can apply it towards your rent," he said, waving toward the canal.

It was perfect. I called Lucy to tell her about it as I pulled away from the house.

"Well, I'm moving in next week," I said.

"Whoa! That was fast," she exclaimed through the car speakers.

"Yeah, but do you know why he's renting it out so cheap? I doubt I'm anywhere near covering the mortgage payments."

"He's big on helping other alcoholics. He must be doing well financially, and he probably just wants to pay it forward."

"Huh." A wave of guilt nipped at me. Pete, despite his junkie past, had treated me with kindness, but he was operating under the assumption that I was a drunk. I was repaying his generosity with a lie. Could I offer to pay a little more since he wouldn't be housing a true recovering drunk? Sure, I wasn't drinking right now. But I could envision Ollie and me living in this house for a while, maybe years.

If I told Pete I was posing as a member of AA, would he relinquish his offer? And would he tell Lucy? One of the chants at the meeting had included the line "Let there be no gossip." And that told me there was a definite gossip problem in that group. Once I decided to have a drink again, I'd feel like a fraud hiding the wine when he came over to unclog the bathroom sink. I hoped I didn't skim past some stipulation in the rental agreement stating that I needed to be sober to live there. But that would be weird, maybe even illegal, wouldn't it?

"What do you know about Pete?" I asked.

"What do you mean?"

"Is he normal?" I began. "Would he, um, I don't know, cross any personal boundaries?" I was trying to find out if he would feel compelled to keep tabs on me, drop by with AA pamphlets, or rifle through my trash.

"Well, he's not normal. None of us with this disease are normal."

You got that right.

"Well, what I mean is, does he seem like . . . ?" I searched for the right word but couldn't find it. "Does he seem like . . . a creep or anything?"

"Why?" she asked. "Did he do something to give you that impression? Goddammit. There are some folks in the program who are still very sick. They gave up the drink, but it didn't cure the crazy."

"Mmm," I replied like I knew what she was talking about.

"Sorry, can you hang on just a sec?"

"Yeah."

I merged onto the causeway. The sky had darkened since I'd left Pete's, and the bay churned and boiled. While waiting on hold for Lucy, I wondered if those crazy AA people just needed to relax and have a drink. Hell, it could cut down on all their gossiping. I was being cynical. The people at the meeting had been nothing but nice and welcoming. But my mind painted the group a little cultish.

Maybe it started when I took one of those alcoholic assessment tests, thinking it would help me to blend in better at her AA meeting. I answered yes to three out of about twenty-five questions. They were:

1. Did you ever have a DUI?
2. Have you ever drunk heavily when you were disappointed or after quarreling with someone? (Both 1 and 2 happened on the night that I found Ollie.)

I forget what 3 was.

My results: "You could have a drinking problem."

Figuring the website was a camouflaged advertisement, I'd written it off. But what if it had been right? Did Lucy see something in me that I didn't?

There was faint chatter coming through my car's speakers now. Was she conferring with Tatiana? I pictured Tatiana towering beside her in a protective stance, monitoring her conversation.

Lucy got back on the phone. "I'm really sorry. Where were we? Oh yeah. I thought Pete was one of the cool ones. Is he a pervert or something?"

"No, no. He didn't do anything. I'm just saying that since he's doing me a favor, would he try to act like my sponsor or something?"

She giggled. "Sponsors have to be the same sex. That reminds me—I've actually met a couple nice, *normal* women who are taking on sponsees."

Sponsee. Is she serious?

"Okay, well, I just got to Reggie's," I said, scanning the wall for the security mafia. They waved to me now.

CHAPTER TWENTY-ONE

Reggie's gate was open when I edged onto his property. The guards must have sought shelter from the approaching storm that was blowing in. A horn sounded, and for a second I thought it might be a city emergency alarm. Then in my rearview mirror I saw a man dashing toward me. He was one of the paparazzi who sat out in front of Reggie's. His shoulders were rounded and he had almost no neck, but he was quick on his feet. I braked and lowered my window.

"Yo!" the man said in a Latino accent. "Got a minute?"

"Yeah, a minute," I said, looking at the charcoal sky.

He stuck out a hairy hand and I shook it through the window. "I'm Angel, and I think you're gonna want to talk to me," he said.

He pulled a manila envelope out from behind his back. "I'm letting you see this before I put it on the market."

I was familiar with these paparazzi tactics. He wanted money. I'd been approached like this before when I worked for Lucy, and most of their claims were worthless. I took out the photos expecting to see a telephoto shot of Reggie hitting a bong by the pool. Like that would be a big surprise to anyone.

"This was taken downtown two nights ago," Angel said. "These show Reggie at an abandoned warehouse in the Wynwood district."

I hid my surprise. When you hear "abandoned warehouse," the first thing you think of is criminal activity—drug deals, sex trafficking, murder. "So?" I said nonchalantly.

"So, I wanted to give you first dibs."

I studied the photograph. "You must have a better shot than this," I said. "The only thing that stands out to me is that you forgot to use your flash." I was bluffing. It was clearly Reggie in the photos. Ham was in the picture, too.

"I heard dogs barking, too."

"Stop wasting my time," I said.

Angel stared at me. "Are you sure that's your answer?"

"Well," I said, thinking better of it. These guys could make your life miserable. "Maybe we can work something out. Are you sure you're the only one with a copy of this photo?"

He nodded.

"If you bury the picture, I won't tell Reggie you tried to blackmail him. Believe me, I'm doing you a favor." I paused for a moment. "Plus I'll throw you an exclusive here and there. You'll be able to sell an exclusive for more than this grainy photo."

Angel just stared at me.

"Okay?" I said, putting my car in drive. "I'm driving away now."

"Okay," he said.

CHAPTER TWENTY-TWO

I'm cold and exposed in a tiny concrete room. Someone's watching me, eyes boring into my body. I must have died when I hit the dog, veered off into a tree or something. Maybe this is hell, and I got sent here for working for a man whom many people consider wicked. The woman strip-searching me seems to be enjoying her power. Shivering is a sign of weakness. If I could just grab on to something to make me still.

I jerked awake, my arm reaching. Velvety fur met my fingers, and I relaxed back into my pillow. There was a thumping on the bed. Ollie was up now, propped on his back haunches, wagging his tail and smiling at me. I rose, shuddering in the air-conditioning as I pulled on a sports bra and a hoodie.

We headed out into the dewy morning. I'd never felt anything other than misery being away from my bed before 8 a.m., but Ollie's exuberance seemed to run through his tether, up my arm, and straight to my core. He chewed his leash as he tromped ahead of me, his ears flapping in the salty morning breeze. When I noticed he'd half severed the leash, I told him no. He stopped gnawing and glanced back at me.

"Good boy."

We picked up speed. Ollie's tongue lolled out and he squinted his eyes, for him a picture of contentment and joy. I tried to think back to the last time I felt that way. Lately, my brain had felt like a balloon. Masquerading as an alcoholic and a PR mogul took up a lot of air. My upcoming DUI trial and the threat of going back to jail swirled around in there, too. *Lucy's lawyer is the best,* I told myself. Somehow the lawyer Lucy hired for me got my driver's license reinstated shortly after my arrest. If he could do that, he could keep me out of jail.

Today was my day off, and I resolved to not spend it worrying. I focused on Ollie, glimpsed the world through his eyes. Even though he had been mistreated most of his life, he saw the world as a place filled with adventure and fun, a delight to the senses.

Jessica the attorney I'd hired for the youth center called as we were finishing our run. She'd been busy over the last twenty-four hours, and she had a slew of questions and action items for me. My anxiety returned. I would never have time to tackle everything she listed off in addition to my regular work responsibilities. I told her I'd meet her at Reggie's in an hour.

As I grabbed my purse and keys, Ollie tilted his head at me, as if confused. As if he knew there was a change in plans. His eyes said, *But I thought we were spending the day together.*

How could he possibly know that? I wondered.

Maybe he felt the shift in my energy.

"Sorry, bud," I said as I shut him into the apartment.

Guilt nipped at me as I drove to Reggie's. Jessica was already there when I arrived. She spread photos and blueprints of three inner-city buildings on Reggie's patio table.

"Of course they'll need renovations," she said. "My contact at the zoning office is standing by to push our requests through quickly." She sipped her coffee, her ice-pink nails glinting in the sun. "And there are several progressive movers and shakers who are interested in being board members."

It couldn't be this simple and fast.

"Jessica, what about Reggie's reputation?" I asked.

She ran her hands from her forehead to her neat blond bun, slicking back a few stray hairs that had popped up in the humidity. "This is going to be quite positive for his reputation."

"Has anyone turned you down?" I asked. "Given Reggie's past?"

"As long as he's not bringing in dog fights or naming the place 'Pussy Palace,' people are going to be on board. He's making a huge financial contribution to this city."

I liked her.

"When can we go check out the buildings?" I asked.

"Now. Reggie told me he wants to see them today."

I wouldn't be getting back to my dog any time soon.

After touring the first site, we stepped out into exhaust-filled air. A jet engine whooshed above us, close enough to blacken the sky for a moment. Reggie stopped on the sidewalk, beaming at me and holding up his palm. It took me a second to figure out what he was doing, and by the time I realized I'd left him hanging for a high five, it was too late. He dropped his hand, his face still alight.

"You like the place, huh?" I yelled over the roaring plane.

"It's amazing," he said. "I was picturing something just like this when you talked about locations. This got to be the one." He backed up so he was standing in the street and squinted at the structure. "It'll need some work, but that loft in there is sick!"

The screeching of tires made me jump. Angel's silver Nissan bumped forward and then back. He leapt out and shuffled toward us.

I'd forgotten to tell Angel to pretend he didn't know me in front of Reggie and Ham. Ham warned me on my first day that I was to inform them of all outside communications regarding Reggie. I was busted.

Doors slammed beside me, Reggie's security coming to cover him.

The ground seemed to shift in the commotion. For a split second, I felt like I was on roller skates.

Angel lifted his camera up to his face. "Fancy seeing you here, Al— "

"Stay back!" I yelled over him. I glanced at my bosses to see if they had heard him, but I couldn't tell because Ham and two security guards had formed a barrier in front of Reggie, their backs to me.

I stayed planted on the sidewalk.

"I'll take that exclusive now," Angel said, smiling at me.

"Shut the hell up," I said, my voice rasping.

"What the fuck is he talking about?" Ham asked, opening the car door for Reggie.

I shook my head at him, suggesting I was just as confused as he was. Then an idea came to me.

"That was my old boss, Lucy. We have no such agreement pertaining to Reggie."

Angel opened his mouth to argue, but I kept talking.

"I might be able to give you a little exclusive if you promise not to bombard us with questions," I said, hoping he would understand he should play along. "You have to promise to give Reggie fifteen feet of personal space at all times."

He lowered his camera. "Sure. Can you get Reggie to give the statement?"

"You'll do what I ask? And no pictures until I say?"

He traced a cross over his heart.

"You sure this is a good idea?" Ham asked as we walked toward the Mercedes.

"We might as well get some buzz going. This foundation's moving like a freight train, and we'll be opening before we know it." I motioned for Reggie to lower the car window.

"I think we should give this guy an exclusive," I said.

Reggie pulled his shades down. "Why would we do that?"

"This is actually great timing," I said. "Why not let everyone see you here scouting a location? It will look more spontaneous than a conventional announcement on TV. They're catching you in action."

He opened the door, and I slid in next to him.

"Yeah, you right. I'll do it."

"Okay. We'll make this fast. We still have two more placcs to scc."

"This the one," Reggie said. "Don't need to see any more. It's meant to *be*."

"You must want to check out the other ones just to be sure, right?"

"Don't need to. Now, what you want me to say to this guy?"

I briefed him, and we stepped out onto the pavement together. Angel had his video recorder at the ready. Surveying the scenery for the best angle and light, I noticed something that sent a chill through me. The building across the street had two broken windows side by side.

I had seen this place before, and so had Reggie. That was the building from the picture Angel had shown me in the driveway.

CHAPTER TWENTY-THREE

Morning came too soon again, and a couple nights of frayed sleep with intense but unmemorable dreams were catching up with me. I zombie-drove to work and then zombie-walked to the kitchen for one of Marcia's muffins and a third cup of coffee. A text came in from Lucy as I was staring into the fridge, having forgotten what I was looking for.

Lucy: *We still on for the meeting tonight?*

"Shit," I said to the orange juice and rotisserie chicken. I couldn't flake out on an AA meeting or Lucy would doubt my commitment.

Yep. See you there ☺

I deleted the smiley face before hitting Send.

I remembered that I wanted butter. I settled in front of my fattening breakfast and checked the entertainment websites on my iPad. TMZ had uploaded the video that Angel had taken the previous day. Reggie had delivered his spiel well in person, but there was no telling how the media would spin or splice it. I took a deep breath and hit Play.

Reggie is well lit, his white T-shirt contrasting against the brick building. Revving engines and growling trucks drown out a word or two here and there, and so does the wind when it hits the mic head-on.

The camera tremors and Angel's voice asks, "Why are you [wind gust] in this neighborhood today, Rottie?"

Reggie crosses his arms and crinkles his forehead. "C'mon, son. It's Reggie now."

A blip sounds, and the film jumps ahead, but not far enough.

"Sorry, Reggie. What are you doing here today?"

"We found a [truck thunders by] that will be a safe place for the kids of Miami. We're working with educators, social workers, and artists to create an environment where kids can express themselves in a positive way. The bus lines all come through here, and that's why we chose it. It's a place kids can come after school and on the weekends instead of [wind gust] and getting into trouble."

"What else you got in the works, Reggie?" Angel asks.
"Well, I got a full-length album dropping early next
year, and I'm working with some hot new hip-hop art-
ists that fans gonna love." He flashes his tooth-whit-
ener-commercial smile and waves. "That's all. Thank
you," he says, walking out of the frame.

Reggie came off well. Poor quality video, but it captured
the gist, and Reggie's delivery was personable, as if he
were addressing a close friend instead of a camera. The
video had more than one hundred fifty thousand hits
already. The warehouse with the two broken windows
didn't appear in the frame.

Not bad for my first go as a media consultant.

The next interview would run in prime time. It was
scheduled for a week from today. We needed to be prepared for tough questions. That meant I had to dive into
every aspect of Reggie's past.

I flashed back to two years ago, when the details of
his crimes took over the media. Denise said she'd cried
for a week. She'd wanted me to come home. It was just
like her to take something that happened to someone
(or something) else and make it about her. I'd told her
to stop reading the articles. "That's what your Uncle
Paul said, too," she had said. "But it's my duty to pay attention. If we turn our backs because it's too upsetting,
nothing will change."

Now it was time for me to face the atrocities committed by Reggie, and I wanted to do it in private. I shut myself into my office for the first time since I'd worked there. I closed the blinds even though there was a beautiful view of the gardens outside. I started to comb through every charge and accusation.

The beatings, drownings, and shootings of dogs that didn't perform well—I already knew all that, but my breath still hitched as I read the details again. When it became too much, I took little breaks. I posted a funny meme on Paul's Facebook page, looked at home design ideas on Pinterest, browsed furnishing and décor sites. I purchased an accent rug on Amazon—I would probably end up returning it.

I went back to the stories and came across one about Reggie that was new to me. One of the dogs in his ring was buried alive. A teenager saw someone shoveling dirt over the animal in a vacant downtown lot. The teen dug up the dog as soon as the perpetrators left. The kid's family ended up adopting the victim and later reported that the dog was healthy and flourishing. That animal's story ended better than some of the others'.

I pressed my knuckles hard into my eyes and plowed forward.

Maybe Denise's reaction wasn't just theatrics. Back then I'd thought that dog fighting was shitty, pointless violence. But it was a passing thought, a vague injustice as far removed from me as the faceless people suffering in foreign countries. Now I was mourning for the animals in my bones. They were right next to me.

Sick and with an overwhelming urge to hug Ollie, I slammed my laptop shut and walked out to the backyard to gaze at the calming water. I thought about the full bar in the pool house and how a neat three fingers of bourbon would numb me enough to get through this interview prep. But then I would have to live another lie. Lucy had started keeping track of my days sober, and she sent me a text every couple of days congratulating me. Those messages already gave me guilt pangs. I imagined how those would feel if I were drinking.

I went back inside to finish the job. I tried to cultivate the objectivity they pounded into us at journalism school.

Reggie is a changed, decent person, I told myself. To get the public to believe it, I needed to believe it. I focused on his relationship with his little girl, pictured him tossing her up in the air, the pure love in his eyes.

But three hours later, reading over my comprehensive interview prep document, I felt like a spin doctor for a dirty politician. Did Reggie deserve the goodwill I was trying to generate for him?

Things were simpler with Lucy. Not that there hadn't been dark days with her. There were times I questioned why I stayed with her. But when Hurricane Lucy had hit the shores of Miami Beach, her destruction was turned inward. She'd never hurt anyone.

And as I said, she'd saved my life.

At age thirteen I was that weird, quiet girl at school who had found her dad dead. It wasn't bad at first. People gave me the right of way in the halls. And one of the cute skater boys stopped and gathered up my books when they'd tumbled from my locker. I was someone to be cared for, protected. None of them knew my secret. If they knew what I'd done, they'd have no sympathy for me.

My classmates' sympathy lasted for roughly a month, and then I started to sense that I was disappearing. Feeling needy, I dropped my pen in the class where I sat next to the skater boy. He watched it hit the ground and continued chatting with his friend.

Our health teacher devoted a class session to a recent school shooting in another state. He said trauma can alter your brain chemistry, and I believed him. But I felt the change in chemistry a little lower, in my center. There was a vacuum in the middle of me.

At first I tried to fill in the blank, feed myself cheeseburgers and fries and Pop-Tarts. But the emptiness only grew, along with my waistline.

Then I discovered my first drug—coffee. It allowed me to subsist on a random diet of baby carrots and graham crackers. This had sent Denise into a tizzy, knocking at my bedroom door with boxes of take-out food. Once I opened the door to find her fanning an open box of pepperoni pizza at me.

The weight came off and then some, but the emptiness remained.

My childish mind dubbed this phenomenon The Hollow. (I was literary—I'd read *The Bell Jar* twice.) I went online and searched for painless ways to commit suicide. I began hiding Denise's leftover bunion surgery painkillers under my mattress.

I planned my death for a Monday. The plan included my absence from school, but then I realized Denise would check on me every hour, and the pills wouldn't have enough time to do their worst. I would need to wait until that night.

On the day that I was going to do it, my French teacher partnered everyone for a conversational skit assignment by having us draw numbers from a bucket. Lucy and I drew the same number.

We knew each other already, but we approached each other like strangers. Our last slumber party had taken place in second grade, just before the friendship between our mothers had ended abruptly without explanation. Lucy had gone on to achieve popularity, while I languished in obscurity.

I slumped at my desk and picked at its peeling fake wood veneer.

"This is stupid," Lucy said, dragging her desk over the worn, electric-blue carpet and placing it next to mine. "Everyone's going to order croissants at a sidewalk café."

"I'd rather kill myself than order a fucking croissant," I said.

Lucy laughed.

Maybe it was because I didn't give a shit anymore. Maybe it was because I was in the mood to shock people before my final shocking act, but I was hit by a burst of creativity.

Our classmates got up in front of the class, stiff and acting out their scenarios in bad French accents. Not everyone ordered croissants—some asked for brie or wine.

We ordered blood. The vital fluid of our classmates.

"Regardez ces étudiants délicieux qui nous déchirer membre par membre," I said. "Look at these delicious students whom we will tear limb from limb."

"Do any of them deserve eternal life?" Lucy asked in French. *"Mais, non,"* I replied, my gaze fixed on the skater who had failed to pick up my pen.

Our teacher laughed and clapped when we were done. *"Très amusant,"* she said.

Our classmates had disturbed looks on their faces while we took our bows.

Lucy and I walked out together at the sound of the bell, friends again.

That afternoon she showed up at my house, helping herself to Denise's proffered take-out box and sauntering into my room, chopsticks and lo mein in hand.

Lucy pulled a coffee thermos full of liquor from her bag. "Drink this," she said, shoving it at me. "You're going to need it."

I screwed off the top and got a noseful of thick black licorice.

"Ew, no," I said. "It smells awful."

She didn't answer and threw my sliding laminate closet door open, not flinching when it slammed hard against the frame and a cat yowled in the other room.

"Fucking overalls?" Lucy said, perusing my wardrobe. "Are you seven?"

I shrugged and sniffed at the dark chemical liquid again. I'd never had alcohol before, except for the time my dad had given me a sip of his beer and I'd spit it onto my pink jelly shoes. How much would it take to get me drunk? A couple sips? A cup?

"Maybe we can make this work, make it like a retro look," she said. "You need to wear something provocative underneath."

I looked down at my threadbare pajama bottoms. "Um, I'm fine in this."

"You're not wearing that to the party. Don't you have any dresses without flowers on them?"

"What party?"

"You're not getting out of this." Lucy grabbed the thermos and poured a shot into the cup. "Trust me, this will make you want to go."

I held my breath and slugged it down. I wanted to want to go—get out of this giant litter box I inhabited. The booze warmed its way down my throat and shot back up to my head like a balloon, pushing out the desolate thoughts.

I wanted more.

We sailed into the basketball team captain's McMansion, and I didn't question for a second whether I belonged there in my overall shorts and cami with no bra. Neither did anyone else.

Lucy's sleek friends became my friends. I was popular. Just like that. I remember thinking that we had something in common again: we were both daughters of single mothers.

For whatever reason, Lucy had taken me under her wing, and in doing so she had made The Hollow go away.

CHAPTER TWENTY-FOUR

Roaring thunder bolted me awake. Ollie had somehow tangled the covers, leaving my bare legs and
feet exposed to the air-conditioning. His head rested
on my shoulder. His fur smelled like Fritos and sand,
making me wonder if I had dreamt I was eating corn
chips on the beach. I tried to finagle my blankets back,
but he had made an overstuffed burrito of himself and
wouldn't give an inch. I pushed myself up on my elbows.
Ollie groaned and crawled on top of me, burying his
face in my neck with urgency. Another rumble of thunder seemed to resonate through his body.

He was terrified.

When had this started? We'd gone running in a storm just the other night, and he'd seemed fine. Maybe if I got him back out there he'd see there was nothing to fear.

But he wouldn't cross the threshold of my front door.

"You have to go potty at least!" He let out a low moan and held his ground. "Ollie, let's go," I said with exuberance, giving his leash a tug. Nothing. "Ollie, come." My voice was stern this time. His brown eyes bulged with fear as his front paw hovered over the thin metal strip separating linoleum from concrete.

My heart clinched, seeing him so torn between his instinct for self-preservation and a desire to please me. "Oh fine," I said with a sigh. Miami storms blow out as quickly as they blow in. Maybe we'd be able to step out after I got ready for work.

As I shut us back into the safety of my apartment, a troubling thought hit me. I stooped down and rubbed Ollie's distraught head. Was this how he had felt before he met me, knowing he could be forced into a terrifying situation at any time? That was most likely where he had come from—a fighting ring. Had he wanted to please his old master, too, even though that person had subjected him to a life of violence?

The things I read the day before about Reggie's fighting ring played on repeat in my head. I wanted to go to work today about as much as Ollie wanted to go out in that storm.

A low whine came from the back of Ollie's throat and he shuffled his front paws, stretching his head toward mine as if telling me what I should do.

Before I could wuss out, I fired off a text and hit Send.

Might have food poisoning. Sorry. Will come in later if it gets better.

Take the day and get well ☺ was Reggie's response.

I almost felt guilty.

Another text came in. It was Lucy. *Come over for dinner tomorrow night?*

I'd just seen her at the AA meeting the previous night. She must have missed me as much as I missed her.

Sure. Yay! I responded.

The sun broke in through the blinds, pulling me from the lull of daytime squabble shows. Morning had given way to afternoon, and poor Ollie had to be dying to go to the bathroom by now. I jumped up from the couch, and my head went light. I froze, waited for the faintness to pass, but my breath started coming in weak, fast bursts. I couldn't get enough air. Ollie dashed to the center of the room and commenced the butt-wiggling salsa number he did when he anticipated a walk.

"It's alright, buddy. We'll go in a second," I murmured.

I let myself fall back onto the cushion.

I looked at my shaking hands, tried to make them stop. But it was no use. The shuddering traveled from my diaphragm all the way to my fingers. I remembered this sensation. This was what my body had done when I'd suffered that brief but harsh string of panic attacks shortly after my dad's death.

My limbs went numb, and the dark spots appeared, wavy at the edges. I assumed the position the school nurse had shown me back then, head low, hands on knees, waiting for it to stop. I thought I'd beaten this a long time ago.

I was vaguely aware that Ollie had started vocalizing, my crippled senses distorting his yowls into low wah-wah sounds. I just had to ride it out. My breath would return. It always did eventually.

After a minute or ten, the sensation returned to my fingers, and my breath fell into a normal rhythm. I sat up and blinked. The spots had dissipated, and Ollie's paw rested on my knee. I rubbed his soft ear between my thumb and forefinger like a toddler does with a beloved blankie.

He sat on his haunches, statue-like, as if he knew I needed him to carry me for a moment. My strength was returning, and the logical part of my brain started working again. The emotions I'd felt when I'd delved into Reggie's past had caused my anxiety attack. It had been years since anything had affected me so strongly. Someone at last night's AA meeting had said she'd been going through life partially numb, and now that she had removed the numbing agent (a.k.a. booze), the floodgates were opening. Maybe my dam had broken just like hers, and without alcohol my feelings were a raging river.

Or Ollie was the reason for this meltdown.

No human would be so affectionate and gentle after going through what he did. It killed me that someone had hurt him.

A margarita wouldn't change that.

I took Ollie for his walk, and then I went out and bought a thick steak to share with him. He nipped at the grocery bag, but I didn't scold him. I stowed the meat in the fridge and jumped right back at him, and we became a frenzy of hair and giggles and barks.

I fed him most of the steak.

It was the picture of a perfect mental health day—exactly what we needed. We went to bed early—too early, because I woke to Ollie's soft snores just before midnight. My mind commenced racing again, going over the evidence from Reggie's trial. I dreaded going to work the next day.

I decided to see if Paul was online.

That green dot appeared next to his name on Skype.

"You can't sleep either, huh?"

"No," I said with a sigh. "Work stuff."

"Thug life got you down?"

I laughed. "Yeah, and on top of it I'm getting ready to move."

"Good thing you never unpacked to begin with." He gestured at the boxes stacked behind me.

Ollie trudged out from my bedroom and plopped at my feet with a grunt. Greta's head popped up into view on the monitor, her pointy ears standing at high alert. She let out a loud bark, and Ollie scrambled up, placing his paws at the edge of my desk. They started yapping at each other, and Paul and I leaned back in our chairs, waiting for them to finish their conversation.

When they stopped, Paul poked at the inside of his cheek with his tongue like he did whenever he was perplexed. "You've wanted to move forever, right, kid?"

"Yeah, but it couldn't come at a worse time." I told him about the house and the cheap rent, leaving out that I most likely got that price by posing as an AA member.

"Why is it such a bad time?"

"I'm having a crisis of conscience or something. When I interviewed with Reggie, he asked me if I thought he was a monster. I'm starting to think he is, and it's really freaking me out. Something's wrong with me."

"Dear girl," he said, stroking Greta's ears. "Nothing's wrong with you."

Ollie plopped himself on my feet. I patted his head, and he grunted again. I never knew if his grunts meant annoyance or contentment. He grunted when I shifted positions and woke him up, which he hated, but he also grunted when I scratched his ears, which he loved. After a second his eyes squeezed shut and he put his head down, so I concluded he was content this time.

Paul leaned into his computer's camera. "This makes sense, how you're feeling about Reggie's past. A dog just came into your life." He paused and gave me a mischievous grin. "You never understand until you have one of your own." My cousin had gushed those exact words during her daughter's bout of colic one Thanksgiving. Paul and I had shared a major eye roll at the time, but in retrospect it rang true—at least as it applied to dog owners. You wanted them to be happy, and you wanted to protect them. Just like a mother who dotes on other people's babies, you feel something for animals that don't even belong to you because you realize just how special yours is.

"You're right, Paul," I said. "I'm not a thug. I've gone soft."

"Are you thinking of quitting?" he asked in a gentle voice.

I bobbed my head, bit the inside of my cheek so I wouldn't start crying.

"Well, only you can make that decision, but think about this: a lot of people have gone down bad roads and come back better for it. Even me."

Even him? What had he ever done? I opened my mouth, about to ask him, but he held up a finger.

"What does your gut tell you about him? Not after reading all that stuff today but before. I remember you telling me how considerate he was to let you sleep during that big bash he threw."

Does Reggie strike me as evil? No, he doesn't.

"He's a loving father. He's kind. He's always respectful. It doesn't make sense. How could someone change that drastically?"

"That's what strong people do."

Lucy popped into my head. I'd been so concerned with how her life change affected me that I hadn't considered how hard it must've been for her. Getting clean had to take guts. "That makes sense," I said. "But what was your bad path?"

He waved his hand. "You don't want to hear about all that now. I'll tell you another time." He paused. "Especially after what you've been through." Whenever he referred to what I'd *been through*, he meant my dad's death. And I'd been thinking about the events surrounding his death more than usual. Especially that horrible thing I'd done around that time. Up until very recently, the memory would crop up every now and then and I'd push it back down. But lately it seemed like several times a day I would come back to it, as if it happened yesterday.

"Well," I said to Paul, "I'm intrigued. You're going to have to tell me about your bad path sooner or later."

"Deal," he said. "But not tonight. Get some sleep."

We signed off. I knew I wouldn't sleep. Once my mind gets going on a problem, even after I find some sort of resolution it's hard to stop the churning. Ollie snored at my feet, and I hated to wake him.

Wade's number sat on my desk, staring up at me from the creased piece of paper that I'd shoved in my pocket at my first AA meeting. He'd mentioned in his talk that he still stayed up late, even without alcohol and drugs. I didn't dare call him. But sending a text was easy enough.

CHAPTER TWENTY-FIVE

"**Y**ou okay? Sure you don't need another day off?" Reggie asked when I presented him with his blueberry smoothie on the patio the next morning. He saw what I had seen when I'd looked in the mirror this morning: droopy glazed-over eyes, lifeless skin that my La Mer face tonic had failed to revive.

Despite getting little sleep, I felt better than I looked. My brain was more fatigued than my body, and I liked it that way. I'd put it through a workout thinking about Reggie's past and wondering what Paul's bad path had been. At 3 a.m. I'd risen and made a list of the pros and cons of sticking it out with Reggie. The pros won for now, and they went as follows: *I am doing this for Lucy. I have the opportunity to run a major PR campaign, and if I prove myself, Lucy will let me represent her. This job isn't forever. I am making a shit-ton of money. Paul gave me his blessing.* And finally, *He's not a horrible boss.*

"I'm good, Reggie," I said. "Feeling much better."

He sipped his smoothie and studied me with one eye closed.

"But I could use a couple days off next week. I have to move."

"Have to?"

In my weakened mental state, I didn't bother to lie. Lack of sleep always acted as a truth serum for me. "My neighbor may have or may have not threatened to report me for my dog."

"You ain't never told you had a dog. What kind?"

"Pit bull."

"No shit." His hand went to his mouth, and he turned his back to me. "You mind going inside and calling Ham out here, please?"

I hadn't expected his reaction. *I guess I don't have to decide whether to quit because they're going to fire me right now.*

I paged Ham, and he shuffled outside. I pretended to do administrative stuff on my iPad as I snuck glances at them through the window. Their faces were somber during the brief exchange, and then Ham trudged through the sliding door.

"Follow me," he said.

Here it comes.

We didn't speak as I trailed after him out the front door, across the driveway. If he was trying to get me out of the house to fire me, it would be for nothing when I had to take a walk of shame to retrieve my belongings. Marcia would purse her lips and shake her head at me. She would do that anyway, though.

The climate changed when we entered the garage, like we'd stepped onto another planet. It was otherworldly and frigid, with giant dehumidifiers droning from the ceiling and a long row of Ferraris and Lamborghinis resembling futuristic spacecraft. I shivered as we walked alongside their mirrorlike hoods, cold and gleaming.

"Where are we going?" My voice sounded small in the great structure.

Ham simply pointed ahead to a door.

"It's storage up there," he said, pulling a set of keys from his pocket and trying a couple before the right one clicked in the lock. He swung the door open, revealing a wooden staircase. "After you."

I hesitated. Why would he take me to the garage's attic? My confession about my dog must have raised a red flag for them. Pit bulls were the very breed that had been rescued from Reggie's dog-fighting ring two years ago. Perhaps I should've feared these men more.

"What you waiting for?" he asked without inflection.

If someone like Ham wanted me upstairs, I was going upstairs one way or another, I reasoned. I'd seen the mobster movies. The doomed person played it cool. Accepted the inevitable.

Maybe he just wanted to scare me a little.

The most reasonable explanation was that he wanted to show me something, and wouldn't I feel stupid explaining why I took off running?

"Sorry," I said, starting up the steps, hoping he didn't notice my wobbly knees.

The loft above the garage was set up just like any other attic. Rows of bins and boxes lined the walls and shelves, many taped up with labels like, "Tupperware, Photos, and Notebooks." I was struck by the commonplace nature of the items. Reggie seemed like the last person who would care about extra food storage options and nondigital pictures. One said, "Mom's China." I wondered if his mother was still alive and in East Cleveland.

Ham heaved a couple boxes aside and then put them back, talking to himself. "Nope, not these. Maybe over here." His back was to me, and he was wiping sweat from his brow. Now was the time to make a run for it if that was what I decided to do. He seemed like he was trying to find something. And it probably wasn't a weapon, because I was pretty sure he already had one on him. Once or twice I'd noticed him patting his hip as if he was checking for something—or protecting something.

He was sort of a lumpy guy, but his right side seemed to protrude more than his left even under baggy pants.

"Can I help?" I asked.

"Naw, think I got it," he said, lifting a plastic bin the size of a coffin and setting it on the floor with a thud. On the side of the container was a piece of tape with MAXIMUS written in capital letters by a thick Sharpie. He pulled out another smaller bin carrying the same label.

"Let's go ahead and open them," he said.

We worked the top off the larger container, unlocking the seal in several places before Ham could peel it off. I peered inside. First, I noticed a giant rolled-up fleece cushion, maybe the size of a futon. He helped me heave it out and unfurl it onto the ground. It was a large oval-shaped bed with bumpers on the sides, big enough for me and another person to sleep in comfortably. "What is this?" I asked.

Wordlessly he pointed to the bin, and I looked inside again. A mess of tangled leashes, thick collars in leather and canvas, black and red chew toys, and ropes with giant knots on each end filled the bottom half of the container. I ran my hand over the thick cords, feeling their roughness and wondering about the dog to which they'd belonged. It must've been a formidable animal.

Ham pried the top from the other box, revealing tennis balls, bags and bags of something called bully sticks, and two metal bowls with black paw prints painted on the sides, along with MAXIMUS written in calligraphy. I reached for a flat rectangular object wrapped in newspaper and held it up questioningly.

"Go ahead," Ham said.

I unwrapped a picture frame and turned it over. My breath caught. A magnificent blue-gray pit bull smiled up at me from Reggie's lap. The dog was larger than Ollie by about twenty pounds but had the same grin. Reggie beamed as he held on to the dog.

"That was Max," Ham said softly.

"Wow" was all I could muster. I stared at the picture again. The items in the bins, the photograph, Reggie's joyous expression in the photo, and Ham's somber manner told me this dog had been well loved. "He's incredible."

"Yep. Take what you want, and I'll bring it to your car." Ham's tone was abrupt, a shedding of sentimentality. He spun around and began fussing with the boxes again. I thought I saw him take a swipe at his eyes before he turned and set an empty bin in front of me.

I chose some things, avoiding the bags labeled "Pig's Ears," and filled my box. Ham stooped and grabbed a couple of tough rubber toys and held them up. One was round like a ball, and the other was a cone with ridges along the sides. "See, you can put peanut butter in the little holes," he said, pointing to the openings on either end of the cone-shaped one. "That'll keep him busy."

CHAPTER TWENTY-SIX

Reggie and I sat at the dining room table the next day for our mock interview. I wanted to acknowledge his gift from the attic, but I hesitated to bring it up. If the subject broke Ham's tough armor like that, Reggie might not want to talk about it. Still, it seemed impolite not to say anything.

"Thanks for all the dog supplies, and sorry for your loss," I blurted.

Reggie drew back in surprise. "Glad somebody gets to use them, and thank you," he said in a measured voice.

"These mock interview questions might make you angry," I said, a poor segue to another emotionally charged topic. "But the purpose of them is to give you practice at staying calm while you answer."

"Yeah, I get it. It gotta be done."

I lobbed him a couple soft questions about his foundation and his music career.

"Okay, you ready for the tough ones?" I asked. "I'm going to pretend to be Andrew Cline right now." I laid the notes down so he wouldn't notice my shaking hands.

His knee jackhammered up and down. "Sho 'nuff."

"Can you tell me the story of how you got started with dog fighting?"

He pounded his fists on the table. "Fuck you, Andrew!"

I jumped. He glared at me, wild eyed for a moment, then busted out laughing.

"Sorry. Couldn't resist," he said. "Alright, seriously." He gathered himself. "I got started as a little kid, going to fights. Then when I was eleven, my dad started having me handle the dogs. He said it would teach me about the hard things I had to do in life."

"Did it work?"

"I didn't see any other choice, so yeah."

"Reggie, I haven't seen anything in my prep about Max, but there's a chance this Andrew guy dug it up."

He nodded.

"He wasn't a fighting dog, was he? Can you tell me why you chose to spare that dog from violence?"

Reggie closed his eyes. "Max was the good part of me. The part that was always in there, but I was afraid most of the time to show it."

I felt like crying. Reggie might have done some monstrous things, but he had been a victim first. Now he was ready to show the world the good part of himself, and somehow I was going to help him do that.

When I arrived at Lucy's for dinner that night, I was pleased to see that Tatiana wasn't there. Lucy and I sat at the kitchen counter stools, legs dangling while we ate and watched the French chef prepare each of our courses. I tried to take it easy on the bread and cheese so I could fill up on Nicoise salad, coq au vin ("The wine cooks out," Lucy said, but I hadn't even considered the alcohol), and dessert of course. We'd done this before, and it felt a little strange without the wine. But it was actually better this way—I could relax instead of obsessively counting the number of glasses Lucy consumed.

We mostly talked about me. "What's the latest on the crazy cat lady?" Lucy asked.

"I'm ducking her calls," I said, "but I talk to her just enough so Paul won't suspect what a terrible daughter I am."

"You're still doing that dance?"

"Always."

"Never mind," she said, taking a drink of lemon water. "I'm the last person who should be handing down life advice. How's Reggie?"

I shrugged. I'd decided not to tell her about the campaign just in case I blew it. "Working on his post-prison album and starting a multimillion-dollar foundation. He threw a house party last week that I didn't even know about until the next day."

Lucy bugged her eyes. "Holy shit! Was he pissed?"

"Not even a little bit."

"Well, I guess everyone drops the ball at some point," she said with a chuckle. "But wow. Did you just want to die?"

"I dropped no such ball," I said. "It was impromptu. I'd gone home already, and he didn't call me."

She let her fork drop and cocked her head at me, mind blown.

Sitting there with Lucy stirred nostalgia for old times when we'd just hang out all day. I missed reading scripts with her. She despised sex scenes. She'd practice them in front of me, fully clothed, overacting, and wrestling with a pillow for my entertainment. Once she surprised me by brandishing a whipped cream can she'd hidden under a cushion and spraying it at me.

How she kept a straight face when her leading man stood in for that poor pillow, I'll never know.

We watched the chef torch our crème brûlée.

"I have an ulterior motive for bringing you here tonight," Lucy said. "And it isn't the kind of thing you do in front of someone else. Not even your AA sponsor."

"I'm still not trying heroin with you."

Lucy guffawed, and a piece of lettuce flew from her mouth. "No, silly. I need to make my amends to you."

"What? No," I said. "We don't have to go through all of that. It's water under the bridge." I waved my hand behind me at an imaginary distant river and overpass. "I'm sure I've pissed you off before, and I've never sat you down to tell you I'm sorry."

"It's kind of necessary for me, though. It's part of my recovery. You'd be doing me a favor."

"Fine. But I want you to know I'm not mad at you or anything."

After we devoured our fill, she dismissed the chef, and we moved to the living room. Mushroom circled my feet, her nose working. Then she jumped on the couch and yapped at me. *She must smell Ollie*, I thought. Was she jealous?

"Mushroom, stop," Lucy said.

Mushroom didn't stop. Lucy picked the dog up and took her to the bedroom.

"Okay. I didn't think I would be nervous," Lucy said as she came back down the hall. She exhaled and whisked her hair behind her ears as she sat.

She lifted her hips and pulled a notebook page from her back pocket. "Here goes," she said, unfolding the paper. "Alex, I tried to think of all the times I've wronged you, and I wrote them down." Her eyes scanned the list for a moment before she placed the paper on the coffee table and met my gaze. "The things that stand out to me are the times I asked you to compromise yourself for me. I had you lie to people for me as part of your job. That wasn't right."

I remembered the worst incident in which I was forced to lie for her. Lucy was a spokeswoman for a cosmetics company. After a night of partying, I called our contact and told him that Lucy was not coming in. I said I was very sorry, but Lucy had a miscarriage. There was total silence on the other end. Then flatly, "So she had her period last week, and miraculously she's knowingly conceived and lost a child since then?" Humiliated, I hung up.

The CEO had called me back and fired Lucy.

"You were put in some horrible positions," Lucy said. "That wasn't fair."

"I'm not the first assistant who's been asked to do things like—"

She raised her hand and stopped me. "You don't have to say anything to make me feel better. It's probably best if you wait until I get through all of this. Not that you're forbidden to speak or anything. But I'm just saying—I need to take responsibility for what I've done, you know?"

I nodded.

"So, I yelled at you in front of people more than once. No one should have to put up with that." The muscles in her arms tensed as she squeezed the pillow. "One time that stands out to me is the pre-rehab party."

I recalled how pissed I had been, having to rush-order custom invitations, laser-cut with an art deco design, imitating Miami Beach's architecture, all so she could have a last hurrah. A bunch of models had shown up at the same time, like a pack of slinky, hungry wolves. The only one to acknowledge my existence said that she wanted her drink blended, not on the rocks. Rob was there and he watched the exchange, to my humiliation. I waited for Lucy to pipe up like she did when anyone treated me like the help. I'd expected her to say that I happened to be her best friend and my name was Alex. But she was oblivious, drawing shapes in cocaine: a heart, a shamrock, Mickey Mouse.

I should have added at least a hint of vodka to her drink, but I went with straight water. She spit it back into her glass. Her eyes narrowed, and her beautiful face rearranged itself into something grisly. She winged the glass at me. I ducked, and it exploded against the wall, sending a shower of glass raining over me. Mushroom scampered from the hallway to see what all the commotion was about, and when I plucked her up so she wouldn't step on glass she bit me. I dropped Mushroom, and she yelped as she hit the floor. Lucy's head whipped around. "What the fuck is wrong with you?!"

Rob made his way to my side, silently picking out shards that had landed in my hair, not making eye contact with me. Lucy leaned down and snorted Mickey Mouse's ear.

That's when I saw an orange ember glowing next to her on the Italian leather sectional. I scurried over and plucked up the cigarette she'd dropped on the cushion, burning my finger.

"Ouch, fuck!"

Lucy laughed as I dropped the butt into her watered-down cocktail.

The words "I quit" stalled in my mouth, but I held on to them.

"I have something to tell you about Rob, too," Lucy said.

"What's that?"

"I think you might know about this already." She squinted at me.

I didn't like where this was going.

I started chewing on my nail beds. A hazy memory of them disappearing together at the pre-rehab party sent a wave of nausea through me.

"Did you guys have sex?" I said. I was chewing on my nails, but then I really bit into the cuticle, got a fleshy piece and pulled. Then the blood started to come. I watched it pool just below my coral nails.

"Oh my god, you're bleeding!" Lucy blurted. "I thought you'd quit doing that!"

"Maybe I need a live-in Cuticle Pickers Anonymous sponsor." I stuck my injured finger in my mouth.

Lucy started to reach for me, but I jumped away from her and pulled my finger from my mouth with a loud pop.

"Alex, I'm sorry. This isn't how I wanted this to go."

"Did you guys have sex?" I asked. "You guys did it. There's nothing else it could be."

"No, we just kissed," Lucy said. "I didn't expect this would upset you so much."

I didn't know if I believed her.

"I wouldn't have brought it up if I'd known it would make you feel this horrible. That's not the reason I'm doing this."

"Jesus Christ!" I said. "What the hell is wrong with you? Why would you even think I wanted to hear about this?"

"If there's anything I can do to make it up to you, just tell me what it is. Anything at all." She blinked rapidly.

I shook my head. "Whatever. Can we be done with the apologies now?"

"Sure," Lucy said, jumping up. "You have every right to hate me." She went to the bathroom and returned with a Band-Aid.

"I need a smoke," I said as I wrapped my finger.

We moved to the patio. I thought about Rob. Who knew how many girls he slept with behind my back? He was a cheater. And Lucy was in a bad place. He probably initiated the kiss or whatever. I was too tired to hold on to my rage. We sat quietly under the covered balcony watching the smoke suspended in the heavy, wet air.

"Rob was a douche anyway," I said after a while. "I was fooling myself if I thought we were going to get married or something."

We ground our cigarettes out at the same time and stood.

"I'd better get home to walk Ollie."

"There's one more thing," Lucy said. "Kind of a big thing." She paused in front of the sliding door. "I've been thinking about this for a few days, and letting you go was a mistake. Would you consider coming back to work for me? I mean after you give Reggie notice?"

My breath hitched. I sat back down. I wanted to say yes, but the words wouldn't come out of my mouth.

My reaction surprised me. At the same time, it made sense—now I was running Reggie's media campaign. And I felt like maybe I could win at it. My greatest accomplishment as Lucy's assistant had been scoring her ayahuasca.

And there was her little moment of passion with Rob. No matter how fucked up she was, it was still a betrayal. At the same time, it made me miss him less. Not that I thought about him much—maybe he'd pop into my head a couple times a day. Then I'd take a breath, breathe him out like a toxin, and he'd flit away for another twelve hours or so. "Thank you for the offer" was the only thing I could think of to say.

"Take some time to think about it," she said. A coy smile spread across her face. "But I really want you to say yes."

I nodded.

She touched her hand to her chest. "I'm so sorry about the Rob thing. I thought I was doing the right thing by telling you about it."

I didn't have much to say on that subject either. "Yeah. You probably were."

"Thank God. I could just see us turning into our mothers, fighting over a man."

She wrapped her arms around me.

I started to process the words. *Our mothers. Fighting over a man. What man? My father?*

"What are you talking about?" I asked her, disengaging from the hug.

She didn't respond. Creases appeared on her forehead.

"What the fuck are you talking about?" I asked again. "Our mothers fighting over a man?"

"Shit. I thought you knew that, too," she almost whispered.

I remembered the fights between my father and mother. And her refrain: *You love her more than me.* Denise wasn't talking about me. She was talking about Lucy's mother. Evelyn.

CHAPTER TWENTY-SEVEN

Lucy made out with Rob. That was a gut punch.
My father slept with Lucy's mother. That was more abstract for me.

And why did she think I knew these things already? I felt stupid. Maybe it was all going on in front of me, and I was holding my eyes shut.

I guess I didn't blame my father for stepping out on Denise. She was a special kind of crazy. He probably just needed to be with someone sane for a while. What surprised me was that I never found out about it. Lucy was the biggest gossip I had ever met. After we became friends again in middle school, I had a running commentary of who slept with whom for the next six years. And Denise knew, but she never told me. That made no sense. She lived for crisis. I couldn't believe she didn't turn this into an extended pageant of misery and victimhood.

As I mulled these things over on the way to work, an even more troubling question jumped into my head: What if it wasn't his only affair?

I tried to focus on the day ahead. Today I was going to see Wade, the actor.

Reggie was coproducing an album for an up-and-coming hip-hop artist called Swisha. Reggie told me Swisha preferred an audience when recording and said to bring my clique.

I'd invited Wade against my better judgment.

I also invited Isabelle and told her to bring a friend. She arrived at Reggie's first, with Colin, the pretty man who had accompanied her to pick up her stuff from Jean-Marc's. Though it was ninety degrees out, Isabelle wore a faux fur vest, as only she could pull off. Wade showed up when we were halfway through the grand tour of Reggie's house, looking dashing in slouchy gray jeans and Adidas sneakers. He kissed me on both cheeks, and I introduced Isabelle and Colin.

"Can you believe that our Alex works in this huge castle?" Isabelle asked Wade. She'd been oohing and aahing for the last half hour, and her question told me she didn't recognize Wade. Maybe she only watched foreign films.

"It's pretty sweet," Wade replied, a hint of a smirk on his face. I wondered what his castle looked like. I wondered a lot of things about him.

"Muthafucking shit. It's the *Blue Flame*," Reggie said when we all walked into the studio. Blue Flame was the superhero Wade played in a wildly popular film franchise.

They slapped hands.

"I always wanted to meet you, man," Wade said.

"Yeah? Well it's mutual. You didn't happen to bring your suit, did you, brother?"

"It's in my trunk actually."

They laughed.

Marvin, Reggie's uncle, had moved to Reggie's side with the pent-up energy of somebody waiting for a starting gun. Wade gave him a wide berth.

"We're almost ready to lay down this track," Reggie said. "You all just sit back and watch the magic happen."

Marvin gestured for us to sit with him, and I led our group over there.

The guys who had been at Reggie's recording session, the one where I'd embarrassed myself by calling him Rottie, nodded as we passed them.

"I can't believe that I am here," Isabelle said.

When we sat, Colin pulled an e-cig from his pocket and blew a thick plume of vapor into the air, which looked blue against the white walls.

I needed to get one of those contraptions.

Wade patted my thigh, and a surge of excitement ran through me. I'd told myself this was barely a date, because technically this was a workday for me. But sitting this close to him set my skin abuzz.

Marvin started making small talk, rocking toward the glass booth as he commented on how amazing Swisha was. Then he switched to the topic of new responsibilities with Reggie, nudged my arm, and said, "Told you so." Wade caught my eye and gave me an amused look, presumably finding Marvin entertaining, too.

Swisha's mic wasn't on, but he appeared to be practicing, mouthing words and punching at the air. He was short, stocky, and you could see muscles bulging under his green Philadelphia Eagles jersey. The top of a tattoo peeked out just above the shirt's neckline, and he wore his hair so short that his scalp reflected the light.

The red light above the booth blinked, and the music kicked up, a bass-heavy beat interwoven with sinister-sounding music that could've been sampled from a horror film score.

Swisha placed his hands over his headphones and planted one leg behind the other. In a low, clear voice he rapped:

She see I'm a go-getter/ I said let's get together/ Them crazy eyes/ Gap in the thighs/ I shoulda known better I need a girl who ain't stupid can keep up with me/ She said, "Daddy I ain't witchu just for your money"

How can I know if she ratchet or she on the level?/ She said, "Ima make your dreams come true/ Show you how I'm special"
Thought she'd be a girl I'd take home to my momma/ But she a whore/ Smell like a liquor store/ Got her phone from Obama
Told her it was off/ She come by with a Glock/ Said "I ain't fakin"/ I took her piece/ Threw her down/ Cuz she just messed with Satan
It'd be murder one I'm facin'/ That's how hard I be ragin'/ Can't go back to prison, so I best be disengagin'
But her neck, it feel so good/ My fingers wrapped around it/ I pull them tighter/ Like a spider/ All clamped down on it/ I'm so excited/ Can't deny it/ If I'm bein' honest
Her eyes bug out/ Without a doubt/ She got seconds left/ I take her right up to the threshold of a early death
Why can't I find a girl who's beautiful and smart?/ I need a girl who's dutiful/ And loves me with her heart
Why it always come to this?/ Ain't no coincidence/ Bitches got it in for me/ And I get charged with battery

Afterward we all stood and clapped. Wade wolf-whistled. Reggie shouted, "Hell yeah, niggah!" Reggie turned around and smiled at me and my little crew. I shot him an enthusiastic thumbs-up. He rolled his eyes and shook his head at me, still grinning. I could almost hear him thinking, *Corny as hell.* Which is exactly what he said when he asked me which song of his I liked best, and I'd rapped with all the swagger of a white Midwestern girl the lyrics to *Waiting for the Light*:

Road stretches out in front of me/ Green light flashin'/ Everything that was gonna be/
Don't know the right action/ Can't stop, can't go/ Guess I'll just sit in da glow

Swisha swung the booth's door open, and after he and Reggie shared a one-armed hug Reggie shouted, "It's time to throw down!"

Ham went into the fridge and pulled out a case of Heineken, popped some open, and started handing them out. Wade and I hung back.

The party moved downstairs, outside to the pool. I excused myself to the kitchen to figure out snacks with Marcia, who was already on top of things. She stopped precision-chopping vegetables when I entered and whirred past me with bowls of chips and dips. Something wonderful was frizzling in the deep fryer. God, why couldn't Lucy find someone like Marcia?

I left it to her and trotted out the booze cart.

Isabelle and Colin sat by the pool dangling their legs in the water. Wade and Reggie and a few others were standing in a circle, talking. Wade looked back and shot me a wink as I mixed cocktails. Reggie waved me over.

"People can make their own drinks. Hang out with your superhero date. Enjoy the party."

I almost felt like one of them, a star.

I stood there as they went back to discussing football. Wade slipped his hand around my waist. He did it in such a natural way that it took a moment for me to be surprised. Then, with his other hand, he brought a beer up to his lips. I gawped at him.

"You want one?" Wade asked. "Here, take mine."

I thought back to Wade's heartfelt admissions to all his sins: the motorcycle wreck, Russian roulette, his father dying. Then I thought, *He's an actor. These people are actors.*

"You're not really an alkie, right?" Wade asked me. "You were at the meeting because of Lucy, right?"

"I don't know what I am." I paused. "But what about your stories? Your 'by the grace of God'?"

"Going to those meetings helps me keep it under control," he said, tipping his beer toward me. "I meant every word."

"Oh."

"Reggie said you're his new publicist," Wade said, changing the subject. "That's a pretty big deal."

"Did he tell you I have never done this before and have no idea what I'm doing?"

Wade laughed. "I bet you know more than you let on." He took my hand and led me through the backyard. Isabelle gave me a knowing smile as we headed past her and Colin. I realized Wade was taking me to the pool house. What did he think was going to happen in there? Reggie had made it clear that I was invited to the party and not here to work. But still, this was my workplace. I took a swig of his beer. Fuck it, I deserved it.

"I thought there would be another bar in here," Wade said, shutting the door behind him. "And we get a chance to talk on our own." He moved to the shelves of bottles on the wall. "Gin and tonic?"

"No, thanks," I said.

Then a switch flipped. Lucy had just asked me to come back. And I didn't say no, but that's what I was thinking. *No, but thanks.*

I liked my new job. I liked the new people I worked with. And I was good at it. Reggie wanted me to be his publicist. After I worked at that newspaper in college, I decided journalism wasn't for me. I wanted to be a publicist, but I was too lazy to take the extra classes a change in major would have required. And then suddenly it happened anyway. And it happened on a level I could never imagine. Three years ago I would have jumped at the same offer from Carrot Top's lesser-known brother. Now I was a publicist for Rottie *fucking* Wiles.

"Actually, yeah," I said. "A gin and tonic sounds pretty good."

I drank, and it was delicious. My head hummed.

Wade had three to my one, but he seemed lucid, coherent, answering my questions about his acting career.

No, he didn't have to wear that Blue Flame helmet all day. He broke his clavicle last year and that was when he finally conceded that he was too old to do his own stunts. He was in Miami shooting an independent film. He would go back to LA when it wrapped up.

"I'll miss LA in some ways," I said. "But I don't know if I'll ever move back."

Wade took my chin in his hand and kissed me, his breath the smell of Christmas garland. "It would be nice to have you in LA," he said.

The next morning I could've skipped all the way to my new house. But I had to drive some boxes there. I replayed every word Wade said on the way. I'd never met anyone with that level of savoir faire. He made Rob look like a sniveling frat boy.

At the new house, Ollie raced around, slipping and sliding on the tiled floors, crashing into walls. When I took him out back with his leash on, he headed straight for the canal. "No!" I yelled, holding on to him as he pulled toward the man-made river. He stopped short a couple feet from the edge and gazed back at me.

"You stay out of there, buddy," I told him. I'd considered the possibility that Ollie might want to take a plunge in the alligator-filled waters. He'd probably give them a run for their money, but I would keep him on a leash until I could get the area fenced off.

He rose to his feet, nubbin moving on slow-robot setting, and sniffed at the wide wooden beams separating the yard from the four-foot drop to the narrow dug-out river. There was a splashing sound from below, and Ollie jumped back. I leaned over the edge to see if I could spot a gator, but I all I saw were a few silver bubbles on the water's black surface.

It made me feel relieved that he was scared. He pulled me toward the bromeliads flocking the fence line and commenced sniffing. I stood there for a while watching him explore. Then we went back into the house. I still needed to lug in my boxes from the car.

So far I had remained organized, labeling each box with a destination: "Bedroom 2," "Kitchen," or "Bathroom." I'd always started my moves this way, but by the end everything would fall apart. Unrelated items ended up living together in black trash bags. Electrical cords tangled with bras, spilled lotion ruined a set of towels, and I'd lose something important like a favorite shoe or my social security card. This time I vowed not to let my system fall into disarray. I had pulled off seamless moves for Lucy. It was time I showed myself and my belongings the same level of respect.

Each time I brought in a box, Ollie was investigating a new area of the house. First in the corner of the living room, and then nudging at a box of dishes in the kitchen. As I made my way to the bathroom with a box of toiletries, he was nowhere to be seen. I found him lying on his back in the master bedroom closet.

He liked it here.

I unrolled the liner paper I'd chosen for the kitchen cabinets, navy and cream chevron, and began cutting and affixing. The work was mindless, meditative, and I realized I was nesting for the first time, planting vinyl roots.

When all the shelves were lined, I realized it had been quiet for too long. I checked to see if Ollie was asleep in the closet. I found him in the bathroom, his face in the toilet. "Ollie!" He raised his head from the commode and gaped at me, water dripping from his smiling jaw.

"Who will help me move my furniture?" I asked. "You?" Ollie tilted his head as if considering my question. "Rob's out," I said. To my surprise I felt nothing at the mention of Rob's name. "Jean-Marc?" I asked, sniggering at my own joke. Ollie's ears perked.

I clasped Ollie's ears and rubbed. He closed his eyes and leaned into me. "I have no dudes in my life except for you, so I guess I'll have to shell out for movers."

Perhaps I could have another dude in my life, if only temporarily. I wondered if Wade liked dogs.

CHAPTER TWENTY-EIGHT

Reggie's living room looked like Sunday morning in a frat house. The air hung thick with a stale chemical smell. Bodies sprawled on the living room sofas. Swisha and a couple girls from Reggie's music videos were among them. And so was Wade. That familiar sinking disappointment tugged at me, seeing Wade there passed out, never having made it home.

This felt like Lucy and Rob all over again. Did I seek this out?

I had bigger things to contend with, and I couldn't let this get to me. Reggie's interview with the TV reporter was scheduled to start in a few hours. I'd have to reschedule, listen to the producer yell at me through the phone about professionalism and integrity.

Ham traipsed through the kitchen archway. "He need some vitamins," he said, handing me a handwritten list of supplements. "Can you get someone here to give him a B12 shot?"

"Yeah, I know a guy, but—"

Reggie's eyes flickered open. "What it *is*, what it *is*, Al," he said as I started clearing up bottles. I'd always hated being called "Al." It reminded me of a retired deli owner who chewed on cigar stumps. "This bitch cashed out." Reggie pointed down at the girl lying across his lap wearing nothing but a ripped tank top and a thong. It felt wrong to see someone unconscious and half-naked. I wanted to cover her with a blanket.

"I can see that," I said, trying to keep the edge out of my voice.

"I'm thinking the pinstriped Galliani for today," Reggie said. The whites of his eyes burned purple red.

I carried an armful of bottles and an overflowing ashtray to the kitchen. Ham followed, grabbing the ashtray from me. A cigarette butt fell out, and he bent to pluck it up.

"He hasn't been to bed, has he?" I asked.

"That's why he needs them vitamins. I'll finish cleaning up here. You go."

The glass bottles rattled and clanked when I dumped them into the recycling bin. "He doesn't look like he's up for it. Why don't I get in touch with Andrew?"

"I already tried talking to Reg. He *don't* want to reschedule. He's excited about this."

"Has he had anything to eat?"

"No."

I headed to the living room. Reggie stood in front of the TV, his mouth screwed sideways in concentration. He fiddled with his phone, and a rap tune began to play thunderously through all the speakers in the living room. A girl in a damp bikini sprung from a couch and began to dance, her calves grazing the polluted coffee table. Reggie sashayed up to her and placed his palms on her waist, grinding on her from behind.

"Yo. Al," he called over the blaring music. "You get my shit?"

"Not yet," I said. "I'm going now."

"We'll have to keep entertaining ourselves until you get back," Reggie said, raising his hands in the air as he dry-humped the girl.

"You guys hungry?" I asked. "Where's Marcia?"

"Ham said she's gonna be late today. No muffins."

"Oh, that's right. I'll go get you something."

"You the best. You know what? This girl the best," Reggie said to no one in particular.

He escorted his dance partner to the couch, then leaned over the table and picked up a glass pipe. "Somebody give me a lighter."

Nobody made a move to fulfill his request, so I pulled my only mini Bic from my dress pocket and held it out to him. I could see the media campaign crumbling before me.

"Reggie, this has to be the last one if you want to pull this thing off today."

He swiped at the lighter, missing it the first time and seizing it on the second try. "You right. This the last hit." He crouched low, simpering over his gear.

"Promise?" I asked. He rolled his eyes up toward me and nodded vigorously. Then he hit the pipe and the air around him turned blue and hazy.

Wade's head popped up. "Heeeey," he said in my direction, trying to invoke his most charming face. "Fancy seeing you here."

I ignored him.

"Alright, Reg. Ham will help you get ready. I'll be back in a bit."

"You da man."

Ham came over to me, his eyes on Reggie. We watched Reggie hit the pipe again.

"Can you get him in the shower?" I asked.

Ham took Reggie by the arm and led him toward the stairs.

When I got back, Wade was gone. I couldn't help but blame him for Reggie's condition after hearing his AA stories. I really didn't know why Wade wanted to go out with me. He could have met Reggie any time he wanted. He didn't need my celebrity connections.

Wade seemed broken to me now. He probably didn't need a reason for anything.

Andrew and his TV crew knocked, then blazed into the house before I could answer the door. I trailed him and his crew, nerves on edge, as they darted from room to room. It seemed like Andrew was hoping to catch somebody committing a crime. I shot Ham a panicked glance behind Andrew's back as we passed in a hall. Ham closed his eyes, nodded—his chill-out face. I'd worried for nothing because Ham and the rest of the staff had removed all evidence of the sordid goings-on. Essential oils simmered in burners I'd never seen before. The surfaces were wiped clean as a monastery.

Andrew stepped out to the back patio. "The lighting's just perfect out here," he said.

His team began setting up. I went back into the house to check on Reggie.

"He'll be down for makeup in ten," Ham said.

"How's he doing?" I asked.

"That B12 shot made a new man out of him. He's drinking his green smoothie and eating his veggie omelet now."

Andrew barked from outside, "The sun's right in my eyes. How did nobody remember to bring a tent?"

I ducked my head out of the door. "There's an awning," I said, pressing the button. The massive white canvas unfurled with a mechanical whir.

"Excellent!" he said, waving off his makeup artist.

I walked over to him. "Listen, Andrew, I know you're going to have some tough questions, but Reggie would like you to refrain from discussing his daughter. He wants to ensure her privacy."

Andrew took off his glasses and touched the metal arms to the side of his mouth, a theatrical gesture I'd seen him perform on camera.

"Of course," he said, dramatically thoughtful.

The patio door slid open, and Reggie emerged looking crisp and vigorous. He moved in a straight line, but I wondered what his eyes looked like under those sunglasses. "Ready for the firing squad," he said, dusting something unseen from the shoulders of his suit. He'd changed his mind about the Galliani and gone with Brooks Brothers. He shook hands with Andrew.

"We're all set to go," Andrew said.

"Let's get this party started, then."

As the crew fastened a small microphone to his lapel, Reggie called me over and pulled off his sunglasses to reveal clear, unpuffy eyes. "Listen, I just want to say thanks for sticking with me." He covered his mic, inched closer, and spoke into my ear, so I could feel his breath. "I know it's hard sometimes, but just trust me when I say you're doing a great job. I'll get you some help so you can focus on this kind of stuff more."

"Thanks, Reg," I said, taking a step back. All signs of the tweaker from earlier this morning had disappeared, as if his superhero power was sobering up at will. Still, I had to ask, "You sure you're good to do this?"

"Yeah, thanks to you. Believe it or not, I studied last night."

Andrew's producer clapped his hands behind us. "Time to get in your places," he announced.

For some reason—maybe because the occasion called for it—I gave Reggie a slight bow. He grinned, executed a one-eighty on the heel of his designer shoe, and took his place on the white-cushioned patio love seat across from Andrew. I hung to the side, fingernails hovering in front of my lips.

Reggie crossed his legs, unbuttoned the jacket with a flourish, gripped the cuffs, and inched them farther down his wrists.

The producer said, "Five, four" out loud, then counted down with his fingers and mouthed, "Three, two, one."

On "one," a current seemed to shoot through Andrew's body, shocking him into a personality change. He addressed the camera. "Reginald Wiles is one of the most controversial figures of this decade. He's been called many things: a prolific entertainer and music producer, a father." His countenance darkened and he turned to another camera on his right. "An animal abuser—even a monster—and now, a man trying to make good with a justifiably indignant population after his incarceration." Andrew took off his glasses and dipped his head. "Thank you for granting this rare interview and for welcoming me into your home, Reggie."

"My pleasure, Andrew."

"You have a beautiful estate here in Miami, obviously a testament to your success." He motioned to the greenery surrounding the pool, the gulf beyond that. One of the cameras panned the scenery.

"Thank you."

"What have you been up to since your release from jail last month?"

Reggie touched the tips of his fingers together, looked Andrew in the eye. "I've been getting back to business, focusing on the positive. I'm working with some young talent coming up, trying to give them a boost, just like Mad Dirty did for me." Mad Dirty, or MD, was the producer who discovered Reggie and placed him in the spotlight. MD's empire earned eight digits each year, and anyone backed by him topped the Billboard charts within weeks.

"You say you're 'focusing on the positive.' That must be hard. The negative publicity— how has that affected your life?"

"I can't say it isn't difficult. A lot of my fans are still there, but I'm sure I lost some folks on the way. I can't blame them." Reggie dipped his head. "All I can do now is live from today forward and continue to concentrate on the music."

Andrew leaned in and put his glasses back on. I'd always thought people could make a great drinking game out of watching his specials. Take a shot when the glasses come off, and drink again when they go back on. Nobody would remember how the program ended.

I could tell the next question would be a zinger because Andrew made a show of shifting in his seat, crinkling his forehead. If you believed his act, you might think that what he was about to say was something that pained him.

"I have to ask, Reggie. The court records show you ordered abusive and unimaginable acts against animals. What was your level of participation in these torture sessions?"

My ears perked. I had included this question almost verbatim on my prep sheet.

With a neutral expression, Reggie uncrossed his legs and bent forward at the waist. "I wasn't a direct participant, Andrew. But I am responsible for what happened. Being removed from it is no excuse."

Andrew held Reggie's gaze, waiting for him to elaborate, but Reggie left it at that.

"I'm sure many of our viewers have read about the atrocities committed against these dogs." Andrew nodded to a crew member, who handed him a piece of paper. "But I'll go over it for those who are unaware of the details." He began reading in an astonished tone, as if he were learning these details for the first time. "The dogs were kept in cages for up to twenty-three hours per day. Those that didn't win brutal fights were starved, beaten, drowned, and electrocuted." The reporter paused and dropped his jaw in a mixture of disbelief and disgust. "Do you deny these allegations?"

Reggie bowed his head. "If you read the court records, no, I did not."

Nice touch, seeing that Andrew had the court records in front of him, I thought.

Andrew folded the piece of paper. "This is not normal behavior, Reggie. What do you think caused this behavior, this hatred for living things?"

Asshole.

Reggie's posture stiffened a little. His shoulders clenched and his cheeks worked, chewing on the reporter's question like a rotted piece of fruit.

"I don't hate living things, Andrew. I was brainwashed."

"How so?"

It was subtle, but I could tell Reggie was struggling. Someone who didn't know him might have interpreted his body language as alert.

"My dad made me shoot my pet dog in the summer before middle school. I doubt that's something most folks can comprehend."

"I'm so sorry that happened, Reggie."

Reggie nodded, his cheeks still churning.

Andrew continued: "But some would say that a man must take responsibility for his actions." He took a calculated pause. "So I have to ask: How can you live with yourself?"

Eyes at the sky, Reggie brought his palms together as if in prayer. "I can't justify my actions. But I can give you my truth. Dog fighting was part of my culture growing up, and I learned to detach, just like all the men I looked up to. Like any other boy, I felt like I had to do what my dad demanded of me." Reggie's voice cracked slightly. "Today I know what I did was wrong and cruel. Now it's my responsibility to right the wrongs. I wish I'd figured that out sooner, but I didn't. Animals suffered from my actions. And for that I am sorry and ashamed."

I fought the urge to cheer and whoop. Reggie had practically memorized the prep sheet, and he'd delivered the statements with a perfect mix of authority and humility. Reggie could have been a politician if not for his criminal record.

The TV crew started packing up the cameras and lights. I glanced at the window and saw Marcia flitting around the kitchen. I headed in to offer my help. A sweet, spicy fragrance hit me when I walked inside. Pots steamed over blue flames, and Marcia pulled a roasting pan from the oven.

"I made him ribs, mac and cheese, and Caesar salad," she said. Marcia forked several huge racks of meat and plopped them on a cutting board.

"It smells great," I said. "Can I help you?"

"It's my job, miss."

Marcia, I thought, *I am not going to take your damn job. The last thing I cooked was a frozen pizza. And that was two years ago.* I smiled at her.

"And I have homemade bread, too," she said. "You want to try?"

"This looks wonderful," I said.

Ham lumbered inside, patting his stomach. "That's what's up!" he boomed, grabbing a piece of bread from the basket on the counter. He doubled back and threw open the door. "Hey, Reg!" he hollered. "Good food!"

Marcia handed me a plate, and I started spooning side dishes onto it. She topped off my platter with a half rack of ribs.

As I unfolded my napkin and placed it in my lap, Ham returned. "Reggie's gonna eat later."

A forkful of macaroni hovered between the plate and my face. "Thought he'd be starving by now." I shoveled the pasta into my mouth and chewed with my eyes shut. It was perfection—there were at least four kinds of cheese in there.

"He's gonna celebrate first."

I opened my eyes to see Ham shrugging, his mouth creased in a frown.

He loaded up two heaping plates of food and sat beside me. "He does this sometimes. Goes on these sprees." He picked up the entire rack of ribs and took a bite. Most of the ribs fell off the bone and landed partially on his plate and partially on the table, but he didn't seem to notice. Marcia scurried over with a dishrag.

"Do you think he's alright?" I asked, setting my silverware down.

"He always alright I guess," he said. "Anyway, you can go enjoy the rest of the day. You did a great job."

We ate in silence. Ham was still eating after I finished. I walked to the sink and rinsed off my plate. Marcia snatched it from me, placed it in among the perfectly spaced items in the dishwasher.

I sat next to Ham again, and he gazed at me from under heavy lids.

"Would it help if I stayed?"

"Naw, he be straight tomorrow or the day after. I'm leaving, too. Going to dinner at my momma's."

CHAPTER TWENTY-NINE

I stayed for a little while longer, not wanting to leave for some reason. I went to the screening room and sorted some Blu-rays.

When I came downstairs, it was dark. I found the living room in the same shape as it was that morning, except with a new layer of debris on the coffee table. Reggie and Swisha bookended a few new girls. One held a cut straw up to her nose and snorted from the dirty table with the intensity of a Shop-Vac. Swisha saw me come down and directed a shaky salute my way.

"Hey, guys," I said.

Reggie stopped bobbing his head to the music and squinted at me. He still wore the suit from his interview, soot marks on the pants, the blazer crumpled and flung to the floor.

"What up, girl?" he said before turning his attention to the white mound in front of him. He moved in slow motion, fumbling for a rolled-up bill. Then he changed his mind and picked up a pipe. When he reached out for the pile of cloudy stones, he knocked a couple onto the floor. He looked at me and made a clicking motion with his thumb and forefinger.

I gave him the same disposable lighter that I'd managed to get back from him that morning.

"Seeeee, this girl an-ti-ci-pi-tates my needs," he said.

One time Lucy, just as inebriated as Reggie was now, told me that I failed to anticipate her needs. At least I was improving at my profession.

Reggie hit the pipe. Swisha's chin fell to his chest, and his eyes fluttered shut.

"Nobody can hang," Reggie said, his voice an octave lower than normal as he blew out the smoke. He grinned, and his eyes crossed for a second. "Aw, Swish gonna lose the bet!" Swisha didn't move. "You my witness, girl," he said to the small woman with powder on her upper lip. She laughed through her teeth, cheeks expanding until she started coughing and fell back onto the couch cushions.

Reggie turned to me. "They dropping like flies." He gave me a knowing look, as if we were in the same fucked-up boat together. "Hey, you want a hit? You earned it."

He scooched over and patted the space between him and Swisha.

"No, thanks," I said. "Gotta drive."

He stood and walked over to me, threw his arm around my shoulders. He tried to escort me to the couch by taking one sideways step for every forward one. The girl's worrisome hacking continued. "Are you okay?" I asked her. "Do you need some water?" She nodded wildly, her eyes bulging.

Grateful for a reason not to sit in front of a big pile of drugs, I walked to the kitchen and filled a tall glass for her. Her coughing had subsided when I returned, but she took the glass from me with both hands and chugged the whole thing.

"You all good, baby," Reggie said to her, reaching over and slapping her back. She panted and clutched her chest.

"Well, I'm going to get go —"

"Damn!" Reggie shouted at the top of his lungs.

He startled me. "Jesus Christ, Reggie. What?"

"I gotta get into something!" He clapped his hands together.

Swisha's eyes fluttered open. "What are we doing, Reg?"

Reggie gathered his paraphernalia from the table and dropped my lighter into his pocket. Then he scraped powder into a ziplock baggie with a credit card. He didn't seem to notice half of it disappearing into the shag rug.

"Where the keys to my Benz?" he asked.

They hung on the hook by the door, as always.

"I'm not sure," I said, trying to look at anything but those keys. "What about a movie? I've organized your Blu-rays for you. I can find any one you want."

"Naw. I need some fresh air."

"Well, don't you want to change out of your suit first?" I asked. While he changed his clothes, I'd arrange a driver for him.

His head dropped and he scanned himself. "Yeah, you right." He turned to the young woman who had been choking before. "Wanna join, baby girl?" She sprung up and grabbed his hand. Together they darted toward the stairs. Reggie stopped at the bottom, scooped her up, and carried her to the second floor.

I picked up the walkie from the coffee table and asked the guard stationed at the wall if anyone could drive Reggie.

"I don't have coverage down here if I leave," said James the security guard.

"Can't you call someone?"

"I'll get back to you."

He sounded doubtful. Maybe I needed to drive him myself. I could run home and take care of Ollie in between stops. Or perhaps Reggie would change his mind about leaving. Ideas flit and in out of your brain like fireflies when you're that messed up.

But he and his dainty lady friend clambered down the stairs about a half hour later, ready to hit the town.

"You find my keys, Al?" He was wearing his grill, and it glinted in the light of the chandelier hanging over the foyer.

"I'm going to chauffeur you tonight, Reg."

He crinkled his nose. "No, you get the night off. You done good. You don't need to be doing this stuff anymore—you're my publicist now."

"It's fine," I said. "I think it will be fun."

"You think I can't drive?" Reggie's face was defiant, and his body twitched with synthetic energy.

"No, you'd probably do great driving." I paused to search for the right words. "But I'm also thinking, why risk it?"

The woman by his side looked up from her pointy manicure and twirled her hair, eyes darting back between Reggie and me.

"It ain't your job to watch over me," Reggie said. "I got bigger guys than you to do that for me." He turned to the side and smiled at no one. "You gonna call the five-o on me or something?"

"Of course not."

"Alright then. See you later."

"Look, Reg," I started, "I have to be in court for a DUI in a week. I might get thrown in jail." Until that moment I had believed Lucy's lawyer would exonerate me. Now doubt took hold. I thought of that frigid, dank cell and the women who had been right at home there. That could be me.

Reggie placed his arm on my shoulder. "Hey, man, you okay?" All the anger was gone from his voice. "You need my lawyer?"

"Yeah—I mean no. I have a lawyer," I said. "I just don't want you to have to deal with this shit, too."

He flung his arms in the air. "Okay. Damn. I won't drive." There was a cockeyed smile on his face.

His friend released her hair, which she'd knotted in a couple places now. "I'll drive!" she said.

Nooooo!

The front door swung open, and one of the guys from the front security marched in. With his rigid walk and black suit he looked like an ex-military type, someone who wouldn't think twice about taking a bullet for his boss.

"Where to, sir?" he asked.

Reggie patted his pocket, full of drugs and paraphernalia. "Just a couple quick stops. Then downtown. Maybe the Pink Fox."

"Yo, Swish!" he called.

Swisha popped up from the couch and jogged past us through the door.

"Call Victor at the Pink Fox and have him clear it out for us," Reggie said. "We're celebrating."

I didn't realize how worn-out I was until I trudged up the stairs to my apartment at dusk. *This is one of my last times making this climb,* I thought. Soon there would be no more avoiding Jean-Marc. No more coming home to boxes, vast negative space adjacent to overcrowded furniture. No more hideous green carpet.

It would feel so good to collapse on the couch, but Ollie was long overdue for a walk. He would have boundless energy after being left alone for so long.

My phone chimed, and I pulled it out of my purse. An artist had sent me the rendering of a custom satin jacket for Reggie, his face embroidered on the back with teeth done in gold thread. I examined the photo as I made my way down the walkway to my apartment, chuckling.

When I reached the door, my stomach lurched. It was cracked open.

PART TWO

CHAPTER THIRTY

The exposed deadbolt mechanism dangled from the splintered door. I pushed inside.

Ollie wasn't at my feet doing his figure-eight greeting dance.

"Ollie!" I called. He didn't come. Maybe whoever had broken in had scared him. I slung my purse off my shoulder and dashed to the bedroom, where he liked to nestle in my heaps of clothes. My eyes searched the sea of fabrics, and I called to him again, but he didn't rise from the pile. I flung back the rumpled bedding. Not there either. The other side of the bed, under the bed. No dog. "Ollie," I said, leaping over boxes and crates to the bathroom. Sometimes he liked to lie on the rug in there. I yanked the shower curtain open and one of the rings snapped loose, fell into the empty tub with a loud clank.

It occurred to me that someone might still be inside the apartment. I almost hoped they were. If I found someone hiding in a closet, I'd ask that person where my dog was and offer them a head start with all my valuables in exchange for that information.

I darted to Ollie's other hiding space—the corner of the galley kitchen. It was empty. My chest rose and fell in bursts and the room spun. Black spots took shape in front of my eyes. I ignored my dimming vision and looked through all the rooms again in case I missed him. I checked the closets and under the bed and inside boxes, even though I knew he was too bulky to fit into those tight spaces.

A surreal sensation grabbed me, like I was watching someone else's bad dream through a tunnel.

As I rounded the corner from the kitchen to the entryway, I stubbed my toe hard on the stone bookend I'd dumbly left there while packing. I limped to the balcony and scanned the well-lit grounds of my building, especially the pool area, where Ollie had tried to drag me more than once. A little white ball moved across the grass to the right of the pool. My breath caught for a moment, but then the light-colored mass started moving vertically up a short palm tree. It was an opossum. Below, two swimmers—a middle-aged couple—bobbed in the deep end, splashing and laughing. Their happy-go-lucky behavior appalled me, as if their world should be in a shambles by proximity.

When I started yelling his name, the couple stopped their water games and snapped to attention. "Is your kid missing?" the man shouted. Their heads flicked from side to side.

"No. It's my dog. Have you seen a dog?"

They both shrugged.

I booked it down the stairs, grasping the rails and swinging down two steps at a time. All the while I hollered out my dog's name as doors creaked open and curious faces poked out.

"Have you seen a dog?" I asked.

They shook their heads.

I chose the route we took the most often on our walks. After three blocks of calling, the pain of jogging in bare feet was too much to ignore. All I wanted was for him to pop up from behind a bush, nubbin tail wagging, happy to see me. If I concentrated hard enough, I could make it real.

When I reached the corner of Alton and Sixteenth, I halted, unsure which street to take. As I stood still, the heavy air descended on me all at once, threatening to crush me. Tears and sweat crawled down my body like wet tentacles. I couldn't keep running like this.

I loped back to my building's parking lot, realizing I didn't have my car keys when I reached my car. I took the stairs two at a time again, my legs aching.

After another quick search of the apartment, I fell to my knees, dumped my purse's contents, and searched for my keys in the pile. I found them and snatched up my wallet, somehow remembering that my gas tank was near empty. Blood streaked the linoleum on the spot where my wallet had been. I froze. Was that Ollie's blood? As I got to my feet, a stab of pain shot through my toe, the one I'd mangled in my collision with the bookend. That had to be the source of the blood, didn't it? I threw on some flip-flops and flew back out to my car.

I started my engine and blew out of the lot, going the wrong way down an aisle and almost slamming into a BMW. The car's horn blared from behind me and echoed in my ears for blocks until the sound of my shallow breaths replaced it.

Think, I told myself. My best bet was to go to the new house. I'd heard stories of dogs finding their way home from hundreds of miles away. Yes. Maybe a burglar came in, and Ollie got spooked and took off for my rented bungalow thinking he'd find me there.

Throngs of pedestrians held me up at the Lincoln Road intersection, and I visualized pressing the gas and plowing through them. An older woman crossing with shopping bags and a small child noticed me screaming and pounding the steering wheel with my fists. Her eyes and mouth formed an O, and she galloped across the street, dragging the kid. After what seemed like forever, I sped through the crossroads and down the side streets to my new place. I pulled into the short drive and leapt from the running car, dashed down the stone walkway leading to the backyard, colliding with a giant shrub. It rattled and scraped at my neck and chest—Fire Bush, Pete had called it, which I had found hilarious at the time.

But nothing was funny now. Ollie wasn't there.

Everything hurt like a bad hangover when I pulled into my apartment's parking lot two hours later. Ollie could have come back to the apartment by now. It made the most sense that he would return here. My crappy flat was the happiest home he'd ever known.

A familiar feeling crept over me as I climbed those stairs. That old ache from years ago, a black hole that started in my chest and ran all the way down to my gut.

This couldn't be happening again. I flashed back to the living room after my dad's funeral. Sitting there with Denise and a few disinterested cats, thinking, *This is it. This is forever.* My lungs, heart, and stomach moved aside to make room for the nothingness.

Jean-Marc was on the balcony. He gazed at me from his perch at his smudgy glass table. "Did you have a burglary?"

"Yeah." My voice sounded hoarse and distant.

"What did the robbers steal?"

I couldn't answer him. In all my frantic circles of the apartment I hadn't taken stock of my belongings.

"Your door was wide open. I shut it for you."

"Great," I said, pushing into my apartment.

I didn't have to call to Ollie to know he wasn't there. The widening hole in my gut told me the place was empty. I looked around for clues. The TV was still on the stand, along with the Blu-ray player, but my computer and iPad, which I kept on my tiny desk, were gone. Somebody had robbed me, but they were too lazy to carry anything heavy. On the way to the kitchen, I crashed into the bookend again—with the other toe this time. I pulled the freezer door hard, slamming it into the wall, reached for the bottle of vodka inside. I screwed off the cap, took a long swig, and felt the reassuring burn in my throat. I needed it if I was going to grill Jean-Marc for information.

For good measure I picked up the bookends and threw them across the room one by one. They both grazed my IKEA coffee table, taking big chunks out of the dark wood veneer and landing with a floor-shaking thud. The destruction gave me no satisfaction.

Another gulp of liquor and I found myself outside, facing Jean-Marc. "Did you notice anyone out here earlier? My dog's gone."

"*Mais, non,*" he said, raising an eyebrow. He pulled out a stool for me, but I continued to stand.

"I know you hated him, but are you sure you didn't hear anything?"

"Ehhhhh." He crossed his arms and scrunched his face as if he was considering whether he should tell me something.

"Tell me!" I wasn't fucking around with this French dickhead anymore.

"I did not think it meant anything at the time, but I saw some men on the balcony this afternoon. I thought maybe they did not live around here."

"What did they look like? Did you see them right out here?"

"Ahhh, they were for a moment talking. I peeked out to see who was making the noise and saw them, but then I stopped watching."

"What were they saying?"

"Sorry. I did not hear what they said."

"How many? Young? Old?"

"Two. Maybe your age. They were African-Americans. Wearing black hoods." He started to reach out for me, then thought better of it and placed his hands on his chest. "Look. I know you felt fondly toward your pet, and I am very sorry he is missing. I do not hate him. Like you said, he has had a troubled life. If there is anything I can do—"

"Okay. Thanks," I mumbled.

I back went inside and scavenged for something to water down my eighty-proof beverage. Plain iced tea would have to do. Who the fuck would come after my dog? I threw open the cupboard. No clean glasses there. The dishwasher hadn't run in a few days. I selected the least dirty cup and mixed my drink.

My mind flashed to Reggie. He had been tweaked out of his mind and was looking for trouble when I'd left him. But no way would he be involved in this. And it wasn't like one of the biggest rap stars in the world could just show up at my highly populated building and expect people not to know about it. But what if he sent his associates?

Don't be silly, I told myself.

I limped around on aching legs and mangled toes drinking my makeshift cocktail, trying to think. The more sips I took, the less my feet throbbed.

Maybe someone had seen me with Ollie, followed us, and found out where we lived. Maybe it was his previous owner. If that was the case, what recourse did I have? What would I tell the police—that someone had broken in here and took my illegal pit bull? But then again, if they caught whoever took my electronics it might lead me to him.

If I was going to call the cops, I needed to figure out if anything else was missing. My fingers moved to my ears, felt the diamond studs adorning them. One and a half carats altogether. Lucy had purchased the earrings at Cartier a couple years ago and gave them to me as a Christmas gift. She'd said they were nearly flawless.

There was also my grandma's gold and amethyst bracelet that I wore only on special occasions. I treaded back to my bedroom and lifted the lid to my jewelry box. The plastic little blond girl with her pink tiara popped up and started spinning to the calliope version of "You Are My Sunshine." A song that had always struck me as happy now carried the most desolate melody in the world. The purple stone bracelet with the square gold chain sat before the dancing figure, untouched, along with $270 I'd forgotten I'd stashed in there a while ago. My insides squeezed even tighter. This robber didn't seem very motivated at all. What if the intruder took the iPad and computer for show but had really come to kidnap Ollie?

I searched on my phone for the Miami Beach Police Department's number. I'd call them and downplay the situation, and they'd conduct a lazy investigation where they didn't go after the perpetrators full force. Just give me the information, and I could take it from there.

CHAPTER THIRTY-ONE

A knock at the door jerked me awake at about 3 a.m. I sat up from the couch disoriented. My head pounded. A moment later the memory came back—somebody had broken in, and Ollie was gone. I winced. The cops were outside, and I had to deal with them in my half-drunk, half-hungover condition.

Two officers stood at my threshold.

"Alex Rader?" said the woman. "This is Officer Ryan, and I'm Officer Marquez."

Marquez, Latina and tiny, wore hastily applied gold eye shadow. Officer Ryan looked more like a stereotypical cop, tall and solid. You could tell he was athletic even if you only saw his face. He shone his flashlight on the broken lock.

Officer Marquez pursed her lips and scanned the room. "Can you think of anyone who might have done this?"

"No idea."

Her eyes landed on the nearly empty vodka bottle on the counter, and then she studied me long enough to make me uneasy. I couldn't tell if the room was spinning or if I was swaying, or both.

"Mind turning on some more lights, ma'am?" Officer Ryan asked. His voice was smooth and low, the kind that would have a calming effect if my nerves were capable of being soothed.

"Sorry." I walked over to my table lamp on the floor in the corner. I'd already moved its perch to the new house. "I'm moving," I said, feeling the need to explain my sparse furnishings. Neither of them responded.

In the light, they began to pace around, Marquez like she was shopping a tag sale, Ryan more cautious and respectful. After a minute or two, Marquez put her hands on her hips and cleared her throat. "Your TV's still here. Was anything stolen?"

"Yes, ma'am." I'd only said "ma'am" maybe once or twice in my life, but something about this woman commanded it. She reminded me of the action figure guard in jail. "My laptop and iPad."

She leaned against the counter and pulled her own small computer tablet from her breast pocket. "Nothing else?"

"I don't think so." I couldn't decide whether to tell them about Ollie. Would I get in trouble for saying I owned a pit bull? My opening to add that piece of information grew smaller as we stood there, eyes locked.

Ryan knelt next to the front door, slipped on a pair of gloves, and pulled open a small plastic briefcase that looked like a toolbox. "Why don't we talk over here so we can give him some space to work?" Marquez said, motioning at the couch as if she were the resident and I were the guest. I spotted my sweat-stained running bra on the floor and hoped Ryan wouldn't notice it.

Marquez made routine inquiries: Had anyone threatened me recently? When did I get home that night? Had the neighbors seen anything?

"My next-door neighbor said he saw a couple guys hanging around." I watched Ryan dip a brush into a glass jar and apply a thin layer of powder around the bolt.

Marquez clicked her tongue, and I turned my attention back to her. "You sure you don't have any ideas on who might've done this? Anyone you've had conflict with recently?" Her expression was hard, challenging, like she didn't believe me.

"No. I can't think of anyone."

"Seems odd that they didn't take more."

Maybe I should just tell her about Ollie, I thought. If they found him, they wouldn't return him to me because he was an illegal breed. But if they found out who broke in, it might lead me to my dog. Reggie and Ham would help me. I just needed a name.

"I, uh . . . don't know."

"Mmm-hmm." She tapped the keys on her tablet and without looking up said, "Where's your dog?"

"What?" She'd thrown the question out fast. It caught me off guard.

My cheeks burned under her laser glare. She knew I'd heard her the first time.

A sharp crunching sound pierced the silence. I jolted, but Marquez didn't flinch.

"Sorry," Ryan said with a grin. He was holding a wide piece of transparent tape that he'd just peeled off the door's surface. "Got a print."

Marquez ignored him. "I see you have a dog," she continued, waving her hand at Ollie's bed and toys in the corner. "Is your dog missing?"

Why hadn't I just told her the truth in the first place? I was strung out. My brain was a ball of lint. Logic had left me hours ago, and the vodka hadn't helped. But it felt too late to change my story now.

"Uh, no. He's at my friend's house."

"Well, that's lucky, isn't it? Why is he there?"

I glanced at the ceiling, then back at her. "She keeps him when I work long hours."

Ryan finished his task and joined us in the center of the room. His good-natured smile made me wish he was the one questioning me instead of Marquez.

"You have a dog? Where is it?" he asked.

"At her friend's because Ms. Rader was working late," Marquez said, sounding annoyed that he hadn't kept up with the conversation.

Ryan took a step forward and placed his hands on his belt as if he were snapping out of friendly guy mode and back into cop mode. "That's good," he said, his voice lower now. Maybe he was her trainee or something.

"Well, guess that's about it," she said, handing me her business card. "We'll be in touch." She marched to the door.

"Thanks so much," I said as they walked out.

"You're welcome, Miss Rad— " Ryan started to say.

She interrupted him. "And don't forget to have your neighbor call us."

"Wait," Ryan said, turning back. "I forgot something."

Marquez sighed. I backed up to let Ryan move past me.

"My kit," he said, bending down to pick up the handled box he'd left by the entrance. "And this," he said, handing me his business card. "Where do you work, Miss Rader?"

"It's Alex. You can call me Alex. I'm an assistant to Reginald Wiles," I said.

"Well, isn't that fascinating," Marquez said from the balcony, pulling out that tablet again and entering something else on the keypad.

I didn't fall asleep again until it was light out. Then I had one of those vivid morning dreams, the kind where you're the puppet master, guiding the action.

Rob and I sat in the Corolla I had in high school, even though I didn't know Rob in high school, but he looked like Officer Ryan instead of Rob. Ollie's head lay on the armrest between us, and we were all headed to the Grand Canyon. When we got out of the car, Ollie took off running into the desert. Panicked, I raced after him, dropping the picnic basket of warm sushi that I'd brought for some reason. In the distance I could see a man jumping off a donkey and grabbing Ollie by the collar.

Then I woke, flooded with relief and happiness. Those feelings quickly faded, and despair overtook me like prickly vines. I threw on some clothes, splashed my face, and headed out.

My plan was to hit the animal shelters. I'd looked up the laws regarding pit bulls and learned shelters had to hold a pit bull for five days before euthanizing.

I arrived at the first shelter just as it opened, stopping at the entrance to text Ham.

Have an emergency. Can I come in late?

I heaved open the heavy glass door and headed toward the front desk. My shoes squeaked on the freshly mopped floor, adding to the symphony of yowling dogs audible through the glass partition beyond the lobby. An overweight orange tabby cat stalked back and forth on the desk's counter, as if to guard the information behind it. A college-aged girl looked up from her computer screen and greeted me with a tenuous smile.

"I lost my dog. May I go in and look for him?" I motioned to the atrium behind her.

"How long has your animal been missing?" she asked as if she were reading the question from an index card. The cat sunk to its haunches and licked a paw.

"Since yesterday."

"If he was brought in last night, then he hasn't been processed yet. So he won't be on the adoption floor," she read from her mental script. "Let me get someone to take you to the back."

She picked up her phone and hit a button on the switchboard. "Donald or Debbie to the front desk please." She plunked the receiver back down and said, "Someone will be right with you." Then she hunched over her keyboard and began clacking away.

I took to pacing the tiled floor and checking my phone every few seconds. Finally, it vibrated and chirped back at me.

OK Reg not here anyway.

I wondered if Reggie had also been missing since last night.

There was a gust of hydraulic doors, and the barks and howls rose a few decibels. I looked up to see Debbie emerging from the back. She wore a too-large outfit consisting of a green men's T-shirt that read VOLUNTEER and cargo jean capris. She reminded me of Denise.

"What's up, Sierra?" she said to the girl at the desk.

"Can you take her to the back to look for her dog?" Sierra asked, pointing at me.

"Sure," Debbie said, and moved toward me with a concerned smile. "Oh dear. What kind of dog?" She took me by the arm and guided me toward the room she'd just come from.

"He's an American bull dog"—another term for a pit bull with a less negative connotation, according to my web searches. "Tan and white."

We advanced into the blaring, echoey gymnasium, my nose prickling from the industrial disinfectant smell. Cages flanked us on both sides filled with spaniels, labs, and poodles jumping and scratching at the glass walls of their tiny spaces.

Debbie kept hold of my arm and I let her lead me, grateful for the support. "He wouldn't be on the adoption floor yet," she said. "Did he have identification?"

"No." My insides clinched. I hated myself for procrastinating on getting a tag for his collar.

"You must be so worried, hon. Let's see if he's here." She pushed through a swinging steel door in the very back that read STAFF ONLY, and the ceiling dropped by about ten feet. Individual cages resembling old-timey jails housed the dogs. Their barks were more formidable than the ones in the atrium, as was the odor. The walls were gray and dank, adding to the prison effect. A Doberman launched at us from the back of his cell, growling and baring teeth. I jumped back.

"Some of these guys are hard cases," she yelled over the roar. "They haven't had loving homes or owners."

I thought of Ollie back here with these dogs, how scared he would be. He hated loud noises, and he shied away from most large dogs. "What happens to them?" I hollered.

"We try to rehabilitate them, but we don't have the resources to help them all. Mostly we try to get them into no-kill shelters. If not, a lot of them won't last long."

We looped around all their pens, passing maybe thirty dogs. Some of them showed their fangs; others barked exuberantly; one German shepherd cowered in the corner, making me want to comfort it somehow. Feces littered several cages, some of it smudged across the floor, dotted with paw prints. I trudged on with Debbie, searching and hopeful despite the hopelessness around me.

We circled back to where we started, and a giant lump formed in my throat. Ollie wasn't there.

"I'm sorry, sweetie," Debbie said, her face full of compassion.

"What's with the scared one?" I pointed at the German shepherd.

"Oh, that's Molly. She's been here about a month. She won't look at anybody, and she gets really scared when someone enters her cage."

Molly obviously wasn't aggressive. "Why is she back here?"

"Nobody wants a dog with that level of anxiety. They either tend to act out or they won't interact at all."

"That sucks," I said, glancing back at her as we left the back room. Perhaps all Molly needed was someone she could trust. That, and quieter roommates.

CHAPTER THIRTY-TWO

My morning of searching for Ollie came up fruit-less. I'd been to three shelters and seen hundreds of homeless dogs. I wondered if I should just call the officers and tell them my dog was stolen. How could I have been so stupid? Marquez had flustered me. Maybe my DUI had given me an unreasonable fear of being arrested. If I told them the truth now, they could nab me for filing a false police report. People went to jail for that, didn't they?

I went to work. I kept going forward but had a nag-ging feeling I was moving toward nothing. Like at any moment I might stumble on a black hole and cease to exist. I couldn't let it suck me in because Ollie was out there somewhere, alone. It seemed highly possible that he had been abducted and taken back to the underground dog-fighting world. Reggie knew all about that scene, and I needed to talk to him about it.

Reggie's voice sounded over the intercom as I was pouring myself a cup of coffee. "Yo, Alex. Come to the master."

Since when did he start calling himself that? I wondered. A beat later it dawned on me that he was referring to his bedroom. I plodded upstairs.

I rapped on the door. "*Entrée*," he said in a raspy voice.

When I walked in, my first instinct was to apologize and leave.

Reggie gestured from his bed for me to come closer to him.

He looked diminished in his California king, his larger-than-life presence shrunk to real-life size now. His dreadlocks had been sheared off, and I couldn't help thinking his strength had gone with them.

"What it is?" he said, patting the small Afro that extended two inches from his skull.

"I like the new do."

Squinting at me, he leaned forward and pushed the sheeny gray comforter down to his chest. "You for real? You sound like you're lying."

"No, I *totally* like it." I heard the hesitance in my voice, too. I had no frame of reference—no hairstyle accentuated a sallow face with puffy, sunken eyes. "And I like your room, too," I said.

I'd never been in his room before. He had it decorated Japanese style, with a huge cherry-blossom-printed rug and dark wood furniture.

He made a grunting sound. His hair sprung back into place when he pulled his hand away.

"I don't know if I like it," he said.

"Which one? The room or the hair?"

He sighed. "Any of it. I don't know anything right now. Feel me?"

Yes, I felt him—more than he could know.

Reggie pointed at an armoire situated against a wall between two doors; the bathroom and closet I presumed. "Go in there for me," he said. "Bottom drawer—there's a little brown box."

I pulled out a shoebox-sized wooden container carved with tribal-looking symbols and walked it over to him.

"This'll get me straight," he said, taking it from me. He opened the box and pulled out a glass pipe and a freezer bag that I was glad to see was filled with pot and not crack. When he unzipped the seal on the bag, a sweet, earthy smell filled the air. He plucked out a bud the size of a fun-size candy bar and examined it with fascination as it glowed like an emerald under the bedside lamp.

I'd wait to ask him my question until after he smoked his weed. He'd be relaxed, less likely to be offended. Yet my heart continued racing as I tried to form the words in my head.

His expression turned to disgust when he picked up the pipe. "Damn. Who the fuck left this shit dirty?" He extended it to me with a shaky hand. "You know how to clean this out?"

"Sure. Bathroom?" I said, taking the pipe from him. He pointed to the left of the wardrobe. I went to turn the knob, but then, thinking better of it, I raised my hand to knock.

"Ain't nobody in there."

I found a Q-tip in a glass canister next to one of the sinks and went to work cleaning the black ash from the bowl, glad to have something to do with my nervous hands. Even the papery cinders left by this high-caliber stuff smelled intoxicating. Once the pipe sparkled, I brought it back out to him.

"You want some of this?" he asked.

"No, thanks," I said. "I should keep a clear head."

He scoffed. "Alright then. You probably got plenty of shit to do. Stay close, though." His way of telling me to leave. My time had run out to bring up my sensitive topic because I was a chickenshit.

"Wait. You got a lighter?"

"In my car. Be right back."

You absolutely have to ask him when you get back, I told myself as I leapt down the steps and then out the front door. The longer Ollie was missing, the more danger he was in. I grabbed an eight-pack of Bics I'd bought and ran inside, back up to Reggie.

He sucked on the bowl hard and held the smoke in. His red eyes didn't look like they could spare any more blood vessels. A caustic smell, not earthy at all, hit the air.

He'd switched out pipes on me.

He exhaled, and a weird smile spread across his face. "You probably don't want to hit this."

"No, but can I talk to you about something?"

"Aw, shit," he said, his smile fading. "You're leaving me, ain't you?"

"Don't worry. I'm not quitting," I said.

"Good. So what's up then?" he asked, firing up the pipe again.

"Um, I'm just wondering about dog fighting."

He sat up and exhaled a cloud of chemicals. "Why you asking? This another interview?" He snorted.

"Well, my dog is missing and I'm just wondering—"

"What happened?"

"Somebody took him, and I just wanted to know if you might have any insight that could help me find him."

His eyes wide, he set the pipe in his lap. "What you saying?"

"I'm just wondering if you could point me in the right direction."

A vein I'd never seen before protruded from his forehead. The next second he threw the covers back and jumped to his feet.

"You think my people took your pit bull?" he asked. "Yeah, because that's what we do—go around stealing good people's dogs. You even check the shelters before you came straight to the source?" His eyes flashed, and he was larger than life again.

I took a step back, directed my palms at him. "No, that's not what I meant at all!" I wondered how differently this conversation would be going if he'd stuck with the pot.

"What you mean, then?" He looked angry enough to choke me. I'd never seen him like this. Those lyrics jumped into my head: *I stay clean for a minute / Then I'm back up in it.* I hadn't realized that song was autobiographical when I'd first heard it in his recording session.

"Of course I checked all the shelters," I said. "All I'm wondering is, uh, based on your past experiences, if you might know where someone with bad intentions might have taken him."

"You think I was involved?" He pursed his lips and hung his head. "I thought you were different, Alex."

I shrunk at his words, but only for a second. I didn't have time to be a screen for his projections. My dog was missing, and Reggie could help me figure out how to find him if he would just take a moment and set down the crack pipe. I was sick of this shit, dealing with the multiple personalities of drug addicts.

"Well, I thought you were different, too," I said. And I walked out.

Reggie called after me through the closed door, through the blood vibrating in my head. I dragged myself to the kitchen, pressing on my hot temples, trying to contain the motion.

Marcia's pastry of the day sat on the counter in a breadbasket, folded into a linen cloth. The scent of pumpkin and sugar set off my hunger and nausea responses at the same time. I needed food to coat my stomach or else I would be sick. They were scones, still warm. Leaning against the counter, I wolfed one down dry. It sat like a baseball in my chest after I swallowed.

I tried to figure out what to do next. Reggie would most likely get over our argument when he sobered up. And I could talk to Ham. I should have gone to him in the first place.

The doorbell chimed, startling me. I crossed the house to answer, but Ham was already there, hand on the knob. He paused when he saw me.

"Didn't know you was here yet. Everything okay?"

The concern on his face set me off, and I felt tears forming behind my eyes, ready to spring. "Just a minute," I muttered, already beelining for the bathroom. Without meaning to, I slammed the door. Then I turned on the faucet and checked the mirror to see how shitty my face looked. Patches of red had popped up on my face like a world map. Old, murky mascara cut black rivers down my cheeks.

Someone tapped on the door. "Alex? You alright in there?" It was Ham.

"Be out in a second," I called, trying to sound light and breezy.

"The tiki guy's here, but take your time."

"Yep." *Shit.* I had completely forgotten that today was the day the contractor started on the structure for the pool. I splashed cold water on my face and toweled off.

"You can do this," I whispered to my reflection. The image in the mirror whispered back, *No, you can't.*

The foyer was empty when I stepped out. I stalked around the corner to the living room. Ham and the contractor stood talking outside the picture window, their backs to me, facing the pool. As I headed to join them, the intercom clicked.

"Ham, meet me in the master, please."

I froze. Reggie sounded annoyed. He was going to talk to Ham about me. I couldn't take another confrontation. I grabbed my stuff and left before anyone could stop me.

That was the last day I worked for Reggie.

CHAPTER THIRTY-THREE

Go back now, I told myself as I got on the bridge leading off Star Island. It wasn't too late. Reggie and Ham wouldn't even know I had left. But my car kept driving away—it wouldn't go back.

I checked my phone, and it showed some new messages. None of them were from the police or the shelters. My thoughts jumbled. A horn blared beside me and I swerved back into my lane, narrowly avoiding an SUV. I waited for the accompanying adrenaline, but it didn't come. I floated outside my own body, watching somebody else drive recklessly until I was home.

My hands trembled as I opened the medicine cabinet and then the pill bottle. I poured the tiny tablets into my hand. Sleep would help. I still had some old Ativan of Lucy's. She'd given them to me the day before she'd left for rehab. "No reason for these little beauties to go to waste," she'd said, pausing while holding the pills halfway between us, as if reconsidering before she handed them over. I swallowed one without water and funneled the rest back into the container. Then I changed my mind and took another one.

In the hot, tiny bathroom, I could smell myself. Dense sweat, the kind that came after a night of drinking, oozed from my pores. I turned up the air-conditioning, slumped on the couch, and flipped on the television. My brain couldn't grasp what the talk show host was saying to the transvestites on the screen. Whatever it was, it pissed me off. Then a tragic image of a bald child, probably suffering from cancer, appeared. That pissed me off, too.

I slogged to the kitchen for a beer, downed half before I returned to the couch. I flipped the channels until I landed on *The Good, the Bad and the Ugly*, but I couldn't follow that either, even though I'd watched it many times with my dad, and then alone. Through the thin slats of my blinds I could see the morning clouds had given way to sunshine, and I wished the skies would cloud over again. The TV droned on as I clamped my eyes shut to block out the glare.

Then something happened. The gunshots and clomping horses on TV seemed to transport from the hard desert to a muffled, snowy field. I opened my eyes and the cruel light from before now streamed toward me in fluffy ribbons, as if someone had rubbed Vaseline on the windowpane. The specs of dust looked like glitter. I started thinking that everything might actually turn out okay. Ollie might be okay, because there are kind people out there, too. Maybe somebody had broken in and Ollie had scared them off and then, spooked, he'd bolted. Somebody would find him and take care of him, let the shelters know they had him. They'd probably found him already, and word would come to me soon.

And then I slept for a long time.

My eyes clicked open. My phone's blue light blinked in the periphery of my vision. I sat up on the couch, dizzy, checked and saw Denise was the source of the flashing blue dot, and deleted her message without listening to it. It was still several hours before dawn. I wandered outside. I couldn't see anything. I went back inside to find a flashlight. The beam illuminated the bay, the trees, my neighbors, all silent and unmoving. Leaning over the railing, I jumped at a rustling sound so tiny it could've been a bug leaping onto a leaf.

The sound spurred me down the stairs. I called to my dog, and someone yelled, "Shut the fuck up!" If Ollie was around, he would run to the sound of my voice. But what if he was injured nearby, unable to get to me? I kept calling his name.

At sunrise I trudged back to my couch, which had soaked up my cold sweat while I'd slept. Instead of going to my bed, I lay on the floor. If Ollie wasn't comfortable, I shouldn't be either. I tossed around for a while before giving up on sleep and taking a shower.

Decontaminated and ready to work the problem, I still had three hours to wait before the shelters opened. I couldn't bear it, sitting there alone. I got into my car and trolled around South Beach in a trance, riding the brake, squinting at every yard and every bush. Not many cars were out at this early hour, so I only pissed off a couple people.

I dialed several shelters before opening time. Only one person answered.

"Did your dog have a microchip?" she asked me.

"Micro what?"

"Microchip!"

"I heard you the first time. I don't know what that means."

A loud sigh whooshed through the phone. "It's an implant that contains their information, so if they're lost we know who to contact. Every responsible dog owner should get one." She talked to me like she was a social worker confronting me about my child's mysterious bruises.

My blood felt like fire in my veins. I wanted to murder her through the phone. "Do you think you're helping anything by treating me like a negligent asshole when my dog is lost?" I asked. "A dog I found in the street and brought home by the way. Your microchipping lecture isn't going to help me find him right now, so can you please check and see if you have an animal matching his description?"

"Well, when you found him in the street, the first thing you should have done is take him to a vet," she said, her voice full of wrath.

"Stop telling me—"

"And the vet would've told you—"

"What's your name?"

"Ma'am, you need to calm down. I don't have to take this kind of abuse."

"You have no idea what abuse is. What's your name?"

There was a click, and then the connection went silent. Had that really just happened?

That woman had taken me from despair to rage. I could work with rage. I couldn't remember which shelter I called, so I did a reverse phone number search on my phone. Then I hightailed it to her location, cursing all the way.

The building, a converted ranch house on a residential street, stood on a shady plot of patchy grass. I charged up to the front door and turned the knob to find it locked. Through the window I saw a middle-aged woman with closely cropped hair milling around. I checked the time. Eight fifty. I sat on the bench outside, rigid and waiting for nine.

A woman moved toward the front and unbolted the lock. Her eyes went wide when she spotted me glaring from the bench, and she spun and disappeared. I rushed inside. A din of yelps and yaps greeted me, and there were no other volunteers in sight. I passed through a small room of cats in stacked cages to a larger area, where about twenty dogs also huddled in stacked kennels. There were large breeds alone on the bottom, little ones sharing the spaces on top. I didn't see Ollie among them.

Rounding a corner, I nearly bumped into a skinny man with a baby face, gray hair, and horn-rimmed glasses.

"May I help you?"

He sounded like a Muppet. Ernie from *Sesame Street.*

"Yeah, I'm looking for the person who I spoke to on the phone this morning," I yelled over the dogs. I wanted the woman to hear me from her hiding place.

He held his palms up to his chest, protecting his body. I hadn't considered what I'd do once face-to-face with the woman. I'd never punched anyone. All my angst from the past thirty-six hours was laser-focused, trained on a voice on the phone.

Ernie took a step back. "May I ask what the conversation was regarding?"

I couldn't help but scoff at the way he shrunk from me like I was wearing a bomb vest. "It's regarding my lost dog. I checked to see if you guys might have him, and she was incredibly rude to me."

"Um, she's actually on another call, so you can leave her a message or I can help you. Do you see your dog?" He gestured around the room.

Ernie made a good substitute target for my anger. "Seriously? You think I'd be wasting my time listening to you talk in circles if I saw my dog in here? Do you have any more dogs anywhere else?" I started marching toward a door in the back that read "Volunteers and Employees Only." Ernie stepped sideways, blocking me. "No, actually. Those are the offices, and they're private." He scratched at his elbow. "I think I'm going to have to ask you to leave now."

I cackled again. "Oh my god. That's rich. She's holed up back there cowering from me, and she convinced you that I'm the one who provoked her! You should've heard the things she said to me on the phone." I could hear how nutty I sounded, but I didn't care. I contemplated running around him into the office.

"If you don't leave now, I'm going to have to call the police." His voice tremored and he didn't meet my eyes.

Someone needed to teach these animal people how to interact with humans in a sane manner. I could have gotten past him, busted through that flimsy "Employees Only" door. But then what would I do once in the office? Hit someone for the first time in my life and go to jail?

"Fine," I said, turning to leave. "But you guys really should work on your public relations skills."

Ernie breathed out a relieved sigh. I knew I'd made a huge mistake, losing my temper. This organization could end up taking in my dog, and I'd alienated two of its gatekeepers. I spun back around to see Ernie's hand on the lock, poised to shut me out of the building.

I tried to sound humble and contrite. "Listen, he's a tan-and-white pit bull. Please have somebody call me if he comes here. He's everything to me. You have my information."

Pity mingled with the fear in his eyes. "Of course."

Still, the bolt clicked behind me after I stepped out, and I suspected I wouldn't be welcome there again. Banished from an animal shelter. Just like my mother.

I wanted this punishing nightmare to end. No matter what I did, things just kept getting worse. It felt like someone was pulling levers and pushing buttons, putting me through this hell. Then it struck me. Maybe someone was orchestrating everything—God or karma or Satan.

Maybe all this was happening because I wasn't a good person, and it was time for me to pay.

CHAPTER THIRTY-FOUR

I sabelle called me just as I finished my rounds of shelters the next day. I'd forgotten that she was supposed to watch Ollie that morning. Her voice cracked when I told her he'd gone missing.

"We will look for him tonight," she said.

That night the air hung lighter and cooler than it had in a while. Isabelle picked me up at sunset and gave me a sorrowful half smile as I buckled my seat belt. I told her I'd exhausted the South Beach search, so we set out for downtown. Pink and orange streaked the horizon as we crossed the bridge, the bay reflecting the sky's colors like a warped mirror. A fantasy about returning later with Ollie sent a brief rush of optimism through me, the kind of hope that dissipates fast and makes you feel lower than you did before.

"Have you eaten?" she asked.

I couldn't remember.

She reached behind her seat for her giant tote and pulled out a Clif Bar. For the first time in at least a day, I ate.

"There are some cheese and crackers somewhere in here," she said, digging into her bag once again as we passed Star Island.

I pictured her lopping slices from an "aging" wheel of cheese with insects hovering around it. "That's okay."

She took us on a tour of the city, slowing in Little Havana, and we passed bars and restaurants, including the Pink Fox, with its disturbing logo, a flashing neon magenta fox's head on a topless woman's body. The downtown air felt different at night, the sooty congestion of the daytime streets rubbed out by darkness. A sparkly group of thirtysomethings spilled from a Hummer limo toward a club, where the attendant unhooked a red rope so they could bypass a line of resentful, less attractive partygoers. Ahead of us a grim woman steered a shopping cart around a corner. A beater car without a muffler screamed past her, but she didn't react. The only dog we saw was a terrier being pulled along the sidewalk by an old man.

We needed a plan. We needed to talk to people. There would be no group of men with "Dog Fight Club" silk-screened on their chests.

"We're just wasting gas," I said. "I mean, what are the chances of seeing Ollie just walking down the street?"

"Hmm." She stuck out her lower lip and blew a breath upward, and her bangs rustled in the breeze. "He found us once—he could find us again."

"If he's out there, he's in a seriously unsafe neighborhood," I said. My heart sped at the thought of asking questions in an area where shootings happened regularly.

Isabelle set her jaw. "Let's go there then."

She didn't know what she was saying. Criminals would zero in on two young women tooling around in a German sports car. "No, we're not doing this," I said. "I'll ask Lucy's bodyguard to take me out tomorrow night." It was a lie. I couldn't wait for tomorrow. I'd go back out tonight, hope to see a sign, maybe sketchy activity, anything that might point to dog fighting. If Ollie was in danger, I'd have to put myself in danger to save him. Personal safety was low on my list of concerns right now anyway. But I didn't want Isabelle to get hurt or die tonight.

Isabelle stopped the car on a deserted street and faced me with crossed arms. "It is easy to see how eager and distressed you are. You have been biting your fingernails and smoking many cigarettes. You will not wait until tomorrow, and you are not allowed to go alone. I am like Ollie's godmother, so I am going with you."

I didn't know Isabelle had a hard-ass side to her. She was normally agreeable, to the point that I'd wondered if she had any opinions of her own. An argument formed on my tongue, but I dismissed it, convinced by the defiant look on her face that it would make no difference.

"Guess we're going to Liberty City then. Make a right."

Liberty City stuck out in my mind as the worst neighborhood in Miami. Anyone paying attention to crime stories in the *Herald* or on the local news knew about it. We didn't say much on the way there.

We crossed Northwest Seventh Avenue and rolled toward a sea of blockish cement apartment complexes with air-conditioning units peppering their facades. Beyond that, plywood covered the windows of several dwellings, their grounds enclosed by iron bars. Litter had somehow made it over the high padlocked fences— broken bottles, fast-food bags, and in one yard a pile of matted clothing.

Isabelle hit a button and the car doors bolted in unison. I took a last puff of my cigarette, tasting the noxious filter before I flicked it outside and shut my window. We sat alert in our sealed vacuum, checking out the terrain. Unlike the rest of lush, junglelike Miami, most plots in this neighborhood bore no grass or plant life, except for a stunted tree here and there. Below one of the working streetlights stood a run-down corner store, its window signs boasting check-cashing services and lottery tickets.

The words FUCK THE 5-0 were painted in thick block letters on the side.

Isabelle stopped at the intersection in front of the store and motioned to the right with a questioning look. I nodded. Just as she turned, a group of young men strolled out of the store and started toward the road, all grins, until one of them spotted us. He tapped another guy on the shoulder, leaned in close, and said something to him. A split second later, all five members of the group froze at the edge of the street, glowering at us. Isabelle stiffened and I held my breath as we drove by, both of us watching them from the corners of our eyes, and then in the rearview mirror. We exhaled at the same time when they started moving again.

Under a glaring yellow streetlight ahead, tiny figures, too small to be adults, were lined up along a fence. As we moved closer, we realized they weren't children at all. They were children's toys—a worn stuffed elephant and several bears, one of them as big as a grand prize you'd win at a carnival game. A thin board was staked in the ground in the center of the menagerie. Attached to the post was a photograph of a child beaming and grinning, her two front teeth missing. Isabelle and I exchanged a solemn look, realizing that we were passing a memorial for someone's dead little girl.

She rolled down the window halfway. "Maybe we can hear something that will help us," she said.

A dog barked in the distance, and Isabelle turned in the direction of the sound. We passed one- and two-family bungalows surrounded by metal barriers, a vacant lot, and another wary group staring us down, this time young women. The barking had stopped, but Isabelle kept on in that direction.

I wondered if this was a waste of time, winding around these mean streets senselessly following noises, too scared to talk to anyone.

Two guys dressed the same in calf-length shorts and slide-on sandals over white socks stood on a corner up ahead of us, passing a cigarette or a joint.

"Let me just ask them if they know anything," I said. "I'll yell it through the window, and then we can just drive away really fast."

Isabelle dipped her head and pressed the gas, not braking until we were right on top of them. One of them flicked the joint or cigarette to the ground.

I rolled down my window. "Hi. Have you guys seen a pit bull? Tan and white?"

Everything about them hardened. Their bodies went rigid and shadows darkened their faces as if the lighting had changed.

"I think my dog was kidnapped." My tone was pleading.

They swaggered our way, holding their cold expressions.

Isabelle's hands clenched and unclenched around the steering wheel. "Should I go?" she whispered.

"Hang on." One of the men looked like he was about to say something.

"What you doing riding here at night?" yelled the one on the right, all five fingers spread and pointing at us.

"I'm just trying to find my—"

The man on the left interrupted, jerking his closely shaven head side to side. "Bitch, I don't care if your *momma*'s lit up on fire in that gutter. You ain't got no business here. Now stop asking questions and get the fuck out of here."

"I'm going," Isabelle said, hitting the pedal and catapulting both of us hard against our seat backs.

We said nothing until we crossed an invisible barrier from dicey to safe, where grass grew and the buildings weren't covered with iron grates.

"What now?" Isabelle asked.

"Let's just go back to your place. I can try the shelters tomorrow." I was lying again. I would drop her off and go back. Canvas more people.

"But I still want to help. Maybe we should not have left there." She moved her hands to the side of the wheel, ready to execute a U-turn.

"I have one other idea," I said. "Do you feel like trying over by the airport?"

"Sure."

I directed her to the place where Angel took the picture, the one showing Reggie and Ham standing in the deserted warehouse district near the site of Reggie's future youth center. I had her park down the street on the opposite side.

She killed the lights and leaned against the headrest. A dump truck groaned past us, kicking up gravel and dust. "Do you think something is going on here?"

"I've heard some things. It's probably nothing, but do you mind if we sit here for a few?"

"Sure," she said. She heaved her bottomless tote from the back seat, raked through it, and retrieved a silver thermos. "You must be thirsty." She removed the lid and filled it with a foggy, grayish-green liquid.

"Dirty martini?" I asked.

"Green tea, silly."

It was silly, but at this point it wouldn't have surprised me if she whipped out a blender and ice cream and made a Mudslide. I sipped the honeyed tea and my stomach warmed.

"Good idea," I said, handing it back to her.

She smiled. "So, what have you heard about this place?"

"Well, Reggie was photographed here late one night. Jean-Marc told me he saw some guys matching descriptions of people in Reggie's crew hanging outside my apartment the night Ollie disappeared. He probably doesn't have anything to do with this, but it's worth checking out."

We passed the thermos back and forth a few times like it was a bottle of Jack Daniel's.

"Jean-Marc asks about me often, no?"

"Yeah."

She placed her hands on the steering wheel and looked straight ahead. "I know you have been having to deal with Jean-Marc. I truly appreciate that you haven't told him where I am living. I know he can be quite persistent."

"Well, he hasn't tried to waterboard me yet or anything like that."

"Pardon?"

"Uh, he hasn't been that bad. I'm betting he was happy that my dog got stolen, but I don't care what he thinks. I just don't want him to come after you."

"Hmm," she murmured. She looked like she was trying to decide whether to tell me something.

"What is it?"

"It is nothing." She slouched in her seat.

"No, tell me what you're thinking," I said.

She blew a breath upward, sending her hair fluttering again. "I don't want to say. It will just make you feel more bad."

"That's not even possible."

"He is such an asshole," she said. "He said maybe your dog ate some bad cheese and got sick."

"You talked to him?"

"I had to arrange to get the rest of my things. Colin took some friends, and they picked them up."

"Yeah?" I smacked a new pack of cigarettes on my palm and unwound the cellophane tab. I lit one and handed it to her. She took a long drag.

"Jean-Marc was having people over, so he ignored Colin." Isabelle offered the cigarette back to me, but I waved it away.

"He always seemed like kind of a grumpy hermit to me. I didn't think he ever had company."

She shrugged and ashed out the window. "Well, he is getting careless."

"What do you mean?"

"With the drug dealing. He always said 'never from home.'"

"He's a *dealer?*"

She looked at me, surprised. "You didn't know?"

"No, but it makes sense, I gu— "

Just then a flicker of light illuminated one of the waxed-over windows across the street. Isabelle saw it too. Her hand moved to the ignition and she gazed at me, waiting for instructions.

"Hang on. Let me think for a second." I hadn't expected anything to actually happen. As far as I'd figured, we were here to rule this place out.

We sat in watchful silence for a minute, scanning the area. The street was deserted except for a parked pickup truck.

"Maybe there is another entrance?" Isabelle asked.

A shadow flashed in front of the window.

"Someone is there," Isabelle said.

Two silhouetted forms moved toward the lighted area on the street. They came into view and faced each other. The person wearing a hat started waving his arms frantically, as if arguing a point. I wiped my eyes and squinted. It was Reggie and his uncle, Marvin.

CHAPTER THIRTY-FIVE

"Holy shit! Get down!" I said, folding myself low in the seat. Isabelle did the same.

I chanced a quick peek through the very bottom of the window. Reggie and Marvin went at it like an umpire and a coach, close enough to exchange spit. They didn't seem to notice our lone vehicle sitting across the road.

"What are they doing?"

"Yelling at each other. I don't think they've spotted us."

"I wonder what they are discussing."

"Whatever it is, it's really pissing off his uncle."

"You think Reggie is still fighting the dogs?"

"I'm starting to wonder," I said. What other possible business could Reggie have in that warehouse? Still, it didn't make sense. Why would he risk it after everything that had happened when he was on probation? It was not like he needed a gambling ring to bring in money. He could slap his name on a can of nausea-inducing body spray and earn millions.

"This is pretty bad, no?"

"Yeah," I said absentmindedly. My brain was trying to form a recognizance plan. "Maybe we can see more from the other side."

"Well, they don't know my car. You can stay low while I take us around the building?"

Instinct told me we needed to get away from them, but we were risking it either way. If we moved, they could spot us; if we sat here, they could spot us. How would we explain ourselves if they decided to investigate our car and they found us crouched here inside?

"Yeah, let's go."

Isabelle started the car and drove away from them. I watched them, and they didn't seem to be paying attention to us. She circled the block, and we arrived at the rear entrance.

Two sedans sat outside of the back of the building. Not quite the makings of a huge gathering, but there was a loading dock where cars could potentially enter the massive structure.

"I'm getting out to take a closer look," I told Isabelle.

Her eyes bulged.

"Just drive down the street a ways. Call the police if you don't hear from me in five minutes."

"You must be joking. I am coming with you."

"No!" I almost yelled, zipping my hoodie to the neck. "Just get the car out of here. It'll stick out—they'll see it before they see me." I reached for the handle.

"Okay, but I will not leave you here."

"I'll call you in a few minutes," I said, getting out of the car.

Isabelle drove away. I crouched and crept toward the dock. When I pulled off my hood, I heard a thumping sound. It was music.

I made my way to a wide path that led to a mechanical gate large enough for two cars to enter at the same time. To the left was a double entrance for pedestrians, its windows spray-painted black. Tiptoeing to the far end of the structure and rounding the corner, I saw a sliver of light shining out. An opening. Either whoever painted the window black had missed a spot or the paint had chipped off.

The gap was above eye level, but there was a concrete ledge that I could use. I hoisted myself up, then rested my forearms on the ledge and leveraged my feet against the wall. Straining, I raised myself up just a bit higher until my face reached the slight opening.

What I saw sent a bolt of terror through me so strong that my nervous system seemed to short out.

My body went slack, and I tumbled to the ground. My chest heaved. It felt like all the oxygen had been drained from the atmosphere.

I scrambled up on shaky legs and clawed at my back pocket for my phone.

"Alex?" Isabelle answered.

"Come get me," I said in a voice that didn't sound like my own. "I'm around the corner from the loading dock."

"I will be right there."

She sped up to me about ten seconds later and threw the door open. I walked toward her with deliberate steps for fear my legs would give out again.

Isabelle fired questions at me, but the screaming disjointed images in my head drowned out her words as we zipped away from the warehouse. I'd seen evil, dark and gnarled like dead vines wrapping around me, squeezing the life out. A sudden urge to destroy something clutched me like those imaginary withered limbs. I threw a fist at the dashboard, somehow expecting the hard surface to give from the force of my punch. My hand connected with an abrupt, painful crack.

Isabelle flinched. "What happened?"

"We have to call the police," I said, trying to retrieve my phone. It slipped through my fingers to the floor, and I watched it slide under the seat as Isabelle took a corner. I felt around down there with my good hand while resting my throbbing hand on the dashboard.

"Your hand is swelling," Isabelle said, nodding at it. "Do you want me to take you to have it checked?" Her eyes darted from the road to me.

"No, it's fine," I said. I found my phone and dialed 911.

An operator answered.

"I need to report dog fighting, over by the airport."

"Okay, ma'am. How were you made aware of this?" the operator asked in an underwhelmed voice.

"I just saw it!" I said. "Can you please send someone now?"

"What did you see?" There was clacking in the background. Fingers on a keyboard.

"There was a ring, like a boxing ring." I sucked air through my teeth as images flashed in my head. "And the dogs had these cages on their faces. The guys took them off, and there were people crowded all around, yelling."

"Took what off?"

"The face cages!"

"Are you sure?" She was doing data entry.
I slapped my probably broken hand on the dash again without thinking, and dizzying pain shot up my arm.

"Why the fuck would I make something like this up?"

"What's the address?"

"Hang on." I covered the phone. "We have to go back," I said to Isabelle.

She braked and made a wild U-turn.

"Ma'am? There are lots of emergencies going on in this city, so I need you to tell me the address right now."

"I got it!" I gave her the future youth center's address and told her it was the building across the street.

Isabelle stopped the car again. "Should we still go back?"

I struggled to think. My knee-jerk reaction had been to flee as far away from that awful place as we could get. But what if Ollie was in there?

"Yeah, we can park a block or two away. I want to see them get raided."

As we drew closer to the scene, a line of cars sped toward us.

"Get down," Isabelle ordered.

I huddled and listened to the vehicles hiss by.

"Don't get up. More are coming," she said when the rumble of engines died down. "Do you think they are coming from the place?" she asked. Another screaming caravan passed us, longer than the last one. "You can sit up now," she said, touching my leg.

Someone must've seen me spying, because there was no other explanation for this mass exodus. I shivered thinking that Ollie could be in one of those cars. "Did you see any dogs?"

She shook her head. "I could not see anything much at all."

The building came into view again, deserted and dark. "Maybe some dogs got out of fighting tonight," I said to make myself feel better. But a wave of sick helplessness crashed down on me. My hopes for retribution were squashed, because the cops couldn't bust people who weren't there. And Ollie could have been within a few feet of me, but I couldn't get to him. Something had to be done, even if we had to do it ourselves. We could be the detectives.

"Let's follow the cars," I said.

Her head moved side to side again. "They are far gone, and it would be too dangerous to try to catch up with them."

I slammed myself against the seat back in frustration. "You're right. Let's just wait for the police."

About a half hour later a lone squad car showed up. A couple officers got out, flashlights blazing.

"I have to go talk to them," I said, leaving Isabelle alone in the car again.

"Hey!" The stouter of the officers gripped the handle of his gun in the holster at his side. The other one shone his flashlight beam directly into my eyes. Unable to see anything, I raised my hands over my head.

"What are you doing out here, ma'am?" asked one of them.

"I called in the dog fighting. Can you please take that light off my face?"

The beam moved to my chest, and I saw bright, floating lights against the dark backdrop for a few seconds.

"We need you to get back into your car." The one who had tried to blind me motioned toward the Audi.

"But I—"

"We'll come talk to you once we clear the area."

I started toward the car, looking over my shoulder as I walked. They appeared to be moving in the right direction, toward the window I'd looked through.

I let myself into Isabelle's car.

"Do you think they will find anything?"

"I hope so."

Two spheres of light came skipping along the ground toward us before we saw the officers. They flanked us on either side, and we rolled down our windows.

"That place is dark," said the short officer with the pushed-out lower lip. "There's no activity in there." He studied my face. "You want to show me what you saw?"

I led everyone to the window next to the garage entrance. "It was through here."

The fitter of the officers pulled himself up past the ledge and hung there for a second. "Nothing," he said. His partner handed him the flashlight, which he shone through the glass. "All I see is a cement floor and some crates." He let himself drop to the ground.

"Can't you get inside?"

"We'd need a warrant for that, miss," said the other one.

"How long will that take?" Once they got inside they would find something. No way those criminals could have packed up that entire operation without leaving behind clues.

"Well, we'd have to show probable cause. Are you two willing to give a sworn statement about what you saw?"

CHAPTER THIRTY-SIX

"I'm not going to tell them Reggie was there," I whispered to Isabelle as we approached the front desk at the police station.

"Why not?"

"Because he's been acting crazy lately. He might come after me if he knew I ratted him out."

"Ratted him?" she echoed.

A familiar man strode our way, shuffling papers. After a second I realized it was Ryan, the officer who had investigated my apartment break-in. He glanced up from his documents and his eyes widened with recognition.

"Hey. Alex, right?"

"Uh, yeah," I said, surprised that he remembered my name.

"What brings you here?" He grinned as if we were fond acquaintances running into each other at a coffee shop, even though it was two in the morning.

"I'm reporting dog fighting."

"Whoa. That was you?" He dropped the papers to his side. He shook his head, a pained expression on his face. "Are you okay?"

I shrugged. "I guess so. This is Isabelle."

They greeted each other, and then Ryan brushed alongside me and leaned over the desk to murmur something indecipherable to the receptionist. He spun back around.

"Officers Kent and McCoy are expecting you. I'll take you back."

We followed him out of the lobby through a corridor with glassed-in offices on either side. The hall opened to a common area filled with low-walled cubicles and sobering fluorescent light. Even in the middle of the night, the headquarters whirred with activity. A group of officers huddled around a computer screen and erupted in boisterous laughter as we passed them.

"Probably watching some cute cat videos to blow off steam," Ryan said over his shoulder.

"Maybe if you stopped sending them we would stop watching them," said a smooshed-faced man wearing a detective badge and jeans that ended mid-ankle despite his stubby legs. He shot Isabelle a wink, and she grimaced at the floor.

"You got me, Pinetti," Ryan said, shaking his head.

We came upon a hollow-cheeked guy cuffed to a desk, the shackles clanking as he jerked at them. I could smell the body odor coming off him, and the scent wafted along with us all the way to the conference room.

Ryan ushered us inside. "Sit anywhere you like," he said.

We plunked down in worn, scratchy tweed chairs and wheeled up to a long wood laminate table.

"As you can see, the stereotypes are true," Ryan said with a grin. "Feel free to help yourself." He gestured at a half-empty box of donuts on a narrow buffet table behind us and propped himself on the table's edge.

I waited for him to start grilling me about what we were doing creeping around near the airport late at night witnessing crimes, but he didn't. Instead he asked me if I had renter's insurance to cover the cost of the items that were stolen from my apartment. I told him I did.

My blood sugar was low. Isabelle and I went over and peered at the donuts through the cellophane lid. They were crusty and stale looking, but I needed to eat one. Isabelle grabbed a chocolate sprinkle, and I took a plain cake.

I stuffed a third of it into my mouth. McCoy and Kent stepped into the room the next moment.

"I'll leave you to it, then," Ryan said, clanging the metal door shut behind him.

Kent went for a donut, and McCoy creaked into his chair, his gut unfurling as he let out a grunt. "We'll take your statement about what you saw tonight, and then we'll have you sign it."

"Mmm-k." Some donut particles escaped my lips.

"Which one of you is Alex Rader?"

I raised my hand because my mouth was still full. The more I chewed, the bigger the food mass grew. McCoy watched me for a moment, then turned to Isabelle.

"Can you each describe what you witnessed tonight?" he asked her.

"She was the one who saw everything inside," Isabelle said.

"Why don't you start by telling me what you saw first, Ms. Naff?" McCoy said.

"Please call me Isabelle. I was going to have Alex tell it."

"We'd like to get both your takes on it. We'll start with you, Ms. . . . . Isabelle," Kent said.

Isabelle glanced at me, cleared her throat, and told him almost everything, starting from when we first noticed lights in the warehouse to the huge caravan of vehicles passing us. She said we saw two men outside but we didn't get a good look at them.

Good job, Isabelle, I thought.

"Okay, do you want to add to that, Ms. Rader?" McCoy asked.

Everyone watched me, waiting. The long bulb on the drop ceiling buzzed in my ears as I pictured my own funeral, complete with Denise throwing herself on my casket. I could only hope Reggie hadn't seen me there.

"That's pretty much it, except for what I saw through the window."

"Back up," McCoy said. "Did *you* recognize the men outside?"

"What? No."

"Tell us what you saw inside the building then."

Slowly, focusing on my folded hands, I described the brief but gruesome glimpse I'd gotten of the fighting arena, the kill-or-be-killed situation these dogs had been forced to endure.

When I stopped talking and peered up at them, their faces had changed from stone to something more pliable, a slight twist that betrayed their firm exteriors.

"That must've been horrifying," Kent said.

McCoy folded his arms and made a whew sound. He pushed the document across the table for us to sign, and then we were done.

Ryan was waiting for us when we walked out. "I wanted to give you my card again in case you lost it."

I hadn't looked at the card he'd given me when he was at my apartment. I scanned this one and saw that his first name was Jacob. Did his friends called him Jake?

Why had he come to my apartment on South Beach if he worked for Miami Police Department?

"Do you work the city *and* the beach?"

"You were my last call on my last day with the Miami Beach PD," he said.

"So you don't work with Officer Marquez anymore?"

His lip twitched. "No more Marquez." He must not have liked her either.

"Well, thanks," I said, starting toward the exit, Isabelle on my heels.

"And don't worry," Jacob Ryan called after us. "They'll get that warrant. I've been in that judge's chambers. She has a framed picture of her chocolate lab in there."

I turned and faced him. "That's good to know," I said.

McCoy sidled up, our affidavit in hand. "Just one more quick question for you, Ms. Rader."

"Yeah?"

"Can you give us anything that would help us identify those men? It'd really help us save those animals."

I closed my eyes for a second. My hands started shaking. Once they got inside the building, they'd probably find something that connected the crime to Reggie anyway. But that was leaving it up to chance—possibly leaving Ollie's fate to chance. After a moment I nodded. Isabelle took one arm and Ryan took the other. They didn't let go of me until we got to the conference room, where I revised my statement.

CHAPTER THIRTY-SEVEN

B y the time I settled onto Isabelle's couch, early-morning light was already streaming through the sheer curtains, and the streets below vibrated with commuters.

My mind still turned. Reggie had snowed me. Not only had I eaten up his lies, but I helped to feed them to the rest of the world. When his interview aired, millions of viewers would believe that he was reformed, too. They'd be sucked in by his charm, just like I had been. They'd think he was a victim of his upbringing.

Until the cops caught him. He couldn't run an operation of that size for very long, especially if he continued along his current drugged-out path.

But that didn't make me feel better. I'd blinded myself to the truth in order to have a career. Maybe if I'd paid attention to the facts that were right in front of my face and let that paparazzo Angel take that incriminating picture to the tabloids, some dogs might have been spared suffering.

The words of that woman who had yelled at me in front of the hotel had been prophetic. I could very well be an accomplice to murder. If I found out Ollie was among those dogs, I'd never be able to live with myself.

Isabelle joined me in her living room, wet haired and looking like she'd gotten as little sleep as I did.

"How is your hand?" she asked, eyeing my bruised, swollen knuckles.

"Fine," I said, even though it was still throbbing. "I made coffee."

"Thank you. I will get some in a moment."

We planted our heels on the coffee table and stared out the window, where long, green palm tree fingers moved the sunbeams to and fro.

"What now?" she asked.

"Keep looking I guess."

Her face crinkled with worry. "Maybe you should try to rest more. I am sure the people at the shelters will contact you if Oliver is brought to them."

"You're right." I scrolled through my missed calls. I didn't recognize one of the numbers and felt a glimmer of hope that maybe someone had found him.

Isabelle shuffled to the kitchen for coffee, and I dialed my voice mail.

Voice mail one: two days ago, Ham. "Hey, where'd you go? Call me."

Voice mail two: yesterday, unknown number, Ham again. "We're really worried about you. Please call either me or Reggie. He ain't mad at you."

Voice mail three: today, Lucy. "Hey, Al, did you think about what we talked about? Want to hit a meeting later? Call me."

Voice mail four: today, Denise. "Sweetie, I know you're busy, but I wish you would answer your phone sometimes. I miss your voice."

I moved on to the texts. Just as I was opening Ham's series of messages, my phone chimed.

Ham: *We checked the hospitals and your apartment. Reggie needs to speak with you urgently.*

I tossed my phone onto the table as if it had suddenly caught fire.

"What's wrong?" Isabelle asked from the kitchen.

"Reggie's looking for me. They know."

"You should not go back to your apartment."

I fished Jacob Ryan's card out of my wallet and dialed the number. The phone rang a few times before a click and then an official-sounding outgoing message asking me to state my business.

"Hi, uh, Officer Ryan. This is Alex Rader, and I'm just wondering if anything's happened yet? Okay . . . thanks . . . bye."

Isabelle was hovering over me when I hung up.

"I have a photo shoot soon, and I will be gone for several hours," she said. "Will you be okay? Why not order a pizza and watch a film?"

She'd stayed up most of the night with me. And she had a photo shoot. She was still going.

"Sure," I said, though the mention of food annoyed me. I hated having to deal with biological needs at a time like this.

I slept for a while longer, until midafternoon. I ordered a pizza, and the delivery guy gave me someone else's pie. I might've smelled it when he handed it to me if my sinuses weren't clogged from all the smoking and crying last night. Inside the box was something resembling a murder scene, with anchovies, onions, and extra sauce. I tried to pick around the toppings, but it still tasted like a fish corpse.

I couldn't just sit here doing nothing.

On my way out I tossed the pizza in the dumpster.

Driving to my apartment, I told myself not to expect Ollie to be there. I just needed to grab some clothes and head to the new house. In traffic, under the late-afternoon sun, I searched every face in the cars around me. One guy held my gaze for too long. Another looked away too quickly. I suspected everyone was following me. An big Buick trailed me for several blocks. I took a turn leading me away from my apartment and saw the molded coif of a little old lady in my rearview, turning in the opposite direction.

I circled the block and the parking lots until I was convinced that nobody was after me and then ran up to my apartment.

It felt like a vacuum in there, even though the door hadn't been properly sealed in three days. I sat on the floor among my boxed belongings, paralyzed, staring at Ollie's short white hairs in the carpet. By the time I got up to leave, it was dark.

I didn't take any of my things with me.

CHAPTER THIRTY-EIGHT

My phone booted up with a moan, and I sat at a stoplight watching for the notifications to appear. A horn sounded long and shrill, and I spun my head expecting to see men in ski masks. It was just an angry guy in a suit. The light had turned green.

The voice mail notification chimed, and my heart jumped when I saw that Officer Ryan had called. I dialed him back and he answered, "Jake Ryan."

"I'm following up on the dog-fighting case," he said, "and I just wanted to give you an update. They got the warrant, and they're running partial fingerprints now. What they found is circumstantial, so we haven't made an arrest. But it might be enough to keep the investigation open. Sorry but that's all we have right now."

"Thanks for letting me know."

"Are you doing okay?" he asked after a pause. "Have you seen anybody suspicious hanging around your apartment or anything?"

"I moved."

He asked for my new address so their records would be up to date.

I wandered into Target and grabbed a cart. It was stupid of me to be here when everything I needed was at my old apartment, but it was easier to buy duplicates than drag myself back there right now. Out of habit I started to bypass the apparel section, but then I stopped. Normally I wouldn't be caught dead in these cheap polyester blends, but the only change of clothes I had belonged to Isabelle, and I was wearing them.

My mind went over my conversation with Jake Ryan. What if they didn't have enough evidence? What if they had to close the investigation? Where would that leave me? Because Reggie knew. Why else would everyone have fled the warehouse immediately after I'd spied on them?

My cell went off as I paused in home accessories, looking at, but not seeing, the trinkets and fabrics on display.

"Hey. Are you okay?" It was Paul. I'd told him about Ollie the previous day.

"Not really," I said, navigating down the bedding aisle. Paisley had made a comeback this fall, and the busy patterns hurt my head. I touched my fingers to my temples and realized I was still wearing my sunglasses. When I pulled them off, the glaring fluorescents hit me like a nuclear bomb. I shoved the sunglasses back onto my face.

"Have you heard anything?"

I'd seen and heard a lot—Reggie outside the warehouse, the grisly scene inside, the police investigation. But Paul would worry if he knew about those things.

"Not much. They're still investigating the break-in."

"Why don't you get out of town for a bit? Come back home."

I moved to an end display and knocked two burlap pillows stamped with turquoise seashells into my cart. "I don't know."

"What don't you know? You shouldn't be alone right now. You can fly out tonight."

"It's not that simple." I steered over to electronics. "Ollie might come back."

As I said the words, I realized they weren't true anymore. If Ollie returned to me, he wouldn't show up on his own on my front stoop. It had been too long. He was being kept by someone else, or he was dead. The floor seemed to drop a couple inches beneath me at that thought. I tightened my grip on the cart handle.

"There's a flight at noon tomorrow. I'll get you an open-ended return ticket," Paul said.

I didn't respond.

"Isn't there someone there who can keep watch on your place for you?"

"Can you give me a day?" I asked. "I can't figure that out this minute."

Paul said he would call me tomorrow.

I gawked at a Disney movie playing simultaneously on all the display TVs, aware that I resembled an asylum escapee, walking around the store in my sunglasses, mouth hanging open while watching animated characters dance across the row of screens. *Fuck it. Might as well get the 50-inch.* I hoisted the giant box and struggled to balance it in my cart.

Paul called as promised just as I reached the humane society's lobby the next morning.

"I just can't do it," I interrupted when he began firing off flight options.

"Guess we'll come to you then," he said.

My body tensed at the prospect of Denise descending upon me. "But Mom's afraid of flying. You're not driving, are you?"

"No, my bad. It's hard to remember he's gone sometimes."

He was referring to Uncle Eddie, who had died of cancer two years ago. They had always been a *we*, extensions of each other to the point that I hadn't distinguished which of them was my blood relative until I was in the third grade.

"Same here." I felt tears coming, but I swallowed them.

"I'll move some things around. I can be there in a few days."

"You'll have a terrible vacation with me, Paul," I said. "I don't even have a bed at the new place."

"Well, that's an easy fix."

We hung up, and I headed into the noisy atrium, nodding at Sierra, the girl who manned the front desk. She returned my nod with her usual thin-lipped smile and half wave. Debbie, the volunteer I'd met my first time there and had seen nearly every day since, rushed up to me before I reached the back room.

"Alex, you had a white pittie, right?"

Realizing that "pittie" was another term for pit bull, a surge of electric joy zipped from my heart to my toes. I took off sprinting past her to the back, crashing through the metal doors. Debbie bounded through after me.

"Is he here?" I yelled, checking the cages.

"Sweetie!" she yelled over the barking.

I didn't stop to answer her or to say hi to Molly, the scared German shepherd mix I'd met on my first visit, who now trusted me enough to let me pat her head through the bars of her jail.

"*Sweetie!*" Debbie yelled again at the top of her voice. "I'm sorry!"

My sneakers chirped as I skidded to a halt. The dogs, roused by the commotion, started to howl and yelp even louder.

Debbie raced up to me, cupping her mouth, eyes saucers.

I froze. "What's going on?"

She shook her head and took my hand. "Come with me."

She led me back to the atrium and faced me. Her eyes blinked rapidly, like she was trying not to cry. Whatever she was about to tell me, I didn't want to hear it. My mouth opened to speak, but all that came out was a watery croak. She nodded as if I had said something coherent.

"Okay, honey, I'm just going to say it."

I shook my head. She didn't need to say it.

"If it was Ollie, he passed on."

It felt like the blood was being drained from my body. I placed my hands on my knees to steady myself.

"How?" I said.

"I've been asking everybody, keeping an eye out for him. One of the vets was out of town for several days and just got back. She said a dog matching his description came through here last week."

I'd tried to prepare for this. Made myself imagine that he was gone forever and feel all the pain that came with it, but only for a minute at a time. If the worst was true, this was forever, millions of minutes.

"Where's the vet?" I asked, letting go of my knees and staggering backward.

Debbie took my arm. "Do you need to sit?"

"No, take me to the vet, please."

She took me to a hallway that I didn't know existed.

"It probably wasn't him," I said in a stiff voice as she raised her hand to rap on the door.

Before she could knock, a lanky blond woman wearing a tight ponytail and a white coat appeared in the door's window and let us in.

"What's up, Debbie?" she said. Her voice had a clipped but not unfriendly quality.

The vet unlatched a kennel gate, plucked out a miniature schnauzer, and stood him on a metal table. The room smelled like bleach. Wet streaks, murky at the edges, ran across the floor.

"Melanie, this is Alex. The white pit bull last week—that might have been hers."

Melanie's face registered no expression as she pressed on the schnauzer's stomach.

"He had light tan markings, too," I said. If only I'd done that microchipping thing that deplorable woman from the other shelter had talked about. Or even an ID tag for his collar. The machine at the pet store had been broken the last time I was there. I should have gone to another store, not been so lazy.

Melanie stopped poking at the tiny dog's abdomen and regarded me for the first time. "Green collar? About eighty pounds?"

I tried to swallow, but I couldn't. "Yes."

"Yeah. He came through here," Melanie said, hooking the small gray dog with her arm. Debbie grabbed a folding chair from the corner and stood it up for me.

I didn't sit. "Is he dead?"

"We couldn't save him," she said as she carried the miniature schnauzer back to his kennel. "He was septic. His organs were failing."

"What do you mean, septic?"

"He must've gotten into something toxic. Poison." She latched the little dog's cage.

My stomach pitched as if I too had ingested something toxic. I squeezed the hand that had hit Isabelle's dashboard hard enough to make it throb again.

"What do you think poisoned him?" I asked the doctor as I let myself fall back onto the chair.

She shook her head. "Not sure, but whatever it was, it did a lot of damage. I'm sorry."

I wondered if Ollie had been done away with for not performing well in the fighting ring. I covered my face, fought back the urge to scream.

"I'm so sorry," Debbie echoed.

"How did he end up here?" I said into my palms after a while.

Melanie skidded another chair across the floor and sat almost knee to knee with me. "I was told a young woman found him in her yard, very sick, and she brought him in. She didn't have the money to take him to a traditional veterinary office."

"Did he suffer?" My voice sounded like it was coming from a ghost at the other end of the room.

"He was barely conscious. I think it happened quickly. He just went to sleep."

Debbie laid her hand on my shoulder. "Let me get you some water," she said.

My stomach roiled again, more violently this time. I sprung up and ran out the door, down the hallway to the restroom, where I slammed into a stall and latched myself in. Standing over the toilet, I began coughing deep and hard with my entire body, but nothing came out.

There was a hiss and a creak, then footsteps on the bathroom tile. "Alex. I'm so sorry."

"Okay. Thanks," I said to Debbie as if she'd just passed me a bag through a drive-thru window. I hoped she would go away.

"I know you're hurting," she said.

"Can we talk later?" I asked, slumping down on the toilet seat.

"You probably shouldn't be alone right now. Stay where you are, but just listen to me. I've lost dogs, too, but I got through it. You can too."

She sounded sincere, like she felt my pain.

"Hang on a sec," I said, unspooling some paper from the roll and placing the wad over my face. Leaning forward, I unlocked the door and pushed it open.

She rushed toward me. For a second I thought she was going to hug me right there on the commode, but she stopped short and ran her fingers through her haphazard curls.

"When I was very low—I mean, *very* low—I got up one day and decided to put all my energy into helping those who were right in front of me," she said. "It saved me."

I wiped my nose again and put my hood up as if it could insulate me from everything. "I can't do anything right now."

"Yes, you can," she said matter-of-factly. "Two employees called off today, and no volunteers have shown up. The dogs are messing in their cages because they haven't had their walks." She squatted down and met my eyes. "You can help them. You have experience with a traumatized animal. Not everyone can do it, but you can."

I didn't feel like I could move, let alone clean poop and wrangle those burly animals. But then I considered the alternative. Going home and sinking into nothingness, retreating under the covers for a week. Even driving myself home to bed seemed like a monumental task. Maybe I could just rest on this toilet seat forever.

My options sucked. But unlike the dogs in the back room, I had choices.

"Where do you keep the leashes?" I asked.

CHAPTER THIRTY-NINE

Paul stood on my front stoop, clutching flowers and wine, a sorrowful look on his face. My eyes filled with tears when I saw him. I charged him for a hug. In the process I knocked the wine out of his hand. It shattered on the cement, spraying red onto our pants legs.

We stood there hugging, making no move to clean the mess.

"I don't have a broom," I said.

"And I didn't pack one."

"I'm out of wine now, too."

"We'll have to get some more, then." Paul stepped back to look at me. "When was the last time you had a good meal?" And without waiting for my answer he said, "I'm taking you out for a nice dinner."

The prospect of going to a restaurant sounded almost as depressing as the places I'd frequented recently— crime-riddled neighborhoods, shelters for unwanted animals, and a police station. I imagined siting among jovial people as they ate and toasted their happy lives.

I went to get ready, and Paul did a double take when I came out of the bedroom wet haired.

"So you are obviously very upset," Paul said, looking at my sweatpants.

"All my clothes are at the apartment," I said. "Are you buying me dinner or not?"

"Burger King or McDonald's?"

We walked to Nexxt Café.

"Every time I come to Miami, I feel obese," Paul said, glancing at the well-toned diners at the tables around us.

"Half these people have had surgery, and the other half are freaks of nature," I said.

The food was good. I felt almost human. Between bites of Cobb salad, I assured Paul I was okay. I told him I was volunteering at the shelter, which made him smile.

He kept the conversation light. He didn't treat me like someone with a terminal illness just because I was grieving. I appreciated that.

He pointed out a towering woman in a tight sheeny dress pushing a stroller. "It's obvious that she's just using that poor child to keep herself upright in those hooker shoes," he said.

I let out a chuckle, remembering seeing the woman here before and thinking the same thing.

"Would you look at that?! The kid's jammed so tight in there that the lady must keep Jaws of Life back at her brothel."

"Time for her to get knocked up again," I said.

When we returned from dinner, we sat on the deck, the only furnished area of the house, on the set of Adirondack chairs that came with it. I brought out a six-pack minus one beer from my fridge. My body already hummed from the wine I'd had at dinner.

"I had the yard fenced in for Ollie," I said. "It would have been such a good place for him."

Paul put an arm around my shoulders. "Can't say how sorry I am, kiddo."

"Thanks."

"Your mom has been grieving for Ollie like he was her own."

My skin went prickly.

I had been feeling better, almost enjoying myself for the first time since I'd lost Ollie, but the mention of Denise killed that sensation. Good old Denise, trying to make the death of my dog about her.

"Oh, has she now?" I said. "Bet that gets her a lot of sympathy."

Paul didn't say anything.

"And it's not like she's grieving hard enough to fly down here," I said. Some malignant spirit had taken me over, controlling what came out of my mouth. That was the only explanation, because I would never say these things to Paul of my own accord.

"She wanted to, honey. She was going to get a prescription so she could get on a plane. I talked her out of it."

"Why would you do that?"

"I don't know," Paul said. "Guess I thought it might be too overwhelming for her."

"There it is," I said. "She's too fragile to ride on a plane. Every other goddamn person in the world can figure it out. But she wasn't too fragile to walk all over my dad and drive him away when he was alive. Everyone thinks, *Poor Denise.* Everybody feels sorry for her. That's how she keeps you right where she wants you."

Thrashing Denise sent a rush through me, bringing back some human feelings. I wanted to keep riding this adrenaline. It felt like the only thing I had left.

But somehow I stopped myself, opened my eyes wide, and blinked, as if the demon had just handed my consciousness back to me.

"I'm sorry. I don't know what I'm saying." It was true. The possibility of Denise visiting had horrified me, yet here I was, acting wounded because she hadn't come.

I had never talked about Denise this way in front of Paul. I held my breath, waiting for him to speak.

"Alex, you should never be sorry for how you feel," Paul said.

"No, Paul," I said. "I should apologize—"

He held his finger up. "There's something I need you to know."

"Okay," I said. "What's that?"

"I'm the one who owes you an apology." Paul paused for a moment, searching for the words. "You're right about your mom. I have blinders on when it comes to her, and I should've realized how that affected you— growing up in a house like that. In a house with thirty cats shitting all over the place. She's a hoarder. She has a problem. And I never acknowledged that it was wrong or strange, because I thought that would only make it worse for you. But that wasn't right. It probably made you feel confused and alone."

I almost gasped when he said the *h* word. He'd never used the term and it sounded harsh—almost like profanity coming from him. At the same time, hearing him say it flooded me with relief, validated some of my bitterness. I wondered why it took him so long to come out with it.

"I know how close you guys are," I said. "This can't be easy for you."

"It's not," he said. "I'm protective of your mother because she's had a hard life, and I feel partially responsible for that."

This I did not understand. If anything, she made *his* life harder. He took care of her for the last ten years. He paid for everything.

"How could you possibly be to blame for her problems?"

He waved his hand. "Sadly I am. But she didn't want you to know about what happened with me."

Another mystery.

I needed answers. It seemed like I'd been living without closure on so many things lately. I'd been swirling between possibilities and tried to predict outcomes. Now that I knew that Ollie was dead, I moved on to the other uncertainties in my life: Was I going back to work for Lucy? Would we move back to LA? Were the authorities ever going to bust Reggie? Would Reggie find me and kill me? Would I live the rest of my life looking over my shoulder?

I didn't need any more uncertainty in the mix.

"You're an adult now," Paul said, as if he were grasping this fact for the first time.

He started talking about my grandfather, who had died when I was in kindergarten. My memories of my grandfather consisted mostly of images—him smiling from his wheelchair, telling stories, the smell of his cigars and iced tea. I remembered sitting in the old man's lap and feeling content.

Paul said my grandfather's personality changed dramatically after his stroke. I was just a baby when that happened. Being raised by him wasn't always easy, Paul told me.

"Especially for someone like me. Dad knew I was different, and he decided it was his job to correct me. Sometimes he would get violent."

"What? He beat you for being gay?"

Paul nodded.

"And here I thought he was a sweet old man," I said.

"You're not wrong. I choose to remember him as he was at the end. We came to an understanding, and I believe he loved and accepted me . . . at least for those last few years before he died."

"Fucking asshole."

"Don't say that," Paul said. "I want you to keep your happy memories of him. He was a good person in a lot of ways."

Maybe so, I thought. *But it took brain damage to make him into a decent person.*

And there was more to the story, Paul said.

One day Denise stepped in front of a punch that was meant for Paul. It broke her nose. Shortly after that, Paul left home. He was aimless for a while, bouncing from job to job until finally he didn't have one. Paul got into drugs. He didn't value his life at all, and he didn't care whether he knew what he was taking or not. And then he discovered heroin. He slept in homeless shelters, vacant places downtown.

I couldn't process any of this. I could never imagine Paul as anything other than upstanding, strong, and together.

"You're serious?" I asked. "You were a junkie?"

"Oh baby," Paul said. "What I just told you, that's the made-for-TV version. The stuff I did—I don't like to put it into words. But I have come to terms with it. It's behind me." Paul's voice started to quaver. "And there's one person who I owe everything to." Now Paul was sobbing and talking through the sobs. "Your mother, Denise, was always there. Even when everyone else left me. She was there. She loved me. She brought me food and clothes. And eventually she somehow made me see. She got me on my feet again. And I'm not saying that she did this for a week or a month. She did this for years. It was a miracle what she did for me." Paul brought his hands up to his face and wiped his eyes, but the tears kept coming.

I cried too. And I hugged him. But in my mind I couldn't reconcile this with the Denise I knew. The one who only watched Disney Channel and Animal Planet because real life upset her. I'd figured the most traumatic thing she'd ever been exposed to was a cartoon witch in *Sleeping Beauty*.

Maybe that was what made her go crazy. Maybe people got a lifetime allotment of strength, and she'd used up all of hers. The Denise I knew was afraid to leave the house.

Paul swiped at his eyes, and I kept hugging him. "You must be so disappointed in me," he said.

"No, Paul," I said. "I love you. I love you no matter what."

We let go of each other. Paul started laughing out the last of his convulsions. "Oh Jesus," he said. "That's why I hate to talk about it."

I smiled at him, but he got me thinking. And before I knew it, what I had to say was ready to burst from me. There was no more holding it in.

CHAPTER FORTY

"I hated Denise," I said to Paul. "For a long time I hated her, and really I still don't like her. I just pretend to."

I didn't even look at him for his reaction. He was quiet.

I wrapped my hoodie tighter around me even though it was warm and humid out.

"It was those fucking cats. I mean, when I was younger, I thought it was pretty cool that we had eight cats. Or however many she started out with. But she kept taking them in. I mean, I lived in a house with thirty to forty cats from the time I was thirteen until I moved out."

I felt myself trembling.

"They shit in my room. They sprayed on my clothes. They ruined everything in the house. It was a fucking nightmare. Whenever she was gone, I would open the door and get as many of them out as I could. But she fed them. And it didn't matter. They all came back. The whole house smelled like a port-o-potty. Everything I owned was covered in hair. I smelled like a homeless person. People at school noticed that. Of course, I couldn't have any friends over. I was so ashamed. I would scream at her to stop, but every day she would bring in a new one.

"There was this one, a kitten. I think she thought I was her mother, because she wanted to be with me all the time. She was cute, but when I fell asleep she would try to make a bed out of my hair. I wouldn't have minded if she just wanted to sleep next to me, but she was always in my hair."

My scalp tingled thinking about that cat's claws shifting, digging, ripping. Maybe that was why I had been so terrified of Biggie in the pool that day.

"I'd put the kitten out into the hallway, but the door didn't latch, so she would push it open and nestle again. One night I was in a deep sleep and she stepped right on my face. It scared the crap out of me. I got so pissed that I picked her up by the scruff and threw her. Except I didn't mean to throw her so hard."

The memory made me shudder.

"I remember saying, 'Fuck you, Denise,' and I tossed the poor cat across the room, right into my dresser. She hit the dresser hard and then fell to the ground. She hit it so hard that the boom box fell off the top. It fell right on her. She was probably already hurt, and then this boom box came down and crushed her head."

I started to shake and cry. "She made the most horrible noise when it hit her. Like she couldn't believe what was happening to her. I know that's stupid. But I can still hear that noise she made."

I held my breath, waiting for Paul to say something.

He reached out and touched my arm. "It was an accident."

I shook my head. "It was no accident. I was pissed and I took it out on a fucking kitten. Like a demented person."

I started to tell Paul the rest.

I went over and lifted the boom box. I could still remember how deformed the kitten's head looked. All I could think was I wished I had a sibling to blame this on. I can remember saying, "I wish I had a twin." I literally said those words out loud. I wanted someone who could share this with me. I wanted them to take part of this burden, and Denise acting crazy, and Denise and my dad arguing.

I wrapped up the kitten in a towel and took it out in the hallway. Denise and Dad were arguing in their bedroom. I heard Denise say, "How could you do this to me again?"

I couldn't decipher my dad's reply. I went outside. I laid the kitten down in the bushes at the bottom of the porch steps and retrieved a shovel from the garage.

Once I got back, the cat felt stiff. I walked it to a spot beneath the pines and oaks, to the side of the house.

Six feet. That's how far down they buried a body. I had to go at least three. The ground had started to harden, since it was the middle of November, and there had been a couple of freezes already.

My face was gritty and salty with dried tears by the time I returned to the house.

The lamp flipped on. My dad was sitting in the corner chair. I started bawling again as soon as I saw him. And I told him everything.

He didn't say anything. At one point he walked across the room to make a drink.

Normally when I came to my dad with a problem, he would listen intently. He would talk me through it, help me figure it out. But he and Denise had been fighting that night. He seemed to have gone somewhere far away in his mind. He never sat in the living room with the TV off in the dark.

After I finished telling him, he said he was disappointed. That was the only thing he said to me.

I didn't see him the next day even though it was a Saturday. He stayed in the garage for twelve hours. He didn't come in for dinner. And he went to bed early.

I stayed in my room to avoid Denise. All I could hear in my mind was the helpless sound the kitten made when his head was crushed. It made sense that Dad would look at me that way.

Denise searched for the cat the next day but didn't find her, of course. I should have just left it at that. She'd had cats run off on her in the past, so it wasn't like she hadn't dealt with this before. But I went and told on myself to my dad, and I ruined everything.

I found Dad before sunrise when I went to the kitchen for a drink of water. The harsh light from the open refrigerator glared yellow on his unnaturally splayed body as he clutched his chest.

How could I not feel that way?

My dad's words played like a record in my head all my life anytime I screwed up: running late for work, dating drug addicts, failing to notice that my boss was still torturing animals. *That disappoints me.*

And now, talking to Paul, my greatest fear was that he would say the same thing to me. I turned to him and said in a wobbly voice, "I'm so sorry I let you down. I'm not a good person."

Paul rose from the bench and dropped to one knee so we were eye to eye. "There is no way in the world you could ever let me down. You are a *great* person. I'm always proud of you. Your family has always been proud of you."

I closed my eyes and nodded over and over as understanding sunk in. I knew why I had been so terrified of letting Paul down. He had been the closest thing I had to a father for so many years. Maybe my thirteen-year-old brain equated disappointment with hurting Denise—and even death.

Though my logical brain understood now that these things weren't related, the association somehow ingrained itself in the dark corners of my mind at a time when I had been more impressionable.

My feelings toward Denise made more sense, too. It wasn't all about the cats; it was also about me. I understood why I wanted to set her on fire whenever she gave me a compliment: I thought that her praise was undeserved after what I'd done. It wasn't her fault. She didn't know any of this. She was trying to be a mom. Even if she sucked at it, she was trying.

CHAPTER FORTY-ONE

Paul held the door for the movers as they brought in the boxes from my old apartment. He'd hired a company and supervised the move, while I stayed back in the relative safety of my new house.

"You have a lot of cops patrolling here," he said as we watched a police cruiser glide by. I thought about the conversation I'd had with Jake Ryan, when he'd asked for my new address.

"Looks like it," I said, the ends of my mouth turning up. *Maybe I have a guardian on the police force*, I thought.

The moving truck pulled out of the driveway, and a moment later Paul's Uber pulled in.

"Thank you so much for everything," I said, hugging him. "Did you happen to see my weird neighbor?" I figured Jean-Marc—jobless, shirtless, and curious—must have poked his head out at some point while the movers were working. I told Paul about him on several occasions. Now Paul got to put a face—and a big orange belly—to the name.

"No," Paul said. "The apartment next to yours was vacant. The door was open and they were painting inside." He smiled at me.

"Wow." Jean-Marc hadn't mentioned that he had planned on moving. Maybe he wanted to get away from memories of Isabelle.

"I'm a little disappointed that I didn't get to meet the notorious Jean-Marc."

We said our goodbyes and hugged again. His visit had put things into perspective for me, freed me of some of my old guilt. New guilt had taken its place of course, but somehow I knew I could get to the other side and be okay eventually.

I strolled inside, planning to unpack, but instead found myself putting my sneakers on so I could walk the dogs at the humane society. I took the trash with me on the way out.

As I lugged the sack toward the garbage bin, Isabelle's Audi skidded up my driveway. She jumped out of the car, her eyes wild. I held the bag out from my side so it wouldn't touch her when she collided into me. As I returned her hug with one arm, I realized she was trembling. Her quaking went through me, making the bottles rattle in the plastic bag.

"What's wrong?"

"I just reported Jean-Marc for selling the drugs."

"Seriously?" I asked, confused. "Why? Did he do something to you?"

She shook her head. "I am just so mad about Ollie that I do not even care what he does to me. It is not right for him to go unpunished."

I'd never seen her so amped up. I couldn't follow her train of thought.

"Wait. Slow down. What does Jean-Marc have to do with Ollie?"

Her eyes pooled with tears, and I could tell she was trying to compose herself and find the right words to answer me in English.

Before she said anything, I understood. The squawking birds, the traffic, and the blazing sunlight faded like someone had thrown a blanket over the world. I remembered what she'd told me about Jean-Marc—that snide comment he'd made about Ollie getting sick from "bad cheese." At the time I'd figured it had been the ranting of a perpetually wine-buzzed jerk-off, but now it took on a sinister meaning.

I let the bag clank to the ground. "You think he did something to Ollie?"

"Yes." She took a deep, trembling breath. "After my friends went to his flat to pick up my things, Colin made an odd remark. He said, 'It seems that Jean-Marc has decided to start making crystal meth.' I asked them what he meant, and he told me they saw . . . anti-freezer?"

I was trembling now, too. "Antifreeze," I said, wringing my injured hand open and closed. I had done an Internet search after talking to that vet at the humane society. Antifreeze was a common poisoner of dogs. It had a sweet smell and taste that attracted animals.

And Jean-Marc didn't own a car.

Rage tore through me. I ran to the house for my car keys.

"Alex!" Isabelle said, running after me. "What are you doing?"

"I'm going to go visit that motherfucker right now."

I tried to get around her, but she stepped in front of me.

"Stop," she said, calmer now. "Just take a breath."

I folded my arms and huffed.

"What will you do when you get there?" she asked.

I realized I wasn't going anywhere, because Jean-Marc's apartment was vacant.

"Nothing. He moved."

CHAPTER FORTY-TWO

Jean-Marc was lucky he'd moved, because otherwise I might have shown up on his balcony to stab him. I checked Miami's arrest records database for Jean-Marc and Reggie dozens of times over the next few days, and as far as I could tell they were still roaming free. Other than that I walked the dogs at the shelter and pretty much avoided everything else. Only there was no avoiding my court hearing for my DUI.

That was the one positive development in my life: the very expensive attorney Lucy had hired got my DUI evidence suppressed, and my case was dismissed. The judge ruled the breathalyzer inconclusive after my lawyer argued that the results of my three breathalyzer tests varied by several points and were therefore unreliable.

When the judged banged the gavel, I should have been dancing down the aisle, but I trudged out of there still feeling like I was serving a sentence anyway.

Lucy kept calling me. She'd gotten a lead in a Woody Allen film and she needed to know if I would be going to New York as her assistant. I imagined I might wander to New York whenever I was ready, maybe a few weeks after she got settled. But she wanted me to forge ahead of her, find her an apartment near the park. "And then you could come back and help with the move," she said. "It'll help you leave all the shit of Miami behind and move forward. Plus you're the only one who knows how I like things organized. I can't do this without you!"

Lucy's calls stressed me out, and I didn't return them.

My phone rang again as I searched for my dog-walking clothes. I let Lucy go to voice mail and located my pants, hanging over the bare shower rod. They smelled like dog, but they didn't smell like a rotting corpse yet. I could go another day before washing them. As I slipped them on, my doorbell sounded.

I stumbled to the foyer, where I pressed my face to the peephole. Lucy, Tatiana, and my landlord, Pete, were all on my front stoop.

I opened the door. "What are you doing here?" I asked, shielding my eyes from the bright morning sun.

"Well, you won't take any of my calls, and we were worried about you," Lucy said, waving her phone at me, my name on the screen.

"We?"

"Can we come in?"

"Sure." I stepped back, and they funneled in past me.

"What's up?" I didn't offer them seats or refreshments.

"We need to talk to you."

"Alright."

Pete pressed his lips together in a smile, and Tatiana wordlessly thrust a to-go coffee cup at me.

"Thanks," I said, wondering if I was really awake or if this was a bizarre dream. A couple slugs of bitter black coffee did nothing to clarify the situation. "Is this about New York?" I asked. "Because I need a couple more days to decide."

She shook her head, and her eyes fell on an empty beer bottle sitting on the counter. Tatiana followed her gaze and then the two of them looked at each other.

"This is because I think you're in trouble," she said, pulling a folded sheet of paper from her jeans pocket. She unwrinkled the page on her thigh, cleared her throat, and brought the sheet up so it obscured her face. "Alex," she said through the loose leaf, "I love you, but I can't enable you anymore."

"What?"

"I'm just going to read this, because this is so hard for me," Lucy said.

Tatiana stepped forward so she was side by side with Lucy. Pete backed up to give them room.

"Your behavior has affected me in the following ways."

Was she seriously going to talk about herself right now?

Lucy cleared her throat. Why did these situations always require a handwritten script? And why was she reading this to me? I couldn't even remember the last time I'd been drunk in her presence.

"I worry about you," she began, her voice grave. "I hardly see you anymore, and we used to be best friends. I feel like you're taking advantage of me. I can't depend on you—you won't give me an answer about New York. And even if you do come, it's not like I can have you drinking around me." She stopped and peered up at me, then back to the lone beer bottle on the counter.

I just stared at her, took another sip of coffee.

"Okaaaay," she said, looking down at her notes again. "Well, your behavior's bizarre. And you're not taking care of yourself." She stopped and looked at my sweat pants, which were covered in dog hair.

I turned my attention to Pete, who had now backed all the way to the edge of the room. "What's up, Pete?" I said.

He pulled one of his hands from his pocket and gave me a friendly wave. I regarded Lucy again. She was gripping her notes like she was resisting a mugging. I wanted to snatch the paper from her and tear it up.

"You fired me," I said. "That's why you can't depend on me. Why is my landlord here?"

"Well, this is his property, and he's had experience with this sort of thing."

"Jesus." I took a step forward. "I can't believe you're fucking *interventioning* me right now!" I knew that wasn't a word, but I didn't care. "You know so little about me!"

She pursed her lips, widened her stance. "You're angry. I was mad just like you when I was confronted."

"What have you told these people about me?" I swung my finger from Tatiana to Pete questioningly.

I'd watched this same sort of scene on cable, and it always involved a subdued but firm mediator. So Pete and Tatiana must be the mediators. If she continued to follow the TV format, Lucy was going to tell me I needed help, and when I told her to fuck off, she'd start in with the threats. Maybe a helicopter was waiting to take me to New Perspectives right now.

"You are so out of touch with what my problems are," I said.

"Really? Why don't we start with the DUI that *I* fixed for you."

Tatiana squeezed Lucy's hand. Why didn't the two of them just ride off into the New York sunset together? Then again, Tatiana probably wouldn't perform all the ridiculous demeaning tasks the job required.

Pete moved closer. "Hey, Alex, mind if I ask a question?"

"Why not?" I said flatly. I was ready to unleash my contempt on him, too, landlord-tenant relationship be damned.

"What problems are you dealing with right now? How can we help?" Maybe he was using some kind of mediator tactic, but he sounded genuine at least.

"My dog died for one."

He ran his fingers through his sparse white hair. "My god. I'm so sorry. I didn't know."

"And I'm sorry too," Lucy said. "But you have to keep living."

"Just a second, Lucy," Pete said politely. He shifted his weight, jutting his hip forward. "Alex, did you see the news yet? A dog-fighting ring just got busted here in Miami."

My stomach dropped. I started for the TV but then remembered I hadn't gotten the cable turned on yet.

"Okay, everyone," Lucy said, a little less stern than before. "Let's get back to the point of why we're here."

All at once her reason for being here became clear to me. This was her desperate maneuver to place me under her control again so I'd obediently accompany her to New York.

"Lucy, I'm busy," I said. "Get the fuck out of my house and take Tatiana with you."

I pointed toward the door. I'd never been so nasty with her before.

Lucy didn't know what to do. She just stood there.

I started searching for my car keys. "Are you that much of a narcissist that you believe I contracted your noncontagious disease just by being with you?" I said. "Or better yet, you think I copied you! Yes, I emulated you so much that I became an alcoholic just so I could be more like you." I snatched my keys from the kitchen floor and strode up to her. "Now you can save me and turn me into exactly what you want me to be! I bet you were just as pleased as hell when I screwed up and got arrested. They couldn't even prove I was above the legal blood alcohol limit!"

My back pocket vibrated, and I checked to see who was calling. I turned my back on my interventionists and answered. "I'm on my way right now, Debbie," I said. I hung up and turned to face them. "Thanks for your concern, but I need you to leave now."

Lucy looked like she was in a trance. "Can we talk later, Alex?"

"Don't call me. I'll call you."

CHAPTER FORTY-THREE

The sky changed from clear to ashen in the time it took me to speed from the beach to the shelter downtown. When I got out of the car, I paused to plug Reggie's name into my phone. I had to know if he'd been arrested.

Wind blusters swirled my hair in my face as I read the search results. Reggie's name didn't appear in any of the headlines about today's bust.

I sprinted inside, through the lobby and atrium, dodging cameramen and newscasters in cakey makeup. The noise turned up louder and louder as I pushed through the big metal divide between general population and the "unadoptables" in the back room. Shouts from volunteers and cruelty investigation workers rose above the patter of nervous claws and barking. All the cages were full, and the overflowing animals were chained to the bars on the outside on short leashes so they couldn't get to each other.

"You can't be in here!" shouted a tall brunette woman in a Kevlar vest.

"She works here," called a familiar voice from across the room. I looked over to see Debbie balancing four bowls of Purina on one arm.

I rushed over to her. "What do we do?" I asked.

"Right now we get them all fed and watered," Debbie said. "You alright?"

"I'm good," I said. I went to the food station and began filling bowls and taking them to the anxious dogs.

Distressed, battered faces peered back at me as I set down the bowls of food in front of them.

"Don't get too close," said a clean-shaven, fortysomething man in a MIAMI-DADE SHERIFF jacket. "They're vicious!" he called after me.

I scowled at him and his crooked name tag, which read "Leonard." Hadn't he seen how the dog brightened up as I moved closer—tongue out, clipped tail swooshing? His kind of thinking was the reason we hear stories about cops shooting people's beloved pets for no reason.

Slowly, a couple inches at a time, I lifted my hand and held it out to the eager animal. He hesitated before meeting my fingers with his nose. After a moment his tongue plunged into my hand, licking every one of my fingers.

Many of the dogs responded in the same way. Within a few minutes they were nuzzling me while I carefully stroked their beaten, scarred bodies. One actually let me rub the orangey-red fur on her belly—a belly distended from the many litters she must have had, its appearance made more misshapen by the stretched-out teats that practically grazed the ground. Her tongue dangled to one side or the other, giving her an adorable, friendly quality. My heart squeezed. I knew she couldn't get her tongue to stay in her mouth because her teeth had been methodically removed. They did this to her so she couldn't fight off the studs they'd bred with her. If I didn't have more dogs to feed, I would have had a good cry. I'd do that later—I was actually looking forward to it.

Some of the new tenants bared their teeth, and a few balled up and turned away from me or splayed themselves flat on the floor, as if trying to disappear. I talked softly to them and hoped they'd eat and drink a little.

"Did the cops say what happened?" I asked Debbie after all the dogs were fed.

She shook her head. "Only thing they said is they came from Doral."

I had expected her to say they came from the airport. Reggie must have moved the location.

"What's going to happen to them?" I asked.

"Broward County's coming for the overflow." She paused and took a deep breath. "It's not ideal, but it's better than where they were before."

"I'll take those two," I said, gesturing at the ones who were pancaked on their cell floors.

She turned to me with bloodshot eyes and a puzzled expression. "Honey, I'm not sure you know what you're saying. Plus you haven't gone through the foster approval process yet. They won't release them to you."

Following the rules was the last thing on my mind. "Those dogs are suffering. That's all I care about right now."

"I know, but what can we do?"

"We can fudge the paperwork, or we can just let everyone assume they got loose."

The rain had come and gone by the time I got back from a pet store with kennels for the dogs I was preparing to steal.

"This is a bad idea," Debbie said as I stowed my back seats to make room for the cargo.

"These guys aren't going to make it in there," I said, frantically lifting the crates into the back. "I can give them a quiet place to recuperate. My mind's made up."

We went back inside to clamoring dogs, their voices now melded into an unbroken, thunderous peal. The Broward County shelter volunteers had arrived, taking leashed animals away and coming back to tether more.

"Should we take advantage of the commotion?" I whispered.

"This is crazy," Debbie said. "But these poor babies are . . ." She looked too exhausted to finish her sentence.

"If they catch me, you weren't involved," I told her.

"Let's just hope they haven't counted the dogs yet."

"I'm willing to take that chance."

We grabbed bowls of food so people would think we were feeding the two dogs. Nobody even glanced at us. We leashed them and guided them to my car. They jumped right up into the open cages, heads down, as if they'd been through the drill many times before.

A low growl sounded from the back as I stuck the key in the ignition.

"You sure you don't want me to follow you home?" Debbie asked through the open window.

I whirled around and the dogs quieted, cocking their heads at me. "Think I'm good. Go get some rest."

"Call me if you need anything."

The ominous snarling began about thirty seconds later. Once I got home, I'd put them in separate rooms, take them out one at a time until they got used to each other.

The sky clouded over again in what seemed like an instant, and a light rain started to fall. The air-conditioning sent shivers through me, but I kept the frigid air blowing on high for my passengers' comfort. They didn't sound comfortable, though. Their voices grew more urgent and guttural, like revving motorcycles.

Buying a moment to gather myself, I braked for a barely yellow light. An angry driver behind me honked a horn. This time when I looked back at the dogs, they didn't go silent. Ears pulled back and fangs extended, they bumped their cages side to side with their muscular bodies.

Debbie would know what to do. I groped for my phone to call her, but all at once giant pools of water slammed into my windshield, blinding me. I slowed and flipped on my wipers, but I might as well have been driving at the bottom of the bay for all the good they did. Leaning forward, I strained to see taillights through the wall of water, figuring I'd be less likely to jump a curb if I kept the cars in front of me in view.

Thunder clapped and the dogs started yowling. I kept inching forward, following the lights. It was too dangerous to turn around with only three feet of visible road in front of me.

"It's okay, you guys," I said in my best Denise voice. They quieted, and I relaxed my grip on the wheel.

But then there was a different sound, like a scraping or sawing. Teeth on plastic. I clicked on my hazards and pulled over. I was still downtown, and there was no way I could get on the causeway in a monsoon while these dogs were trying to eat their way to each other. I wondered if these two had been fighting adversaries.

"No chew!" I said, a command that had worked with Ollie but sounded futile now. The next second I watched as one of the bars broke apart with a loud snap. My heard thumped in time with the battering rain as they continued to gnaw. Why hadn't I bought the metal cages? How was I supposed to keep these dogs safe?

"I can't do this. I can't do this," I said aloud. I snatched the phone from my lap and dialed Debbie. Instead of an answer or voice mail, I got one of those inexplicable cell-phone-busy signals. I was desperate. I needed someone capable to help me. As a last resort, I scrolled through my contacts and called Jake Ryan.

"I'm sorry. I'm such a moron!" I said. "These two dogs in my car are about to kill each other!" Another bar cracked apart behind me. I told Jake where I was parked.

"Just stay where you are. If anyone messes with you, tell them I'm on my way."

He pulled up behind me a few minutes later, siren shrieking, and he jumped out. By this time the dogs had chewed through enough plastic to get their snouts within inches of each other.

"They seemed fine when we left the shelter," I said as he hopped into my passenger seat, drenched. "They're going to break out before I make it home."

He looked back, and I could see the red and blue lights of his patrol car reflected in his eyes. "Why do you have them?"

"I volunteer at the shelter, and they weren't doing well there at all."

He crunched his face as if he were deliberating something.

"Okay," he said. "Let me take one."

"Really?"

"I'd better hurry," Jake said, running his hand through his sopped hair and then throwing the door open and hopping out.

I pressed the lift gate button and followed him around to the back.

"Why'd you get out?" he yelled over the hammering downpour.

I shrugged my now-soaked shoulders.

We huddled under the raised door and regarded the dogs with their snapping jaws.

"I can't tell if one's more aggressive than the other," he said. "Seems they're both equally pissed, so I'll take the bigger one. Get back in your car and follow me home."

He made the transfer and kept his lights flashing as he led me to his house, also on South Beach. The rain had subsided, and to my relief my single passenger hadn't made a sound on the short trip.

We parked in Jake's drive, and I watched him lead the dog inside. Then I climbed into the back of my car and sat quietly next to the mangled cage. Propping himself at attention on shaky front legs, the captive animal wavered between taking glances at me and studying the floor. He had grayish-blue fur, the same color as

Reggie's dog, Maximus. The right side of his face was peppered with holes the width of a standard nail. Some of the punctures were pink and unhealed. He'd lost half of his left ear, but it must've been a while ago, because it had scarred over.

I reached out toward the broken bars and let him sniff my fingers. He let out a sigh and nudged my hand. I rubbed his head, and his eyes fluttered shut.

"Poor guy," I said. "I won't hurt you—I'm your friend."

The rain stopped after a while. Soon after that Jake barreled out the front door in dry jeans and a T-shirt.

"Good. You're still here."

I motioned toward the house. "How's he doing?"

"I got him to go outside, and he even went to the bathroom," Jake said. "He's just sprawled out in the pen now."

We drove separately to my house and got my dog inside. He slunk in the corner of the living room, while Jake went out to get the kennel. When he set it on the floor, the animal lunged for it, panting.

"Maybe he needs to hang out in here for a while so he can get comfortable with his new surroundings," he said, opening the gate.

"Good idea," I said. "Let's put him by the back door so he can see outside."

He was right. My rescue rushed right into the crate, and his panting slowed as soon as we latched the door.

Once the dog was bedded down, Jake ordered us some food, and we sat on the deck with containers of pad Thai in our laps. I turned to see the dog through the glass door, lying on his belly, resting his chin between his front paws. Now that the dognapping operation was complete, my myriad questions came back to me.

"So, were you part of the dog-fighting bust?"

"Yep."

"And I heard you guys found them in Doral, but that can't be true, can it? It was at that warehouse by the airport, right?"

"Nope, it was Doral. But that's all I can say."

"Then those fucking criminals must have moved their operation."

A bite of food hovered in front of his face. He dropped his hand, letting the noodles flop back into the box.

I remembered the brief glimpse I'd had of the dog fight, those five seconds of horror before my arms gave out on that window ledge and I slid to the ground. Jake must have seen so much more, because he'd entered the building, made arrests. It was almost a relief to know that Ollie hadn't been among those dogs today. That he never had to fight again. The comforting thought passed quickly. If he were one of those dogs that made it out, he might be sitting here with us right now.

"So, Reggie's in jail then, right?"

"Nope."

"What? Why not?"

"Sorry, but I can't really talk about his involvement in the case either."

So, Reggie was involved. But then why wouldn't they arrest him?

"What can you tell me?" I asked.

His face brightened, smile lines indenting his cheeks, making him look boyish and mature at the same time. "It's good to see you again."

It was hard not to ignore the stirring inside of me, strong opposing emotions battling for space: grief and— a crush? I'd already registered my attraction to him in a hazy way, but now it was right in front of me.

"It's good to see you, too, even though we keep meeting under horrible circumstances."

"Maybe we'll have to change that," he said.

I nodded and pretended to concentrate on my noodles so he wouldn't notice me blushing.

After a few bites, Jake poked my arm with a chopstick. "So, did you have a death wish or something, driving around with two animals trying to kill each other?"

CHAPTER FORTY-FOUR

I checked on the dog several times in the wee hours because he hadn't used the bathroom during his brief visit to the backyard before I'd gone to bed. At 6:30 a.m., while the light was pink and my street still quiet, I put on some coffee. The dog stirred when I clanked a mug, but he kept his head down, and only his blue eyes followed my movements in the kitchen. Maybe he was used to being penned up for long periods with nobody treating him to prompt morning walks. He was likely met with anger if he tried to ask for anything like food, water, or affection, so he'd learned to go without. But this morning he would get all these things without having to ask.

I coaxed him outside and dropped his leash at the edge of the yard. He gazed up at me warily, not moving.

"Go ahead," I said in my Denise doppelganger voice. He ventured forward but stopped every few seconds to look back, as if asking for my approval. "It's okay," I told him. Finally, he let himself move forward, surveying the land tentatively at first and then with curiosity. He paused at the fence and sniffed the flowering plants, just like Ollie had done.

I wondered if Jake and his charge were doing as well.

On my way inside to pour another cup of coffee, my phone chimed with a text from Jake: *Jerry just fetched a ball in the yard! Couldn't believe it! How's your pup?*

You named the dog Jerry? He freaking fetches?! I typed back.

His last name is Seinfeld because he cracks me up. He shredded the ball instead of bringing it back, but that's still good, right?
Ha!

Mind if I come by after my shift? he texted.

Sounds good.

Meanwhile a message had come in from Debbie: *How's it going?*

Had to give one over to my cop friend because they were going to kill each other, I replied.

A cop!?
Don't worry. He's cool

I named my foster dog Kramer after the *Seinfeld* character, inspired by Jake. The dog's icicle-blue eyes clouded over when I put him in his kennel. He whined, but when I opened the door, he wouldn't come out. So I brought some blankets to the living room and lay next to him, his head pressed against the grates. I gave him one of Ollie's toys. When I woke, the little stuffed fox was disemboweled, and white tufts clung to Kramer's muzzle.

My phone rang, sending Kramer into a barking fit.

"You didn't tell me you stole these dogs," Jake said over the phone. "They have footage of you. We have to give them back."

I felt the acidic burn of the morning's coffee rising in my throat.

"Are you at your house?" he asked.

I swallowed hard. "Yeah. How did they get—?"

"That place was crawling with cameramen," he said, his voice agitated. "But it won't air. The detectives quashed it because it would interfere with the ongoing investigation."

"What if we take them back and they end up putting them to sleep?"

"They won't do that. There's lots of media surrounding this. It would be terrible PR to put these dogs down." He sighed. "But seriously, what were you thinking?"

This was good news, but tears started pooling in my eyes anyway, thinking of them in that scary environment. I had no choice—they'd take them anyway the minute they arrested me. Maybe I could go on the run, but where would I go? Traveling five miles with these dogs packed together was impossible.

"Will I get arrested?"

"You should get arrested." His voice was edgy, harsh.

"I'm so sorry I misled you."

He was silent for a moment and then he continued in a softer tone. "Well, they won't charge you for tampering with evidence if you surrender it today. I'm making sure of that."

"Thanks."

"We'll go together," he said.

CHAPTER FORTY-FIVE

The house felt ghostly and desolate when I returned from giving back Kramer.

Jake wouldn't be coming by later, I knew. He'd texted me after we got off the phone, saying he thought it would be better if we dropped the dogs off separately. When I had called him to apologize again, his phone went straight to voice mail.

I kept thinking of my *Seinfeld* crew back in those cold cages after we'd made so much progress with them in only twenty-four hours. It was too much. Back in my living room, after failing to distract myself with a bestseller and then my current favorite TV show, I swiped my keys from the counter.

I had scrammed from the shelter quickly and wordlessly not two hours ago, afraid I'd run into Jake or start bawling in front of the shelter agent when I handed off Kramer. Now, busting through the metal doors, I wasn't quite sure what kind of reception to expect. But even if the cops and humane society workers treated me like a criminal and banned me from the building, I'd still get to check in on my rescues for a second.

Everyone's kindness surprised me. They gravitated toward me with smiles, nods, and comforting pats on the back. Somebody across the room, whom I recognized but couldn't place right away, waved and mouthed, "You okay?" It was the cop who had yelled at me the day before about getting too close to the dogs. He had returned, out of uniform, and it dawned on me that he was there of his own accord to make sure the dogs were taken care of. My heart lifted a little.

I found Kramer by himself in a cage facing the back wall. "Hey, bud," I said.

His head raised and his ears perked.

My ringtone sounded. I didn't recognize the number, but I answered.

"Alex, this is Detective Roger Denton," said the voice on the other end.

"I'm sorry I took the dogs," I said flatly.

"That's not why I'm calling. I some have questions for you. Can you come down to the station?"

Kramer had turned sideways, and he was peeking at me from the corner of his eye. "C'mon, buddy," I said coaxingly.

"Pardon me?" the detective asked.

"Nothing. Can you just ask me over the phone?"

"Well, we'd really prefer it if you would come in."

"I can't make it today."

Kramer stood on quivering legs and moved a little closer to me. I opened the gate to his cage and plunked down next to him. He'd peed in there, but I didn't mind.

"Alright," the detective said. "We'll talk now, then. How did you know to lead the police to the sight of the dog fighting by the airport?"

"A paparazzo showed me a photo of Reggie outside the building. My dog went missing, and I decided to check it out, just on the off chance that Reggie had started another ring. I honestly didn't expect to find anything. Do you want the photographer's contact information?"

"That'd be great."

"Is there anything else?" I was anxious to get back to Kramer and clean out his cage.

"Just a couple more questions. You spent time inside Reginald Wiles's home," he began. "And I'm guessing you interacted with his father, Marvin Wiles."

"Marvin's his uncle, not his dad."

"Ma'am, that's not what Marvin Wiles said when we arrested him. He told us a lot of things that lead us to believe he ran the operation on his own."

I fell back against the metal bars of Kramer's cage. My brain thrummed. "That doesn't make any sense," I said.

"Miss Rader, it's pretty straightforward," the detective said. "Your name came up. I'm calling to find out what you know."

Marvin seemed harmless—fidgety, sure, but a nice enough guy. I liked him—what I knew of him. Was he even capable of this? Or was he trying to protect Reggie? Would Reggie let Marvin do that for him? Even if he was a criminal, Reggie seemed like he had his principles. But had he lied about how he and Marvin were related?

"Based on what you're telling me right now, we're looking at two very different pictures," I said. "But ask away."

"Did you have any knowledge of the dog-fighting ring when you worked for Mr. Wiles?"

"Not at all."

Kramer's ball of a tail shifted back and forth, and he rested his head on my knee while I ran my fingers through his fur.

"Was there anything mentioned by Reginald or his father—anything you saw that might lead you to believe either of them were involved in criminal activity?"

I remembered their heated discussion in the screening room. "They were arguing one day. I only caught the last part of it. Reggie was saying he didn't need the police looking into him. That's all I heard. I figured it was about something else. Not dog fighting."

The detective was silent on the other end of the phone.

"I'm sorry. I should have said something earlier," I said, my voice starting to tremble. "Maybe this could have all been prevented."

"I don't think anyone saw this coming. Marvin's confession was a big surprise to us."

"How are you so sure Reggie wasn't involved?"

He let out a thick sigh. "Reginald Wiles was the one who called it in."

CHAPTER FORTY-SIX

I didn't call Reggie. I just drove over there. Angel sat in his usual place at the bottom of the driveway, and I stopped to let him know a detective would be contacting him.

Ham opened the door and immediately squeezed me into a boa-constrictor hug. I froze for a moment, then put my arms around him and hugged him back.

"C'mon," he said softly, and I followed him to the studio. The light outside the door shone green, and we walked in.

Ham pointed at the glass booth, and through the clear divide I saw Reggie slumped over, straddling a bottle of whiskey and a glass pipe. He lifted his head and squeezed his eyes shut, reaching both hands out toward me in slow motion. I let myself into the booth, dropped down on the floor next to him, and pulled my knees to my chest. The odor of sweat gone sour replaced his usual Bvlgari cologne scent. He leaned sideways and bumped shoulders with me.

"You heeeere," he drawled. "I'm sorry."

"You didn't do it, did you?"

He wobbled from the waist up and held the whiskey out to me. "Naw."

I took it from his hands and threw back a gulp. "You never did it, did you?"

He shrugged. "Well, it don't matter what I say now. It three strikes anyways so whatever."

"That wasn't your fault back then, you know."

He looked at me with glassy eyes, pins for pupils. "I participated then."

"You were just a little kid," I said. "You wanted to please your dad. And then you went to jail for him. That last time would've been his third strike. He'd get a life sentence."

He nodded slowly, then started rapping in a small voice: *"Road stretches out in front of me/ Green light flashin'/ Everything that was gonna be/ Don't know the right action/ Can't stop, can't go/ Guess I'll just sit in da glow*

"That's my favorite song of yours."

He nodded some more. "I shouldn't have gotten so angry with you," he said. "And I'm so sorry about your dog, man. We looked for him. I know how bad that shit feels."

Maximus.

This man with the commanding presence morphed into the twelve-year-old version of himself. A boy who saw grisly things. A boy who wanted his dad to be proud of him.

"Thanks."

He touched my hand. "I should've turned Marvin's ass in sooner. I thought I could talk him out of it. You know, he's my dad."

I nodded, took another shallow sip of whiskey, and handed the bottle back to him. "You knew I was at the warehouse by the airport that night. I saw you."

"You was there?"

"Yeah. I figured you knew because everybody took off before the police came."

"They took off because I drew my piece on them," Reggie said. "I don't know what it was, but I was ready to shoot some motherfuckers."

I pictured the guns in Reggie's panic room. One of them might have saved some dogs' lives that night.

"Why did you say Marvin was your uncle?"

"I didn't know he was my dad until I was grown. He came around sometimes when I was a kid, but I was told he was Uncle Marvin."

The fuzzy picture that the detective had described to me became clear. Marvin must've decided to tell the truth about how they were related when Reggie got famous. Got rich. That must've felt shitty.

He reached for the pipe and brought it to his mouth. Lifting his seat, he produced a lighter from under him. "I gotta keep track of my own lighters now," he said with a sad smile.

"I've been checking on the dogs," I said. "I even stole a couple of them, but I got caught."

His head jerked and he met my eyes. "You took some of them dogs?"

I nodded.

"How they doing?"

"A lot of them are actually doing alright."

He set the pipe down, and I scooped it up and placed it to my side so my body was between it and him. His eyes followed my movements, but he didn't protest.

"All I see is death," Reggie said, his face contorting. Then he plunged his fist into his thighs, hitting hard enough to bruise. "These drugs are only making it worse. I wish could I do something. Would go back and change everything if I could."

We sat together, stayed silent long enough for our breathing to fall into sync. I wondered when he'd last seen his daughter, Mackenzie. I hoped he was smart enough to stay away when he was in this kind of state.

He bolted to his feet and studied me, one eye shut. "You."

"What?" I asked. I thought maybe his mood had flipped and he would start accusing me again.

"You," he said again.

"Reggie," I said, holding my hands up. "It's okay. I'm here as a friend. I don't want to cause any trouble. I can leave if you want me to."

"Naw, man." He shook a finger at me. "You could do something about this. You're dedicated. You don't want to do it for show."

"You mean, like helping animals?" I asked.

"Yeah, like helping animals."

"I don't think I have any special skill or anything," I said.

"No, it's how you approach the thing. You're not some person trying to show how caring you are. You just care."

"That's a great compliment, Reggie," I said. "Thank you."

"It's more than a compliment."

I wondered if I had helped anything. There were so many suffering dogs. I had tried hard, but because of circumstances they'd slipped in and out of my arms so quickly that I didn't know if they or I were any better off for it.

"I don't know, Reggie."

"But you can!" He swerved out of the booth to the intercom unit. "Yo, Ham, grab me my checkbook."

I pushed myself up from the floor. "Hang on," I said. "You're tired. Why don't you sleep on it?"

Reggie didn't acknowledge what I'd said.

Ham appeared moments later with a leather-bound ledger. He handed Reggie a pen and held the book level as Reggie made swooping motions across the paper.

"Rip that shit out and give it to her," Reggie said.

Ham handed me the form. The check was for two million dollars. My breath hitched.

"I can't take this," I said.

I started out of the studio but turned back when I reached the door.

"Can I see your phone, Reggie?" He handed it to me and I typed in Pete's number and gave it back to him. "Alright. Call this guy. He's a good listener, and he's been through some of what you're going through."

"Pete," he said aloud, looking at the screen. "Dude sounds white as hell."

"So am I."

He chuckled. "Wouldn't it be a trip if I could come volunteer at your shelter someday?"

I scoffed. "Sober up, will you? I'll talk to you soon."

CHAPTER FORTY-SEVEN

I couldn't bring myself to talk to Reggie the next few days. I wanted to give myself time to think, but I didn't do much thinking. I knew I was unemployed for real and would run out of funds pretty soon. When I'd worked long hours for Lucy, staying nights at her place, I'd dreamed of the situation that I had now, living in a comfortable, charming house with plenty of light and having time to enjoy it. But with Ollie and now Kramer taken from me, my new beautiful home felt tainted. No amount of cleaning or happy memories could make it shiny again. I hadn't even used the reading nook for its intended purpose, though I did sit in it to cry once.

The only place, the only thing that made me feel okay, was the shelter.

Not that the shelter didn't hold bitter memories for me. It was the place where Ollie died. If only I had known, I could've been there with him. Those last moments would have wrenched my soul, but at least he wouldn't have been alone.

Debbie gave me a big green shirt that said VOLUN-TEER on the back, and I wore it twelve hours a day while I took care of the seized dogs. Walking them cheered me up. Some of them liked to stroll at my side sniffing the wind. More often they ran out in front of me, as if following an invisible skittering rodent, bolting in every direction but straight ahead. To my astonishment, a few of them tried to drag me back to the building.

"Why would they want to go back to their kennels, where they spend twenty-three hours a day?" I wondered aloud to Debbie.

"Sad as it is," Debbie said, "it's the safest place these guys have ever known."

I continued bonding with Molly, the scared German shepherd who had cowered in her cell when I first met her. I made sure she didn't get lost in the shuffle with the new dogs that came in from the bust. Molly, who had tried to disappear around people, now bounced in circles when she saw me, just like Ollie had.

Even though I'd promised myself *never again*, I woke up in the middle of the night convinced that I needed to adopt Molly. It was as if someone had whispered the words in my ear as I'd slept.

The next morning my new house felt bright again rather than like someone had died within its walls after suffering a long illness. The spirit had flown.

I slipped into my green VOLUNTEER shirt and headed to the shelter, almost laughing as I thought about how I'd never have to shut Molly's sad face into a cage and say goodnight again.

"You look peppy today," Debbie said with a wide grin when I burst through the metal doors. The dogs started barking their heads off as usual.

"I am!" I yelled. "Where did they move Molly? She's not in her kennel."

We stepped outside to get away from the noise like we always did when we needed to have more than a three-word conversation.

"Good news!" Debbie said. "She was adopted this morning."

My hand went up to my mouth. "What?"

"And the best part is, the couple who took her is way into outdoor sports—biking, running, hiking, you name it. They were specifically looking for an active dog."

"Oh my god," I said. "That's amazing." My heart crawled toward my throat.

"I know. Most people ask for a dog they won't have to walk."

I tried to catch her enthusiasm, bobbing my head, forcing a smile. But it felt bittersweet. Mostly bitter.

I heaved up my heavy arms and wrapped them around Debbie. My eyes watered.

Debbie patted my back. "You worked extremely hard to get her socialized. This wouldn't have happened without you."

I couldn't feel anything but sorry for myself.

My phone buzzed in my back pocket, and I checked it. Jake Ryan. I hit the Reject button and shoved it back into my jeans.

Debbie's eyes gleamed, and she placed a fist over her heart. "We churn through a lot of emotions in this place, and this one makes all the sorrow worth it."

"Yeah," I said. "Guess I'd better go check on Kramer now."

As Kramer and I walked, I imagined Molly galloping alongside her new owners as they rollerbladed down a beach path. I smiled.

Jake Ryan called again, bursting my serene picture bubble.

"Maybe they'll let me adopt you someday," I said to Kramer before I answered the phone.

Jake seemed out of breath. He didn't even say hi.

"We recovered a dog from a drug dealer we arrested today. I think it might be yours."

I stopped midstride, surprising Kramer. He let out a yelp.

"My dog's dead."

"Listen," Jake said, "the dealer was an associate of your neighbor, Jean-Marc Marchaud. We got a tip that Mr. Marchaud was selling coke, so we surveilled him and nabbed him. He cut a deal with us, and he informed on his supplier. Last night we raided the supplier compound. That's where we found this dog. He said he took the dog from Mr. Marchaud's apartment."

I squatted down, held my head in my hands. Kramer crouched beside me.

"You still there?" Jake asked.

"Yeah," I whispered.

"We think the dealer got the address wrong. He was the one who broke into your apartment. He thought he was breaking into Marchaud's. His prints match the ones I got from your door."

"Do you have a picture of the dog? Can you send it?" My voice shook.

"Yeah. Hang on."

A moment later the photo appeared in my texts. Joy whipped through me. My head went numb. I'd recognize that Joker's smile anywhere.

"Is he okay? Where is he now? Can I come get him?" I looked all around me, as if Ollie were going to just appear.

"I'll meet you at your house with him," Jake said.

"Oh my god. Thank you . . . thank you." I sprung up, started running with Kramer.

"Can I ask you something?"

"Yeah," I breathed.

"Why didn't you tell me and Officer Marquez that he was stolen?"

I reached my car and stopped, realizing I had to take Kramer back to his kennel.

"You still with me?" Jake asked.

"Yeah," I said, running back to the shelter now. "I lied because it's illegal to own him. I didn't think Officer Bitchy would allow me to have him back."

Jake chuckled. "Maybe not. But when you help the police, they help you. You helped us bring down a dog-fighting ring. In the process we busted about a dozen known felons. No cop in Miami will ever bat an eye at you or your pit bull."

EPILOGUE

A year and a half later

It's weirdly hot for an April day, even in Southern Florida. Standing at the edge of five acres of fenced-in land, I stare at the redbrick complex on the other side. *Hope we're ready for this,* I think, kicking off a flip-flop, rubbing my toes over the coarse blades of grass. A possum catches my eye far across the field, and I watch him scurry toward the exposed roots of the giant strangler fig tree and disappear into a dark nook.

I hold my hair away from my neck and stoop to rub Kramer's head and then Ollie's. All four of their ears are standing at attention. They must've seen the possum, too.

"Don't be nervous," Jake says, kissing my cheek while he fans my neck.

A car door slams in the distance. People are starting to arrive.

"Can I just skip this part?" I say. "I don't know if I can get through it without bawling like a baby."

"No can do. It was hard enough to talk Lucy out of setting up a stage and bringing in Beyoncé."

Reggie reaches us first. "The day's finally here," he says, looking at me with clear eyes and pulling me into a quick embrace. "How you feeling?"

"Hot."

Ham and Pete amble up behind him. Pete draws his hand from his pocket and extends it toward me. "Good to see you, kiddo," he says.

Lucy, Debbie, Isabelle, and a few others join us. As I greet them, I hear another car, and I turn to see Paul and Denise walking across the field. I'd expected Paul, but not her.

"She got a plane? Why didn't you guys tell me?" I put my hand over my mouth, and my eyes flit from Jake to Lucy.

They both shrug. "We didn't know," Lucy says.

Denise crouches and scratches my dogs, then lets them both lick her chin as I watch, bewildered. "Oh hello, sweeties," she says in that voice of hers I adopted. The dogs wriggle and push themselves into her legs.

Paul pulls us in for a three-man hug.

"I guess that's everyone," I say, my voice shaky.

The chattering group grows quiet, waiting for me to speak.

"The green light's flashing for you, Alex," Reggie says.

It's time for me to make my little speech. A lump travels to my throat, and I swallow hard. "Okay. I'll keep it short so I don't lose it," I begin, clasping my hands in front of me. "Without each of you, this dream wouldn't have become reality. I want to thank you for your hard work and support, your generous contributions, and for putting me in front of all your ridiculously rich friends so I could get the funding for this thing."

Everyone laughs.

"But most of all, your love for these animals made this possible." I pause and linger on each of their grinning faces.

"Most of the dogs don't get here until tomorrow, but I thought we could have this little dedication ceremony before the chaos arrives. So welcome to the Dogs in the Back Animal Sanctuary. Thank you all for giving these guys another shot at happiness." I pause, gathering myself for the most emotional part of the ceremony.

Lucy sees that I'm struggling not to melt down, and she steps up to the blue tarp that everyone's been eyeing. "Ready?" she asks, pointing at Ham and then waving him over. "Can you help me with this?" Together they pull the cover away to reveal a life-sized stone statue of a pit bull on a three-foot pedestal. There's an inscription on the platform. "Can you read this for us, Alex?" she asks.

"I doubt it," I say to more chuckling.

"Aw, I got this for you, Alex," Ham says, bending to read the simple words: "'For Maximus and Ollie. Your friendship led us to this place. Your boundless love touches all who dwell here.'"

The group is silent for a second. Then Reggie rushes up to me and pulls me into a giant hug. Our friends and family whoop and clap.

When the cheering dies down, I walk over to Denise.

"I'm so proud of you, and your father would have been, too," she says.

"Thanks," I say. "That means a lot."

I squeeze her hand and an idea comes to me. "Mom, what do you think about staying in town for a little while? The next few days are going to be pretty busy, and I could use all the help I can get."

THE END

ACKNOWLEDGEMENTS

This is for you, Chad, and your brilliant literary/logical mind. You sacrificed so much for me. Thanks for working so hard to support my hippie artist's lifestyle. You stayed up way past your bedtime cycling over characters and plots with me, and you never told me to shut up. When I had the crushing realization that my six-month foray into a nonlinear timeline was a huge waste of energy, you left work and took me shopping. That was huge. I cried when you didn't tell me my first draft was absolutely perfect. Thank God you didn't lie. (And thanks for saying my final draft was amazing.)

Louis Greenstein, I'm so glad I met you. Thanks for your generosity and your advice: "Write the story you don't want to write." You are a true mentor and friend.

To my writers' group, the fabulous Grandview Grind Crew— Leah Reynolds, Aline Pusecker-Taylor, Daniel Best, Paulita Kincer, Angie Romines, Emily Taylor, Lora

Hilty, Karen Kaufman, and David Breithaupt—you guys are my teachers and my second family.

Thanks Robin Hyde, Joan O'Donoghue, and Jeff Branche for reading the clunky early drafts and giving it to me straight.

Friends and family, thanks for encouraging me and listening to me talk about my progress with genuine interest. Fulton O'Donoghue, Thea O'Donoghue, Pat Spoerndle, Maggie Spoerndle, Alex Spoerndle, Steve O'Donoghue, Bob Bond, Melanie Bucher, Brian Bucher, Sarah Hennessy, Brendan Hennessy, Erin Hufford, Julia Rice, Thaddeus Durlin-Meeks, and Shane Durlin-Meeks, you make life worth living.

Finally, thanks for the great edits, Marcus Trower. You were awesome to work with.

ABOUT THE AUTHOR

Erin Adams quit her day job several years ago to focus on writing full-time. As a kid, she read and wrote stories and poems so obsessively that she neglected her schoolwork. Not much has changed. Other than a little freelancing, she's basically an unemployed novelist now. She's beyond lucky to have a brilliant, cool, talented group of writer friends who are willing to read her work and give her the honest (and sometimes painful) truth. Erin has a B.S. in journalism from Ohio University. She lives in Columbus, Ohio with her husband, Chad and her two dogs, Mr. Chilly and Liz Lemon.